Secret Love

F. Burn

ISBN 978-1-914301-07-0

Published 2021

Published by Black Velvet Seductions Publishing

Chapter One

You read about teachers developing inappropriate relationships with pupils and you wonder how it all happened. At what point did they finally decide to cross that line? Whose fault was it? Ultimately the responsibility lies with the adult they say, but when is the student considered an adult? You imagine yourself in that position and you tell yourself that you would never do that, but I found myself in an impossible situation.

It all started when I saw a job vacancy advertised at St. Paul's Catholic Secondary School for Boys in Kensington. They were looking for a Learning Support Assistant with a particular interest in dyslexia. I did have an interest in dyslexia and had been on the lookout for a chance to develop a specialism. They offered training and a generous benefits package. I'd also had enough of working in primary schools and fancied a change of scene. I wanted something that would challenge me intellectually. This seemed like the perfect opportunity, so I decided to apply.

After spending hours filling in the forms and writing up a statement, which sounded like complete waffle to me, I submitted the application. I didn't have too much hope as it was a private school and I wasn't Catholic. Even though I had been baptised as a child, I had decided years ago that I was actually agnostic. However, I described myself as a non-practising Catholic and emphasised the importance of Catholic values. A few days later, I ended up being shortlisted for interview.

The interview consisted of three parts: a short literacy and numeracy test, a tour of the school and a formal interview. The tests were fairly straightforward and I made sure that I was friendly and communicative towards the students giving the tour. The interview that followed consisted of a panel of three senior members of staff, which was a bit daunting at first, but went really well. They seemed impressed with my experience, qualifications and the answers I gave, so I felt that I just might have a chance.

Later that afternoon, I waited anxiously for the outcome. My enthusiasm waned with each hour that passed. I'd almost given up on hearing back that evening, when my phone rang. Jumping out of my skin, I dived towards my mobile. To my utter relief, I'd been successful. I eagerly accepted the position which would commence in September.

Once I had received all the relevant documents in the post, I returned them in person to try and speed up the process. After signing the contract, I officially handed in my resignation.

I don't know how I managed to do it, but I survived the rest of a particularly difficult summer term. Perhaps the knowledge that I was leaving helped motivate me. By the end of it, I felt so drained, and I needed a holiday. There were no tears on my last day because the thought of a long summer holiday ahead was enough to comfort me. Part of me was glad to be leaving – no more HR screw-ups. But the other part would miss the staff. I was also a little bit nervous about starting a new job. I'd have to form new relationships and get used to the layout of the school all over again. Undoubtedly, I would discover cracks in a seemingly perfect school, as one always does.

Once the summer holidays started, I planned lots of things to keep myself and my partner, John, busy. We couldn't afford a big expensive holiday, so we went on day trips to Calais and Brighton, as well as doing things in London. I spent a lot of time catching up with family and friends and even got involved in some sporting activities.

As the weeks went by, I began to dread the thought of returning to normal working life. My excitement about starting a new job was replaced with apprehension, and I found myself worrying about silly little things. I decided to research as much as I could about dyslexia to prepare for the role and this seemed to help a bit. The holidays seem to pass in the blink of an eye, and before I knew it, I was starting at St. Paul's.

My first day at St. Paul's began in the staffroom. Despite my fears about snobby staff, they seemed friendly enough. They all do at first. We had to attend morning mass at St. Paul's Church. Listening to sermons and singing dreary hymns was not my cup of tea. I didn't do listening for long periods of time or singing in public very well either.

The teachers and learning support assistants then separated to attend training. It was actually quite useful, but everyone looked half asleep. I can only describe it as that 'deer in the headlights' look. Once the summer holidays end and you return to work, it's like an electrical shock to your system and you suddenly have to switch your brain on and come to terms with having a job again.

After lunch, I finally met with my line manager, Sue. I recognised her from the interview. She was the special needs coordinator. I was feeling positive until she said, "Due to your experience, we've decided to have you support Richard Cunningham. He's in Year Eleven and has a statement for severe dyslexia. He's entitled to twenty hours of one-to-one support per week. He also has behavioural and emotional difficulties."

I was not happy. Not another bloody difficult student. But, wanting to make a good impression, I just nodded and said, "No problem."

"He's two years behind due to repeating Year Seven and now he's retaking his GCSEs. He'll be finishing his GCSEs at age eighteen, which means he's below age-related expectations. Obviously, he has some issues with his self-esteem and acts out from time to time."

Interestingly, though, last year he managed to pass maths, DT and music. Surely he couldn't be that bad then? This year, he was retaking English, science, history and geography and had chosen art as an additional subject. I was pleased to see that he was going to be doing art, as I was particularly good at art and hoped that would enable me to form some kind of bond. Considering that he'd studied music previously, I imagined he would have a creative side.

And so the following day, after a restless sleep, I started officially. I was introduced to the two other students that I would be expected to support: Joseph – a charming Year Seven boy with Asperger's, and Stuart – a quiet boy with global delay. I then met the infamous Richard. I'd already heard staff speaking about him in the staffroom. Apparently, he was moody, miserable and volatile, often didn't respond to adults and liked running off. *Great*, I thought. But I had to judge for myself. It's all too easy to pigeonhole and label. I'd had some success with difficult students before and hoped that I'd be able to manage the situation.

I was led to one of the Year Eleven classrooms during registration. The form tutor kindly brought me over to Richard. He was holding a pen over an open notebook and he was staring at it, as if lost in his thoughts. I stood next to his table, and then he finally turned towards us with a slightly puzzled expression on his face when his tutor spoke to him, or rather, rambled on nervously. His gaze turned to me while I patiently waited to be introduced. The whole time, he made it obvious to me that he was staring. I wasn't really sure at what, though. To break the awkwardness of the moment, I interrupted by quickly introducing myself.

"Hello. My name is Miss Gabel and I'll be supporting you in class. Nice to meet you." I reached out to shake his hand and he shakily took mine. He studied my face as if trying to gauge what kind of person I was.

"Nice to meet you too," he replied in a quiet voice. He spoke slowly, as if he was unsure of himself. He also seemed incredibly shy. I just hoped he wasn't as bad as they said he was. I guess I got some comfort from the fact that I usually build good relationships with students who had speech and language difficulties – to the point where they don't shut up.

The bell went and I managed to navigate through the hallway to the English class where I'd be supporting Richard. I ended up being a few minutes late, and unfortunately almost everyone was already seated. There was an empty seat beside Richard. As I walked towards him, it suddenly dawned on me that he was actually quite handsome and looked older than a seventeen-year-old. I got a little bit annoyed with myself for noticing that he was handsome, as it was kind of unprofessional.

"Do you mind if I sit here?"

"No, I don't mind," he replied softly. I hesitantly sat next to him, wondering if it was a good idea or not.

He seemed uncomfortable at first – twitchy and fidgety. I wasn't sure if it was because he was self-conscious about sitting next to an LSA. I averted my vision and kind of kept a watch on him from the corner of my eye. Eventually, he seemed to settle down.

The teacher began the lesson by discussing colloquialisms and the differences between formal and informal speech. They had to discuss with their partners what they thought. I assumed that I was Richard's partner.

"So, what do you think?" He just sat there and, after a while, I thought he wasn't going to respond. To my relief, he started to answer the question.

"I think that, ummm... formal speech is more for school or work, and informal speech is how you speak to your friends."

"You've pretty much summed it up there. What exactly is a colloquialism?"

"I think it's a word that you use when you speak informally. Am I right?"

"Yes, you are."

Well, he seemed intelligent enough. The students were presented with a written paragraph, which they had to rewrite. He just stared at it like it was written in Latin. I'd been told that he found reading difficult and would often become unresponsive if he felt he couldn't do something. I'd also been told he was extremely self-conscious about reading aloud in front of others; apparently, he read slowly and often confused words. I imagined that would be worse today, especially because we had just met. I'd read that dyslexic people often understood verbal information better than written information, so I gently asked if he'd like me to start reading it. He gave me a pained expression, blushed, and nodded.

It was at that very moment that I looked into his eyes that I noticed how unusual they were. Like kaleidoscopic gems. Mostly green, with amber and almost yellow highlights around the pupil area. Slightly embarrassed, my face grew hot and I swallowed, hoping that he hadn't noticed. I tried to avoid eye contact and focus on the task at hand. He was able to complete his work with my support.

At the end of the lesson, I was about to leave when I felt a light tap on my shoulder. When I turned around, Richard was standing behind me. "Thank you for your help." He said earnestly.

"You're more than welcome," I said, and I thought, *Well, that was a pleasant surprise. Maybe it won't be that bad after all.*

When I arrived home that evening, I thought about that lesson a lot. I didn't know what had got into me when I had looked into his eyes, but that night I kept seeing his face in my mind.

***

That first week went by without incident. In class, he was usually very polite and respectful. Some days, he could be quite sullen. But, I didn't want to push him, so I never asked what was wrong. I supposed that he might tell me in his own time. I would wonder when the horror stories I had heard would come true and hoped they wouldn't. No matter how morose he appeared to be, he always responded to my questions in class. One thing I couldn't stand was an unresponsive student. It made life extremely difficult.

He didn't speak much at this point, but he did seem to listen to me ramble on — a 'method' I used with students who had problems communicating. I found that a lot of students would open up to me once they had got to know me a bit. I usually tried to find some kind of common ground. After looking at Richard's timetable, I noticed that he had tennis club once a week. I was a little uncertain as to whether it was too soon to take an interest in his extra-curricular activities but decided to go and watch him play.

During the second week, on a Tuesday, I was on my way out and then I remembered that Richard had tennis club. I thought I'd pass by the court briefly to see Richard play. I wasn't sure how he would react, but I was curious. I sat at the far end, so he wouldn't really notice me, as I didn't want him to feel uncomfortable. I watched and came to the conclusion that he was a pretty good player. All that frustration he may have was being worked off and it would help him to stay fit, both physically and psychologically.

I got caught up in the games and ended up moving closer to watch. That was when he noticed me. He did a kind of double take, peering questioningly as if he was wondering why I was there. I just hoped he wouldn't mind me watching. He must have realised that I was there to see him, and to my surprise he tentatively gave me a small wave. I smiled and waved back. When the matches were over, he came over to me, but didn't say anything. I spoke first.

"You were very good, Richard."

He shrugged his shoulders modestly and replied, "Guess I'm okay. Got to work on my backhand though."

"Maybe, but it was good to see you playing. I actually really enjoyed it. Would you mind if I came to see you play again some time?"

"No, that would be nice." Even though I wanted to stay and chat some more, I could see how much he was sweating.

"Well, I guess you better hit the showers. I'll see you tomorrow."

"Thanks for coming, miss."

***

The following week, there was a trip to the British Museum. They were going to look at Greek mythology in art for a project. I was asked to go because Richard would be going. You could visibly see the relief on the teachers' faces because they wouldn't be alone with him, though I had yet to see what was so awful about him. The art teacher wanted Richard at the front, so I suggested that I lead the way to the station.

"Richard? Come here for a second." He walked up to me.

"Yes, miss?"

"I'm going to be leading the way, but I'm probably going to go in the wrong direction. Can you help me? Be my partner?" I hoped my strategy would work.

"Yes, of course, I'll help."

It was clear that he felt awkward in social situations. Throughout the whole trip, he stood near me on the train and in the museum. It was painfully obvious that he had no friends, so I discussed ideas with him whilst we looked at the pieces. I decided to try and sketch one of the monoliths myself.

"So, what do you think?" I said, while showing him my sketch.

"Wow, that's really good. Where did you learn how to do that?"

"Nowhere in particular. It's something I've always been good at. You're pretty good yourself." He gave me a look of disbelief and slight confusion.

"Me? Really?"

"Why? Is that so hard to believe?"

"Maybe. I don't know. Maybe you could give me some tips," he replied, still not convinced.

We continued to sketch some of the pieces and record ideas for the project until lunchtime. We sat in a dining area especially designated for school visits. I deliberately sat next to Richard, as this was a good time to get to know him a bit more. I smiled at him when I sat down, and he gave me the barest hint of a smile.

"I can't believe I've forgotten my water bottle," I complained when I looked through my bag.

"You can have mine if you want."

"No, thanks. You need it."

He took a few sips and put the bottle in front of me.

"You have the rest.

"Okay, thank you."

***

After that, we became a lot more comfortable around each other. I began to really care about Richard's education, because it was his last year in high school and he needed the grades to progress further. I had no idea how he'd cope in the future as he had real needs. It was frustrating because it was obvious that he was trying hard. I began to suspect that the staff hadn't given him much of a chance and that he was misunderstood. It seemed as if they'd written him off. His grades wouldn't affect the school's results, because he had a statement of special educational needs.

Although I'd had a fairly good start at St. Paul's, I did find the staff to be quite cliquey. That was normal in schools, though, and probably in other employment sectors. I mostly kept myself to myself and juggled with the idea of eating with the students in the dining hall. Lunch was free when you sat with the students, which would mean I wouldn't have to prepare lunch for work in the evenings. The only problem was that staff usually gained weight eating school dinners. They were often stodgy and the portions were too large. Sometimes there would be huge amounts of cheese or pastry and I would end up wondering how schools were promoting their healthy eating policies. I hoped that the menu would be better here.

Chapter Two

It was October when the first incident occurred. I was on early lunch break in the staffroom, as I had to cover lunch duty for an absent member of staff, when Sue approached me with a panicked look on her face.

"I'm afraid we need you right now."

"What happened?"

"Richard attacked Michael at the end of English and ran off. Can you help find him and coax him back inside? His mum has been called in for an emergency meeting."

A short while later, I found him sitting on the bench outside the drama block. I didn't say a word. I just sat next to him. He had tears in his eyes, and in that instant, I really felt for him. Eventually, I had to break the silence.

"Whatever happened, I'm here to support you. You don't have to go back inside yet. You can take your time." Oh, how much I wanted to reach out and wipe those tears off his face. I had this overwhelming feeling of wanting to comfort him. I waited patiently until he responded.

"Sorry," he finally said, as he stared into the distance.

"Sorry for what?" He hadn't done anything to me.

"Sorry for disturbing you during your lunch break."

"Don't worry about that. It's boring in the staffroom anyway. I'm more concerned about you."

He put his head down and mumbled, "Do you really care?"

"Well, of course, I do," I responded a bit too sharply.

"Why? Nobody else does."

"I'm sure they do. You're a good person." I really wanted him to believe what I was saying.

"Do you really believe that?"

"Look at me, Richard. Yes, I do believe in you. Working with you has been a pleasure." I did reach out to him at this point. I gently touched his arm. He looked down at my hand like he desperately needed human contact. "Tell me what happened."

"Michael said something and I lost my temper. I had to get out of there or I would have killed him."

"What did he say?" I probed gently.

"He said... You know what? He's right. I am stupid and dumb. I'm two years behind and I always need support. I can't do anything by myself."

"You're not stupid. You're actually an intelligent guy with dyslexia. Even I had to retake some of my exams back in the day. Okay, yes, you do things at a slower pace. But who's to say that's abnormal? Everyone learns differently, and maybe you haven't received the support you needed. I'm available if you need any extra help with anything."

"I already have a tutor, and I know my mum's fed up 'cos I haven't shown much improvement."

"Is your tutor any good?"

He just shrugged his shoulders.

"I tell you what. I'm not really supposed to do this, but I can give you my email address. Contact me any time if you need to." I knew it was wrong, but I felt like I really needed to reach out to him.

"Okay, I will. Thank you, miss."

"And if there's anything I can do differently – like not sit next to you in class, if it makes you feel uncomfortable – just let me know."

"No, you don't have to do that. I focus better when you're around."

We spoke for around twenty minutes and then he agreed to go to the Learning Support Unit to wait for his mum. I went to do lunch duty, and then I was asked to attend the meeting. Apparently, Richard had refused to go unless I was there.

His mother was definitely a high maintenance woman. You could tell from her appearance that she was well off. Stylish hair, manicured nails, expensive clothes and what looked like a diamond watch. She barely acknowledged me at first. Her expression said it all. Annoyed that she'd had to come to this meeting. From what Richard told me, she was hardly ever around. They even had a housekeeper.

The meeting was painfully awkward. His mum accused the school of singling Richard out and only now finally getting him the support he needed. She finally acknowledged me, when asked if she was happy with the support. She was more than satisfied with the support I had given so far. Richard must have said something to her. In a way, I found it surprising. I guess I had preconceptions about middle-class people.

The meeting went on for ages and it was almost home-time when it was over. They had decided not to exclude Richard because Michael had played his part. What followed was totally unexpected, though. She approached me at the end of the meeting.

"You seem to have a good connection with Richard. I'm looking for a new tutor to help him in the evenings or weekends. Do you have any tutoring experience?"

"Some. It's been a while, but I am familiar with what he's studying. I'd be more than happy to tutor him. Not sure if I'm allowed to, though."

"Don't worry about that. The school doesn't need to know."

And that was how I got myself into deeper trouble. She offered a generous rate that was too good to refuse. I wanted to save up, as I had been considering moving overseas in a couple of years. I was a bit nervous about spending time alone with him. Whether or not I wanted to admit it, I knew I was attracted to him. At this point, I had no intentions of crossing the line, though. To be honest, what the hell would he see in me anyway? He was young, handsome and well-off and he could probably get any woman. I was approaching thirty, had acne and a really boring taste in clothes. The worst part was that I had a boyfriend, and he would be mortified if he could read my thoughts.

It was weird. I wanted to help him in a sort of motherly way, but sometimes I wanted to touch him in that way. At times, I longed to run my fingers through his curly blond hair, to caress him, to hold him, or to just be in the same vicinity as him. I'd have to try really hard not to notice his lovely eyes, his strong build or his full lips from now on. In two weeks, I was to start tutoring him after school at his house. So I had two weeks to get my act together.

***

It was Monday. School had just finished. I saw him waiting for me outside the school gates. And he was smiling. He hardly ever smiled, but when he did, my heart literally skipped a beat. It was then that I came to this conclusion: not only was he handsome, but he was beautiful. I guess some would say he was kind of androgynous. His facial features were almost feminine, but masculine at the same time. Sort of ethereal.

He stood there wearing his navy blazer and tan trousers, carrying his messenger-style bag.

"Hi, Francesca."

"Hi, Ritchie."

"My house is just a short walk away."

He called me by my first name now, and I'd given him a nickname. For some reason, delightful shivers ran down my spine when he said my name. We walked and talked. I mostly blabbed on about my family, skipping from one subject to another. I also mentioned that I had a boyfriend.

Then, I just blurted out, "So do you have a girlfriend, Ritchie?"

There was a long pause.

"No, I've never really had a girlfriend before," he replied.

I was about to respond by saying that he could easily get any woman, but just then, we arrived at the house. It was huge.

"So, this is where you live? You've got a lovely house."

"Thank you. It's nice of you to say." He then cheekily added, "Even though, technically, it's not mine."

"Are you being sarcastic?" I accused him mockingly.

"Me? No. Never."

While we stood in the entrance corridor, he asked, "Would you like to work in the dining room or in my bedroom?" He looked at me expectantly. It felt like some sort of test.

"Do you have a desk in your room?"

"Yes, quite a big one, and all my stuff is upstairs."

"Well, I guess we can work in your room then."

"Okay. You can hang your coat up here if you want," he said, pointing to three empty coat hooks. As I took my coat off, I saw Ritchie's eyes flick downwards to my chest. At first, I assumed he was looking at my necklace, but then I realised he was looking at my breasts. I was wearing a fairly snug-fitting, red V-neck top and sometimes it rode downwards, though I often pulled it up to prevent that. It definitely wasn't inappropriate, as some of my colleagues wore clothes that were way more revealing than mine. I usually went for comfort rather than what was fashionable. However, it was hard to hide the fact that I had what some might consider to be large breasts. Feeling a little self-conscious, I adjusted my top, and he realised that I had seen him looking. He cleared his throat and asked if I would like a drink.

We got some juice from the kitchen and walked up to his room. His bedroom was spacious with a minimalist approach – another way of saying it was cold and clinical. He threw his bag on the bed and we sat down at his desk, which was by a large window. The sun was setting just then and we both looked out at it. I was about to say how nice it looked but became distracted by how the orange-red light made his eyes look both stunning and unearthly.

I know he saw me staring, as he turned toward me and smiled shyly. I immediately felt butterflies in my stomach, but managed to shakily get out, "So, let's have a look at the coursework that's due and try to come up with a timetable."

We looked at his diary, coursework requirements, homework due and revision needed. We decided to focus on homework for this first session, until he had done a bit more research for his coursework. Throughout our session, we ended up sitting closer and closer. I was very aware of his cologne and I could smell his hair. I manage to play it cool, trying my best to focus on his work.

Before long, it was six o'clock. I was tempted to stay longer, but I really needed some fresh air.

"Can you come on Wednesday, Francesca?"

"I thought I was only coming twice a week – Monday and Thursday?"

"Mum said you can come more often when I have assignments due, if that's okay? She'll pay you."

"Okay, if she doesn't mind. Oh yeah, before I go, I've been meaning to ask you something. Have you said anything about me to your mum?"

"Yes. I told her that you've helped me a lot. I don't hate school so much now."

"Did you really say that?"

He nodded in response.

"Can I ask – do you hate school that much?"

"With a passion. No one likes me and I've got no friends. I'm the weird, quiet guy with special needs and emotional issues. Lunchtimes are the worst."

"Well... I was thinking about sitting in the lunch hall from now on. Staff can get a free lunch if they sit with the students. You're more than welcome to sit with me if you don't think it's too lame? I don't really like sitting with the staff anyway."

He looked at me like he couldn't believe what I'd just said. Like no one else had given him the time of day.

"It would be nice to talk to someone at lunchtime."

"Well, I would really like to talk to you at lunchtime."

It was almost like we'd arranged to have a first date. I felt nervous like a giddy schoolgirl with a crush. The question was whether or not he liked me back? And that was when it occurred to me. I wanted him to be attracted to me too.

For weeks after the incident, I made sure he sat as far away from Michael as possible. Every now and then I would catch Michael giving Ritchie cutting looks. I wished he would just leave Ritchie alone. During parts of the lesson where discussion was involved, Ritchie seemed a lot more animated. He had more of a spring in his step, and he presented me with a tub full of luscious red strawberries and a custard tart at lunchtime. I must say, I felt quite flattered that he'd bought me something.

"I'm sure you're trying to fatten me up. My partner does this too, but he does it so I can be as fat as him."

He laughed a real genuine laugh – the first time I'd ever heard him laugh out loud. People looked at him like he had three heads when he laughed. Obviously they'd never seen him laugh before either. The next minute we were both laughing for no apparent reason, just for the joy of it.

"It's great seeing you smiling and laughing. You have a lovely smile; you should do it more often," I couldn't help but comment. Then I realised that I may have said too much, as his face turned a light shade of pink.

"Thanks," he said, almost hesitantly. "You've got a nice smile too."

"No, I look like a chipmunk when I smile. My big, fat cheesy smile."

He laughed again. "You do not look like a chipmunk!"

"Look, I'm at peace with my chipmunk cheeks, so let's leave it at that."

We were finally being ourselves around each other. The rest of the week was good and Ritchie was really coming out of his shell. I was so pleased. His teachers had even commented on the change.

***

A few days later, I was approached about accompanying students on a residential trip. Apparently, Ritchie had signed up and paid a while back, Due to his unpredictable nature, they felt that they needed someone to supervise him, and it was unlikely that his mum would be willing to come. The member of staff who was going didn't know Ritchie all that well and was a bit unsure of how to deal with him. So Philip, who was normally not particularly likeable, was unusually polite when he started a conversation with me randomly in the staff room. I immediately thought, *What do you want? Get to the point?* He eventually explained the situation and then, after a whole lot of waffle, finally asked if I'd like to go.

I answered honestly, saying that it depended on the facilities and that I had certain conditions. I insisted that I either get paid for the overtime or get a day off in lieu. I liked to be difficult sometimes. He hastily agreed to the latter, obviously relieved.

Ritchie's face lit up when I shared the news with him, telling me I was the best teacher ever. Although I wasn't technically a teacher, I guess we were all educators anyway. I couldn't help but feel a small rush of pride.

After my conversation with Ritchie, I officially confirmed that I'd go. I thought it slightly odd that they hadn't asked a male member of staff to supervise him, but the other teacher going was male – the PE teacher, Steve Clapham.

They didn't give me much time to prepare; we would be going on Monday, which was three days away. I was determined to have a relaxing weekend in preparation, but as is always the case, nothing goes to plan.

On Monday morning, Ritchie lugged his suitcase towards the coach, making sure to say hello to me. Then he offered to bring mine to the cargo hold. When we began to board, Ritchie asked, "Can I sit with you?"

I couldn't quite hide my enthusiasm or my delight and answered, "Sure – unless I'm told to sit elsewhere. Hopefully, they won't say anything." They shouldn't really have anything to say about it. After all, I was there to support Ritchie, even though I was getting way more enjoyment out of it than I was supposed to be.

"Thanks, miss," he responded, with a bashful smile on his face. I felt like he could sense the butterflies in my stomach as we locked eyes. He definitely saw me swallow nervously in an attempt to control my feelings.

The journey was fairly short, just over two hours. At first, we just spoke quietly about this and that, finding that we liked a lot of the same movies. Being a bit of a science fiction geek, I got a bit carried away, forgetting about the boy behind us who was about to be sick, but managing to pass the sick bag just in time. As the journey continued, I caught myself stealing quick glances in his direction. Every time we made eye contact, the intensity increased. The few times we unintentionally made physical contact, it sent a jolt of pleasure through me.

I noticed quite a few looks coming our way, as some students overheard our conversation. They had either never seen Ritchie speak much, or they'd never seen a member of staff speaking so openly and humorously.

As soon as we arrived, we were shown to our cabins. I was quite pleased with mine, despite the lack of toilet paper. I even had access to tea-making facilities. We only had a minute to drop off our bags, then we hurried off to lunch, which wasn't too bad, considering how hungry I was. It wasn't particularly healthy, but there was a good choice of salads and fruit. Ritchie waited for me to sit before deciding where to sit. I found his mound of beef casserole, potatoes, rice and salad amusing.

I was in the middle of enjoying the lemon cheesecake when Ritchie suddenly disappeared, reappearing with another lemon cheesecake which he gave to me. After a while, I began to feel self-conscious, because he watched me eat it. I felt a bit paranoid, so I talked about everything and anything. The funny thing was that he sat and listened intently. A few minutes later, three other students were listening to me waffle on incessantly as if I was actually interesting.

Back at the cabins, we unpacked our bags. I stood outside the cabins to assist Steve with making sure the boys were doing as they were told. There were three cabins of six boys, and some of the boys had discovered that their shower wasn't working. Steve decided that it would be okay if they used our showers, but only if theirs hadn't been fixed by the evening.

The week before us would be packed with activities such as abseiling, rock climbing, camping, raft building and so on. I doubted that I'd be trying many of the activities, though. Although teachers didn't normally accompany the boys during their activities unless they wanted to, I was expected to supervise Ritchie. I didn't mind, as I wasn't too keen on hanging out in the teachers' lounge anyway. I knew that Ritchie would be up for everything, but anything involving teamwork could be an issue.

That evening was a bit manic because the shower still hadn't been fixed. Steve felt it was best that we weren't alone in our rooms while the boys used our bathrooms, so we both sat in my cabin as they either used his shower or mine. Despite Steve suggesting this, he left me to supervise alone while he left to pick up the Wi-Fi password.

By some bizarre twist of fate, Ritchie happened to be one of the boys who needed to have a shower in my room. Initially, when I heard the knock on the door, I assumed Steve had returned to tell me something, but it was Ritchie. It was almost as if our meetings were prearranged by someone or something outside our control. I couldn't help my intake of breath when I saw him.

He fumbled nervously with his bundle, which consisted of a towel, shower gel, aftershave, a razor and a toothbrush. He dropped everything, due to having too many things in his hands. He quickly bent down to retrieve the items, which now lay by my feet. As he slowly began to stand up again, he ran his eyes over my legs, groin and waist, and they lingered on my breasts. We stood but inches apart, yet I didn't take a step back. He blushed.

Something passed between us.

An understanding.

This was definitely more than a student-teacher relationship. There was something in the air between us. I had felt it a few times, and I knew for sure that he felt whatever this was too.

I cleared my throat, breaking the spell. He dropped his eyes in what appeared to be embarrassment. I decided to release him from my gaze.

"I guess you've come to use the shower?" I tried to say it cheerfully to lighten the mood.

"If you don't mind?"

As if I would mind.

Doing a mock bow, I replied, "Welcome to my bathroom."

He smiled at me and stepped in. I stood outside the door, unable to move at first. I wanted to open the door. I wanted to watch him undress.

I then heard a noise and I quickly took a step back. Remembering that I'd promised to post some photographs on the school website, I sat at the desk with my phone, flicking through the better-quality ones. I stopped when I came across a photo of Ritchie completely unaware that he'd been captured. I didn't want to share that one; it was for my eyes only.

After a while, I wondered why Steve still hadn't returned and what could possibly be taking him so long. Not that I wanted him back sooner, because I enjoyed the thought of Ritchie naked in my bathroom. Thinking again about the way he looked at me brought heat to my face. I found the wrongness of it strangely arousing.

The bathroom door opened and out stepped a fully clothed Ritchie, much to my disappointment. I stood up to let him out, even though I didn't need to. I noticed a few blood spots on his chin. He stood very still as I touched his soft skin, tenderly wiping the blood away with my thumb.

"You're bleeding," I said.

Glancing down, he said shyly, "I cut myself shaving."

For the second time, I got the impression he'd never felt this kind of contact before. Had anyone ever shown him compassion, tenderness or affection?

He looked up, meeting my eyes. His expression changed and he reached towards me. I stopped breathing.

"There's something in your hair," he said as he reached to retrieve what looked like a leaf. Yet again, neither of us backed up or made a move, despite the proximity of our bodies. We found ourselves frozen in this strange moment.

On more than one occasion, I had felt that there was hidden meaning behind many things that were said or done, but I was unsure of whether it was just a feeling of paranoia. Maybe it wasn't.

The sound of Steve's voice emerged. He'd returned. We both immediately took that long overdue step back, like we'd been caught doing something wrong. As Ritchie walked towards the door, he said, "Goodnight, Francesca."

I didn't want him to leave, and I gave him what must have looked like a longing look. Sighing heavily, I replied, "Sweet dreams, Ritchie."

The showers were soon repaired, so there were no more shower-related encounters. I did accompany him while he and his group completed activities and challenges, deciding not to participate myself most of the time. Although I did have a go at less daring sports such as archery and laser tag. Ritchie, on the other hand, threw himself into every challenge, doing as well, if not better, than his classmates. His success did fuel some jealous looks, but he didn't seem to notice.

***

Wednesday night was camp night. I wasn't planning to actually camp out with them. I was just there to supervise the pitching of the tents but decided to stay a bit longer. We sat around the campfire and Ritchie handed me a toasted marshmallow on a small thin branch. The camp leader played a few songs on his guitar and we sang few songs. The boys told scary stories while Ritchie and I exchanged looks of scorn, rolling our eyes in jest.

I had just removed the last marshmallow off my twig when Ritchie dropped his. After convincing Ritchie that I didn't want mine, he comically detached the sticky mess off my fingers. Enjoying the fumbling physical contact, I just sat there, watching unhelpfully.

As he proceeded to eat it, I licked my fingers, realising that he was watching me yet again, and I continued to do so somewhat provocatively. His eyes bore into mine uncompromisingly and seemed to emit the message that he knew.

The time finally came for the boys to settle into their tents. They sorted themselves into groups of three, apart from Ritchie who had to be put into a three. A look of apprehension cast its shadow upon his face, and I got the feeling that he'd find it difficult that night, although Steve reassured me that he would supervise him.

Mid-sleep, I was rudely awakened by the sound of my phone ringing. It was Steve. As soon as I heard his voice, I knew it was something to do with Ritchie. He explained that Ritchie had left his tent and seemed upset. As I wondered where he could possibly be, I heard a familiar knock on my door and I groggily got out of bed, threw on my dressing gown and opened it. It was him. My immediate concern was how I looked, which I knew was absurd, but I didn't turn on the overhead light. The dull glow of the lamp was enough. He walked in and slumped down on the bed, and I sat beside him.

Finally, he said, "I didn't mean to wake you."

"It's okay. What happened?"

"They were asking me things."

"Asking you what?"

"Um, weird questions about..."

He looked down at his hands, obviously uncomfortable. Eventually, he managed to muster the courage to say, "About sex." And then it all clicked into place. He hadn't experienced this kind of situation before.

"Oh, I think I understand what you're saying. Do you want me to have a word with them?"

"No, this is really embarrassing. I've never had a girlfriend – I wasn't sure –"

"It's okay, you don't have to explain. You know what, though? It is *normal* for boys your age to talk about stuff like that."

"I know, but..."

"Most of them are in the same boat as you." I studied his features while I waited for this to sink in a bit. It was incredibly endearing how his creased brow faded, and the tenseness was replaced with uncertainty. He looked up, making eye contact.

"Really?" His expression was expectant, as if I knew all the answers.

I think he wanted more information, to ask more questions. Naturally, he was curious, but it was the wrong place, the wrong time, and I was certainly the wrong person. It was sad that he had no one else he could talk to.

"Yes. I better call Mr. Clapham. I'll just say that you were finding things difficult and needed time out."

After calling Steve, Ritchie's eyes followed me as I removed my dressing gown and put on some shoes and a cardigan. He never took his eyes off me, and I thought it unnerving how openly he stared. I felt prickles down my spine, and I realised that I found the discomfort somewhat enjoyable.

Against my better judgement, I sat back down beside him. He turned towards me and said, "Thanks for understanding." Before I had a chance to respond, he affectionately patted my leg completely unexpectedly. Muted, I sat transfixed by his hand on my thigh.

I willed myself not to give anything away, to keep my expression neutral, and hoped that would calm my beating heart. I tried to get my mouth to say the words I was trying to form, but nothing came out.

I abruptly stood up, unable to retain control. I stood stiffly until I was able to say, "I'll walk you back now."

Halfway there, I realised that I was freezing. I'd stupidly thought that my cardigan would keep me warm enough. Consumed by the presence of Ritchie, I'd forgotten how cold it was out here at night. Of course, Ritchie noticed, and he took his jacket off and placed it over my shoulders. I considered giving it back, but I was genuinely very cold. So I shrugged my arms into the jacket and zipped it up. I felt oddly swathed in the feel and scent of him. It was quite intoxicating.

When we arrived, Ritchie asked, "Do you know the way back?" He'd noticed my confusion and lack of coordination on the walk there.

Not wanting to seem pathetic, I replied, "Yes. See you in the morning."

He looked unconvinced. As I started to take off the jacket he said, "No, keep it for tonight."

I wandered back to my cabin, unsure of whether I was going in the right direction. Slowly, but surely, I made it back.

I gave myself a mental reminder to return to camp early and give Ritchie back his jacket. I ended up bringing it into bed with me that night, giving into my urge to smell it. Inhaling the fragrance of cologne, fresh leaves and a slightly earthier odour, I fell into a deep sleep.

***

It wasn't until our last night that things got a bit heated. It was disco night, but Ritchie was reluctant to attend. It wasn't compulsory for staff to attend, as camp staff would be there.

"I'll go if you go, Ritchie," I said in an attempt to convince him. "But I warn you, I might cramp your style," I added, in reference to the fact that there would be a number of attractive young ladies looking his way. Of that I was sure.

"Would you really do that? Teachers hardly ever go."

"Of course I would do that. I even brought some clothes for the disco, but I didn't realise teachers didn't normally go."

"Well, some do, but they just sit at the side or pop in at the beginning. I'll go because you're going. And you won't cramp my style. I have no style."

"Come on, you have style. The strong silent type of style," I joked. He chuckled in response.

Later on that evening, I tried to put together a decent outfit from what I'd brought. I wore a sheer grey sparkly top with black jeans and red shoes. I shook my hair loose from the bun it was in and it hung in waves down my back.

I made my way to the disco wondering how I would find Ritchie in the dark. However, soon after I stepped in, I spotted him lurking against the wall by the drinks stand. It was the hair I noticed first. The disco lights glinted colourfully off his blond locks.

He didn't see me approach and I was almost glad it was too dark to see all that well. I had begun to feel that the outfit I had put together was mediocre at best. I gently rubbed his arm to alert him to my presence. He almost jumped when he felt me touching him.

Standing close to him, I said teasingly, "Aren't you going to dance? Isn't that why you came?"

He shook his head profusely, refusing to dance. Then he moved even closer, so much so that his hair brushed my cheek. He smelt fresh, like he'd just had a shower. My heartbeat increased unexpectedly.

"But I can't dance, Francesca. I'll look like a complete dork."

We spent most of the night standing in a corner, drinking Pepsi and, with amused fascination, watching a crowd of boys surrounding a group of girls. I began to worry that they would make fun of Ritchie if they saw me standing beside him. Luckily, they were so preoccupied, and it was so dark, that I didn't spot anyone looking. Still, no matter how much I wanted to grab Ritchie and dance, I didn't. We managed to find an even darker spot and kind of just nodded our heads to the music.

We were about to leave when a slow dance song started, which was what I assumed was the last song anyway. Just as we left the disco hall, he quickly looked around and took my hand, leading me to a deserted corridor upstairs.

"May I have this dance?"

I laughed and nodded. That explained all the secrecy. He gingerly put his hands on my waist and started to slow dance. He was right about not being able to dance. I didn't want to even think about how I was dancing, because all I could feel were his warm hands on my waist.

I rested my hands on his shoulders and we swayed side to side to the music. When I finally gathered enough courage to look up, his eyes were already on mine. A surge of heat pushed its way through my body. He held me even closer, his hands lowering, feeling more of my hourglass figure.

The air was so charged that you could practically smell it. As realisation dawned on him, he immediately took his hands off, his face red.

"I think we better leave," I whispered.

We left before the end of the song and made our way back to the cabins. The stars and constellations were a worthy distraction. As soon as I spotted the Summer Triangle, I stopped in my tracks, craning my neck and trying to get a better view. As we were in the countryside, the sky was black and the Milky Way stood out against the clear sky.

Ritchie followed my gaze to see what I was so intent on seeing. "Wow, there are so many stars," he said, awe-inspired.

Pointing up towards the constellation of Cygnus, I said, "You see that group of stars there? Look closely and you'll see the Milky Way."

He looked up for a long time, letting his eyes adjust to the darkness. "Oh my god, I think I can see it. Is it that blurry looking cloudy bit?"

"Yes, that's it. Beautiful, isn't it, Ritchie?"

We stood there caught in the moment. Glad to share the moment with him, I let it go on until I heard the music from the disco end. We hurried down the path before it was filled with over-excited teenagers.

It was quiet when we arrived back at the cabins. I rubbed his arm affectionately and said goodnight. That was about as much as I could do.

It was all over too quickly, and by Friday afternoon we were back in

Kensington. A cab came to pick him up, his mother apparently abroad and unable to greet him. We said a quick goodbye, and when he was driven away, I felt hollow inside. An emptiness that I wasn't accustomed to took hold.

Chapter Three

It was the beginning of November. I had been working with Ritchie for almost three months. It was his birthday on Saturday and I was wondering what to get him. I wasn't meant to buy presents for the students, as it showed favouritism. But we obviously shared a bond. I decided on making a beaded hematite bracelet for him with gold findings.

Thursday night, I sat down with the crimping pliers and the cutting pliers and made the bracelet. I put it in a box with a note. I was planning to give it to him Friday lunchtime.

He was sitting where we normally sit, by the window, and as usual he had a tub of strawberries waiting for me. We began eating, and my heart nearly jumped out of my chest when his fingers accidentally brushed mine when he reached for a strawberry. I was so preoccupied that I forgot to give him his present. I didn't remember until home time. I would be tutoring him that night anyway, so I thought I would give it to him then. We decided this Friday would be a good evening for tutoring, as neither of us had any plans and he desperately needed to study for mock exams in December.

As soon as I saw him waiting outside the gate, I said, "Oh, I completely forgot to say happy birthday, Ritchie. You've hit the big eighteen!"

"It's not until tomorrow, though! And how do you know it's my birthday?"

"It's on your file. And I won't see you tomorrow, that's why I'm saying happy birthday today."

"Oh. Actually, I was wondering… "

I waited for him to finish, but he said nothing.

"You were wondering what?"

"Are you free tomorrow?"

"Think I'm free for most of the day. Why?"

"Um... would you go to the cinema with me? It's just that I don't really have anyone to ask and you're my only friend. Sorry. I'm pathetic, aren't I?"

He looked close to tears when he said this. To tell the truth, he was probably my best friend too. I was just a bit worried we would be crossing the line, as it wasn't education related.

"Would your mum mind?"

"You can say no if you want."

"No, it's not that. She might not approve. I would love to meet up with you tomorrow. You're not pathetic, you're great, Ritchie." I reached over and patted his back. "Please don't get upset. Ask your mum. If she says yes, then I'm there."

"You don't have to meet me if you don't want to."

Starting to feel slightly annoyed, I replied, "What did I just say, Ritchie? I want to meet you; there's no one else I'd rather hang out with tomorrow."

"Not even your boyfriend?"

"No, he's working tomorrow. I'll spend time with him on Sunday."

"Have you told him about me? How does he feel about you tutoring me?"

What a random question. One with hidden meaning behind it, perhaps.

"He thinks it's good, because I'm getting paid for it at a decent rate."

"You're not getting paid for tomorrow though."

I wondered if his self-esteem was so low that he couldn't believe I wanted to see him in my free time.

"He won't mind," I said, hoping that the conversation was over.

***

As soon as we arrived, we went up to his room. Then I remembered the bracelet.

"Oh yeah, I have something for you," I said as I handed the small black box to him.

"You didn't have to get me anything, Francesca."

"I know, but I wanted to make you something. I hope you like it."

He opened it and said, "Did you really make this? You're really talented. Is there anything you can't do?"

That put a smile on my face. Who doesn't like a bit of flattery? "I'm sure there's lots of things I can't do."

"I don't normally wear bracelets, but I'll wear this all the time. Thank you. This means a lot to me."

He stood there indecisively for a few seconds, as if pondering whether to do something. What he did next caught me by surprise. He impulsively kissed me on the cheek and thanked me again. I was completely unprepared. My heart thumped violently and my groin started throbbing. My chest felt so tight that I thought I was going to have a panic attack. I had to take a deep breath and managed to say, "You're welcome."

It was so intoxicating being close to Ritchie. I would often imagine all these scenarios and picture it all so vividly. My mind would drift back to the residential trip, and it seemed like none of it had happened, now we were back to our normal routines. Perhaps I had imagined the whole thing. I sometimes wondered what I was turning into. Was it natural to feel this way, in terms of biology and evolution? To be attracted to a youthful, virile young man? Or was it just downright creepy and weird? Ritchie didn't seem to mind having me around though. In fact, he didn't seem to mind in the slightest. Then again, teenage boys are full of raging hormones, and in most cases I'm sure any female company would be desirable.

"Can't believe you're eighteen now," I commented, to get out of my thoughts.

"I can do all sorts of things now," he answered with a cheeky grin on his face. There was a twinkle in his eye, and I wondered if there was more to that comment.

"Yes, you can."

He took his books out of his bag and switched the laptop on. We just got on with work for a while. I was glad to have a task to focus on, as I'd got a little bit worked up. Ritchie changing his top in the same room really didn't help either.

"Excuse me for a second; I just need to change my top."

I know I shouldn't have, but I watched as he unbuttoned his shirt and took it off. His back arched slightly as he pulled a white T-shirt on. He was fairly well-toned, but in a sort of natural way. I guess swimming club and tennis club helped with that. He turned slightly and I know he caught me looking from the corner of his eye. I immediately looked away.

"Oh no, I didn't realise it was so late. I better go," I blurted out. It was nearly eight in the evening.

"Don't worry. I'll ask mum to pay you the extra two hours."

"No, there's no need." I had to get out of there.

"It's okay, you know." I wasn't sure if he was referring to me watching him change or me accepting extra pay.

"I'm off now. Why don't you give me a ring tomorrow after nine to let me know what your mum says about us meeting? Here, let me write down my number."

I couldn't sleep much that night. I kept replaying the kiss and the shirt scene over and over again. I know I was probably reading way too much into it. He couldn't possibly have any feelings for me, could he?

***

Just before nine, I received a call from an excited Ritchie. When I say excited, I mean slightly more upbeat that usual.

"Mum says it's fine if we meet up."

I was a little surprised, but really looked forward to seeing him.

"Okay, great."

"I think she's glad to have someone babysit me 'cos I'm such a loner."

"Well, maybe she's glad that you won't be alone. I can meet you at the cinema around one-ish. See you then."

I did my housework at the speed of light that morning, so that I would have enough time to get ready. I didn't normally dress up all that much, as I was a bit of a tomboy. That was probably why I had always been accused of being a lesbian during my teen years. I just picked out a nice fitted white shirt and navy jeans. I conditioned my hair and did my nails – that was about as girly as I got. I really hoped he thought I looked nice. I left for the train station.

I nervously stood outside Camden Town Station. I saw him coming out. He hadn't seen me yet, so I took that moment to indulge. I drank in his blue jeans, dark green shirt and sand-coloured jacket. I loved the way his hair swayed in the breeze. He looked fantastic. How did he make everything he wore look so good? I looked dowdy in comparison to him.

Before he even had a chance to say hello, I blurted out, "You look great, Ritchie."

"Thank you. You don't look so bad yourself," he said as he looked at me from top to bottom, which made me feel self-conscious.

As we started walking, I could see him out of the corner of my eye staring at me. I hoped I didn't have snot hanging out or sleep in the corner of my eyes. I turned toward him.

"I just realised how long your hair really is," he said. "It looks lovely. I bet it feels really soft."

That took me right off guard. I just needed a moment to process what just happened. I actually stopped walking. I could feel butterflies in my stomach. *His* hair looked great, especially the way the sun made it shine. I wanted to run my fingers through it. I pictured tugging on it in the throes of passion. Did he *really* think I was attractive? *Play it cool, Francesca. Stop being obvious.*

"Thanks, but it won't last for long. I've got quite a few greys now."

"You don't have any greys. You're too young. I know you're not supposed to ask a woman her age, but how old are you?"

Being way too honest for my own good, I said, "I'm almost thirty, Ritchie."

He took such a deep breath, I thought he was going to hyperventilate. I thought, *Yes, that's the way to do it. Kill him with shock.*

"No, I don't believe it. You look much younger. Around twenty-four or twenty-five?"

"Well, I'm not. I'm an old lady compared to you."

"You are *not* old."

We arrived at the cinema. Ritchie bought us popcorn and slushies and we sat down to watch the movie. I had quite a boyish taste in movies, so I was glad it was an action movie and not some mushy romcom.

I enjoyed the movie, but I was a little preoccupied. All I could think of was how Ritchie's arm was touching mine as we shared the arm rest and how his hand kept brushing mine as we both reached for popcorn. I was too aware of every minute moment of physical contact. He never moved his arm or hand when we accidentally touched. Maybe it was my imagination, but I got the feeling that Ritchie enjoyed it too.

At the Mexican restaurant, we sat at a corner booth. I liked that because it was more private and there was less chance of being recognised. Even though we had chosen an area away from where we lived, it was still a possibility. We chatted about the movie and ordered food and cocktails. We had about two drinks each and they went straight to our heads. I could have sworn that, throughout the evening, he inched closer and closer – so close, in fact, that I felt his knee touch mine. Embarrassingly, I felt myself becoming moist, and that was when I decided we needed to part ways and go home. I was also worried that his mum or someone we knew would see us.

"Look, I'm glad you're enjoying yourself, but we've got to call it a night."

"Oh, come on. This is the best birthday I've had for a long time. It's only nine; can't we stay a bit longer?"

"Sorry, Ritchie. We're lightweights. Your mum would not be happy with me if she could see you now."

"But, Francesca, I'm eighteen now and she doesn't have to know. I won't say a word."

I wondered what he was getting at, but I didn't allow myself to consider the weight of his words and what they really meant.

"I have to go now." I think he sensed that I wasn't going to give in, as his expression changed.

"Okay, okay, you're right. I'll get the bill," he replied sombrely.

"No, Ritchie, let me pay half at least."

"You've done so much for me, so please let me get this."

"If you're sure?"

He softly laid his hand on top of mine and gently replied, "I am."

I felt so touched by his kind words and impressed by his maturity. It was hard to believe he was just eighteen.

As we left the restaurant, I looked around, hoping that nobody we knew had seen us. Losing my job would have meant not being with Ritchie, and that part scared me the most.

Chapter Four

The next few weeks seem to fly by, and before we knew it, it was almost Christmas. Things had been a bit quiet. Maybe it was because his mum had been in a lot more often when I tutored him, and I purposely suggested that we study downstairs. I was partially glad, because he had mock exams coming up and the last thing we both needed were distractions.

The last day of term was December twenty-first and Ritchie had invited me for dinner the following evening. Apparently, he was going to cook Spaghetti Bolognese. I had cooked for him a few times when I'd tutored him – things like steak, pork chops or salmon fillet. I'd also brought containers of food from home that my boyfriend or I had cooked. He seemed to think I was a good cook and said he'd like to return the favour. Of course, I said yes, even though his mum was going to be there.

This was the night that things really changed. When I arrived at the house, Ritchie led me straight into the dining room. His mum was already seated but was preoccupied with her phone. She seemed restless, although she did say hello to me. Then she snapped out of it and offered me a glass of wine. I hardly ever drank wine, but I said yes. I noticed she poured Ritchie a glass too. I wasn't sure if that was a good idea, as he was even more of a lightweight than I was.

"Well, here it is," announced Ritchie as he walked in with our plates. "I'm not much of a cook, but I tried to follow the recipe."

"It looks delicious, Ritchie," I said.

"Yes, it does look nice," added his mum.

We ate in silence, mostly. His mum just picked at the food. In fact, there was a bit of an atmosphere. It was obvious that they didn't usually spend much time together. Although she was the one who broke the awful silence.

"Richard tells me that he's coming along really well with his coursework and revision."

"Yes, he's really putting the effort in."

"If you're free during the holidays, I'll pay you to tutor him for a few days. I just don't want things to slide. He needs the motivation." She spoke about him like he wasn't there. He just sat and stared at his plate.

"Of course, I'd be happy to."

"We're leaving tomorrow for Bath and we'll be staying there until Boxing Day. We have family there, you see. Any time after that would be fine."

She then announced that she was running late and that she'd already made plans with a friend. She said I was welcome to stay a while longer, as it was only six. I helped Ritchie wash up.

"I've got something for you, Francesca," he said, when we walked back into the sitting room. He picked up a box from under the Christmas tree and handed it to me. It was a jewellery-sized box. My heart started to beat just a little bit faster, as I wondered what was inside.

"Open it."

I did. It was a black mother-of-pearl pendant set in silver. I'd been looking for one of those for ages. He must have seen me searching for it online or heard me mention it.

"It's beautiful. Thank you so much."

"Oh, I'm so glad you like it. It's a one-of-a-kind piece, especially for you. I was so worried that you wouldn't like it."

"I love it, Ritchie. I hope you didn't spend too much."

"You're worth it." That meant it was expensive. I wondered if his mum knew that he'd bought the necklace.

"I've got something for you too. It's nothing special though." I had bought him some Blu-rays and a couple of shirts.

"Cool. I haven't seen these movies and these shirts are exactly the right size. Thanks!"

"Merry Christmas, Ritchie," I said as I got up to give him a hug. Next minute he was hugging me back. The hug went on for a bit too long. It suddenly felt very hot in that room, or was it just me? I was the one who broke it. I hoped my expression didn't give me away. I really wanted to hold him again. Why did I break away? I should have waited for him to end it, but I knew I had done the right thing.

"Would you like some more wine?" he asked eagerly.

"No, thanks. I don't really like wine."

"We have spirits."

Oh, to hell with the right thing. "I guess I could have a rum and coke."

"I'll see what I can do."

I sat on the settee, and when he returned with two drinks, he sat beside me. We chatted for quite a while about normal things, and then the conversation became more personal.

"I think my mum thinks I'm gay. She asked me if I liked girls the other day."

"I know how that feels. Everyone thought I was a lesbian at one point."

He laughed when I said this, but then his expression changed. "She's set me up on a date."

"Maybe you'll enjoy it."

"Maybe. I would really like to have a girlfriend, though." He looked down at his drink and uttered, "I get so lonely sometimes."

"You're only eighteen. You'll find somebody one day. Sometimes you have to wait for someone decent to come along."

"No one decent would ever want me. I've got nothing to offer, apart from money, I guess."

"Don't be so ridiculous. You've got loads to offer. Any woman would be lucky to have you."

"Do you really mean that?"

How could he not know how great he was?

"Of course I do. If I was your age, I would have had such a huge crush on you. Not only are you handsome, but you're a lovely person. It's hard to find someone like that."

"You think I'm handsome?" He smiled then, but it faded quickly. He took a deep breath and asked, "Well, how come I've never even kissed a girl before?"

For some reason, I automatically licked my lips when he said this. And for some reason, Ritchie stared right at them unflinchingly, making his thoughts crystal clear. When he saw me staring back, he lowered his head and swallowed hard; his eyes widened slightly because he knew that he'd been caught.

My heart pounded as mixed feelings flooded me. A strange combination of desire and sympathy hit me. His inexperience and innocence made me want to 'teach' him or 'help' him in some way. This, along with the alcohol, gave me courage.

Watching his reaction carefully, I slowly and deliberately asked, "Has anyone ever told you that you have beautiful eyes?"

While staring down at his hands, he opened his mouth to answer, but didn't. This time, I had caught him off guard.

Almost inaudibly, he asked, "Has anyone ever told you that you have beautiful lips?" He slowly raised his head and turned to see my reaction.

I knew this moment would have come eventually. I knew I could have just walked away. We both waited for the other, unsure of what to do.

Leaning in slightly, he added, "I-I'm sorry, I just have to do this."

Before I even had time to comprehend what was happening, his lips were on mine. I sat there frozen for a second, but I couldn't resist his silky smooth lips. I gently placed my hand on his shoulder and pulled him closer. His kisses were a bit stiff at first, but he mimicked the way I moved my head and the way I caressed his lips with mine. The kisses became more urgent and passionate. My groin ached and throbbed. It was too much. I had to pull away.

"No, please don't stop," he pleaded breathlessly. "That was amazing."

"No, Ritchie, I can't do this."

"Why not? I won't tell anyone."

I was annoyed with myself for crossing the line and frustrated that I couldn't control myself. I was seriously in the shit now. If anyone found out, my life was over. I came to my senses.

"I'm sorry. I shouldn't have done that. I've got to go."

"Please don't go. It was my fault. Please stay."

I suddenly felt deflated, sat down heavily on the settee and put my head in my hands. When Ritchie sat beside me, I looked up into his eyes, willing him to understand.

"Look, Ritchie. I'm going to be honest with you. I really like you. And I mean *really* like you. Do you understand what I'm saying?"

"Yes I do, but that's okay, Francesca. I really like you too." He reached over to touch my arm. "You're a beautiful woman."

I almost reeled from the overwhelming wave of dizziness that hit me. I had to focus on breathing as I tried to take in that he'd just called me beautiful. I just didn't have the strength to deal with it then and there. I wasn't used to hearing that – even from John.

"I can't do this." I stood up a bit too suddenly and gathered my things. Ritchie didn't object to my hasty departure.

I never did tutor him during the holidays. I contacted his mum and made up a story about a sick relative. I'd wait until January to face him.

***

Luckily, the first day back was an inset day. That would give me one more day to mentally prepare for Richard Cunningham. I threw myself into work and pretended that the training was interesting and useful. I spent the afternoon trying to help sort out the library. I was almost sad when the day was over. I wasn't quite sure if I was ready for the next day.

Tuesday morning, I was so nervous that I could see myself physically shaking. I normally dealt with stressful situations well, but this was a whole new level of stress. I knew it was my own fault for becoming too attached to Ritchie. And there he was waiting outside English class. Damn, he looked gorgeous. Why did he have to be so bloody good-looking?

We walked in and sat down in silence without saying hello to each other. He kept sneaking glances at me like he wanted to say something. Test results were being handed out. That was when he finally spoke to me.

"Look at my results. I passed!"

"Ritchie, that's great! All your hard work has paid off."

"Thanks to you," he said humbly.

When Michael overheard what we'd said to each other, he gave both me and Ritchie the dirtiest look. He sneered as he said, "You only passed because *she* did the work for you." He actually pointed at me when he said 'she'. All I heard was Ritchie's chair fall to the ground. I realised he was going for Michael. By the time I had processed that, he was grabbing Michael's collar.

"Apologise to her right now!"

"Ritchie, please let him go. I'll deal with him." I observed how his jaw tensed in an attempt to listen to what I was saying.

Through clenched teeth, he replied, "He's being rude to you."

I stood really close to him and looked him dead in the eyes. Using a calm voice, I said, "I know he is, but am I letting it bother me?" He searched my face with his eyes while he thought about this.

"Please let him go." He allowed me to pry his hands off Michael's collar and lead him back to his chair.

"Sir, Richard attacked me!"

"Michael, you provoked him," I accused.

"Don't listen to her. She's just an LSA."

I wasn't going to stand for that, so I retorted, "How dare you speak to a member of staff like that. Hand me your diary right now, so I can give you a detention."

"I will not. Who are *you*?" This was going from bad to worse.

"I'm a member of staff, and when you come to school, you agree to a contract that you sign at the beginning of the year which states 'I will be respectful towards any member of staff and students alike'. Now, hand me your diary." He reluctantly handed me his diary and I gave him a detention. The teacher then sent Michael to the deputy head's office.

When I sat back down next to Ritchie, he asked, "Are you okay?"

"Oh, don't worry about me. I'm fine."

Just then, Ritchie was called to the head teacher's office. I went with him. He seemed really worried.

"Don't worry, Ritchie. You were provoked, and I'll explain exactly what happened."

"What if I get excluded?"

"You won't. You didn't even hurt him." Although secretly, I was also worried that he might get excluded.

Ritchie was asked to go into the head teacher's office alone, but he refused. He would only go in if I went with him. And so I did. He sometimes found it difficult to communicate, especially when he was upset, and I didn't want him getting violent in front of the head teacher. He was improving so much. He didn't need any setbacks. Despite what had happened between us, I still really cared about his education.

Luckily, they decided that Michael was more to blame than Ritchie. However, they both had to attend Saturday detention – every student's nightmare.

At lunchtime, Ritchie hesitantly approached the table I was sitting at with a tub of strawberries in his hand.

"Do you mind if I sit here?"

"Of course I don't mind if you sit here." In fact, I was glad he wanted to sit there.

"I wasn't sure if you'd want to speak to me."

I looked at him with disbelief. If only he knew the truth.

"I couldn't stay from you, even if I tried." There was a short silence while Ritchie absorbed this admission of mine. Then he offered me something in return.

"I thought about you a lot during the holidays, Francesca."

"I thought about you too, but I just couldn't face you. I shouldn't have told you how I felt."

"No, I'm glad you did. Did you mean it?"

To ensure that we were on the same page, I asked, "Did I mean what?"

"You know, that you like me in that way?" He had to come right out and say it, didn't he? I closed my eyes and took a deep breath.

"Yes." I owed him the truth at least.

An endless moment of silence followed. He looked down at the strawberries, as if they had the answers. After some time, he lifted his head and looked at me. I felt like he looked right through me and into my soul.

"When we kissed, I think I knew for sure. I could feel it. I've always been attracted to you too." My vision blurred and I had to blink a few times. Was this really happening? Did he say what I thought he said?

"The big question is where do we go from here, Ritchie? Maybe I should look for another job."

"No! No, you can't leave me. Please stay until I leave. I can't do it without you. Please don't worry. I won't say a word."

"I want to stay, but we've got to put our feelings aside. It might just be a passing thing. It's probably just a crush."

"I think it's more—"

It was Joseph who interrupted that awkward moment. Good thing he had Asperger's, because he was completely oblivious.

"Miss, my friend isn't in today. Can I sit at your table?" Joseph always brought a smile to my face.

"You're more than welcome, Joseph. I'd like you to meet Richard."

"Hi, Richard. I've heard a lot about you. Did you get sent to the head teacher's office today?" he asked nosily.

"Hi, Joseph. Yes, I did get sent to his office," Ritchie replied, whilst giving me a questioning look, wondering how Joseph already knew.

"What was it like? I've always wanted to get sent to the head teacher's office, but I'm too well behaved. I never get told off," he whined. What a character.

Ritchie and I laughed at the same time. It felt like a load had been lifted. Although I was quite embarrassed about what I'd done with Ritchie, in a way, I felt relieved that I had got my feelings off my chest.

The rest of the day seemed to go by really fast, and at home time, Ritchie was waiting for me outside the gate. He was smiling. I hate to admit it, but my heart skipped a beat yet again and I knew things weren't over between us.

Chapter Five

We didn't mention what happened that night for a long time. The whole thing had given me a scare. I'd been careful not to put myself in that position again. Ritchie hadn't pushed, respecting my distance. I even tried to make him lose interest by urging him to take up his mum's offer and she'd actually arranged a date for him. Apparently, she'd been so relieved that he wasn't gay. I have to admit, I still struggled with my feelings. We were still really close, though. I was curious to see whether or not having a young woman in his life would change things. It was for our own good really.

"So, do you think I should go?" Ritchie asked apprehensively.

"Yes. Definitely."

"But I've never been on a date before."

"So? There's a first time for everything." I really wanted him to go and be a normal teenager.

"I kind of know her already, but this is an official 'date.'"

Curiosity got the better of me. "Tell me about her. Who is she?" *And is she good enough for you*, I silently added.

"Her name is Casey and her family have known mine for a long time. They always used to joke that we would get married one day. We're the same age and we hung out a couple of times when we were younger. I haven't seen her for a while, though."

Even though I wanted him to be happy, I wasn't sure if I wanted to hear any more. Part of me wanted him to forget me and move on, yet another part didn't want him to find someone else, afraid that he would forget and move on. So, I just said, "Okay, well let me know how it goes. Good luck."

We finished our lunch and headed to science class. He'd been moved up from the bottom set to the middle set. I was so proud of him. I had to support Ritchie and his table group, as they all needed support in this lesson. I noticed that he became a little possessive when I worked with other students in his class. He was used to working alone or with an adult, but because his behaviour had improved, he was expected to work with other students more. Now I didn't have to focus so much on him. At times, I felt like he asked for help when he didn't really need it. I think it was more of a safety thing. He was still socially awkward.

Sometimes, I still caught him looking at me when he thought I couldn't see him. I pretended that I never noticed. I was still very aware of his presence. I still got butterflies when I looked into his eyes, and my heart dropped when we made accidental physical contact. I noticed that he blushed when these things happened. I put it down to raging teenage hormones. If only he knew how much I yearned for him when I was alone with my thoughts.

The weekend came and went, and I kept wondering how his date went. He was standing outside the LSU when I arrived at work. I opened the empty one-to-one room, which was normally used for counselling, so we could speak privately.

"So, how was it?"

"Okay, I guess." He blushed as he said this.

"Is she pretty? What kind of personality does she have?"

"Yes, she's pretty. Not sure how much I like her though."

I felt a slight stab of jealousy when he said she was pretty, but I didn't let it show. I wasn't going to stand in the way. If he ever did get a girlfriend, then I would have to accept that and support him.

I asked him cheekily, "Did you get to first base?"

"Yeah, we kissed, if that's what you mean," he replied with a slight grin on his face.

"Sounds like it went better than okay then."

"The kiss was okay, but we didn't talk that much."

I was going to offer some supportive advice, but then I got a slightly panicked feeling and decided against it. He was going to slip through my fingers soon, and I had to stand by and watch him drift away. I could feel a lump in my throat forming at the thought.

Robotically, I said, "I'll see you second period in science class, Ritchie." Doing the right thing sucked sometimes.

I was supporting Stuart first thing. He was a difficult one to support, as he had short term memory problems. When you thought he was finally learning something, he'd forget everything you'd taught him ten minutes later. I was in the middle of trying to explain improper fractions when I was interrupted by Sue. I stepped outside, and she explained what had happened. There had been another incident in Ritchie's art class. He'd ripped up his work and run out of class. He still didn't have full control of his emotions, and when he lost it, he really lost it.

I went to look for him. I found him sitting on the stairs near the exit. He was really crying this time. I just sat next to him and put my arm around him. I was aware that the bell was going to go very soon – the hall would be packed, and Ritchie would just find that too overwhelming.

"Ritchie, I know you're upset, but the bell is going to go very soon. Please come to the one-to-one room, where you can have some privacy."

A moment later, he stood up, half covering his face, which was covered with tears.

The one-to-one room was being used, so I brought him to the LSU, which you could partition. I brought him some tissues and a glass of water and led him to a chair. I placed my chair right in front of him. I gave him a minute, and then I held his wrists to try and pull his hands away from his face. He turned his face away.

"You don't need to hide from me, Ritchie."

He allowed me to move his hands, and I reached out to wipe a tear from his face with my thumb. I felt a great love toward him as I did this. I wasn't sure what that meant.

"What happened?"

I was still holding his right hand, so I gave it a gentle squeeze and stroked it with my thumb. He closed his eyes and squeezed my hand back.

"It was that dickhead, Michael. He kept making comments about my work. I tried to ignore him like you said. I tried and tried. I just couldn't take it. I wanted to hit him so badly, so instead I ripped up my work. It was shit anyway. I walked out so I wouldn't hit him. I could fucking kill him!"

I had never seen Ritchie this angry before. He was shaking with rage, and tears of anger still slid down his face. It just wasn't fair. He was always being picked on by this bully. The school hadn't done anything about it yet.

"I know you don't want to hear this, but you did the right thing by walking away. I'm sure your work wasn't shit, though." I handed him another tissue. As he wiped away tears, he asked, "What's wrong with me, Francesca?"

"There's nothing wrong with you. I think you're amazing. You know how I feel about you."

"How come you're the only one who likes me?" There were so many ways to answer that. In the end, I chose the simplest one. "Because they don't know you like I do."

"You're my only friend, Francesca." I felt the sting of tears forming in my own eyes and so I looked away. There were so many things to like about him, and I hated seeing him this upset.

"And you're my *best* friend, Ritchie." He really was. The person I could talk about anything with and spent most of my time with. When he saw that I was upset too, he stroked my hand and became silent for a while. Eventually, he asked, "Why am I like this?"

"It's hard when you feel things so deeply."

"I'm an absolute wreck – pathetic and stupid."

I detested his self-hatred. I could feel my own anger rising.

"Don't you ever say that about yourself. You're a passionate person and you feel things very deeply. If I don't think you're pathetic or stupid, then whose opinion do you value more? Mine or his?" He looked taken aback because I rarely became annoyed with him. But, before he had time to respond, there was a knock on the partition, so I slid it open. It was Sue and Philip.

"His mum is here now. We've called an emergency meeting. Has he told you what happened?"

"Yes, he did."

I could hear Beth's voice in the corridor saying, "I want to see my son." She stormed in and demanded to speak to Ritchie alone, but he wouldn't say anything. So I tried to explain what happened to his mum. Nevertheless, she was not happy.

"This is not the first time that he's been picked on, and if you think I'm going to stand by and watch my son being bullied, you've got another thing coming."

I was impressed. She was genuinely concerned for her son, and you could tell that she wasn't going to back down until they did something about it. Good.

"I want to know why Michael's parents haven't been called."

Sue and Philip looked lost for words, because they knew it was true. They needed to tackle this problem right now.

"We're going to call them now," decided Philip.

Half an hour later, we were all sitting in the meeting room. I urged Ritchie to tell them what had happened, and with some prodding, he finally explained why he had lost his temper. It was meant to be a comforting gesture, but when I touched his arm, I saw how his mum stared at me. I hoped she couldn't see beneath the surface. They were both quite observant sometimes.

Luckily, the staff and Michael's parents agreed that Michael shouldn't have provoked Ritchie. Michael was to attend counselling twice a week, as Ritchie already did, and volunteer as a peer buddy for the Year Sevens. He did not take it well. I laughed quietly to myself when I saw his expression.

***

Ritchie was absent the next day and I felt so lost without him. I was told to adjust my timetable, which meant I was to support Joseph and Stuart all day. I liked working with them, but I kept worrying about Ritchie.

After school, I decided to go and see him. I knew it wasn't a good idea to arrive unannounced, but I had to see him. The housekeeper opened the door and told me that Ritchie was in his room.

He was lying on his bed, staring at the ceiling, as I walked in. Without looking at me, he said, "Hi, Francesca."

"How are you? Were you ill?"

"I don't know – ill in the head maybe."

I stupidly went and lay next to him. We both ended up staring at the ceiling. I knew it was a bad idea, but I did it anyway.

"I missed you today."

"I missed you too, but I just couldn't face school today. I needed to calm down."

"Fair enough. As long as you're okay."

"I'll be okay now that you're here."

"Good." Deciding to try and change the subject, I asked, "So… um, do you have any dating plans this weekend."

"Not really in the mood."

"I thought it might get your mind off things. The last one seemed to go really well."

"She's just not you, Francesca."

"What's that supposed to mean?"

"Sorry, I know we were trying this 'denying how we feel about each other' thing. I've got some bad news – it didn't work. When I was with her, all I could think of was you. When I kissed her, I closed my eyes and replayed that evening in December."

I could just feel the tension building up, and my heart felt like a drum beating louder and louder. I really wanted Ritchie to like me as much as I liked him, but a part of me hoped that he'd come to his senses. Then, maybe, I could have handled this whole thing better.

"Really? But I thought you liked her. You said she was pretty."

"Yeah, well, she is, but she kind of reminds me of my mum. Only cares about herself."

"That's not entirely true. Your mum really stuck up for you yesterday. She does care, Ritchie."

"Well, she's got a funny way of showing it. I still don't wanna be with someone like her."

He turned on his side to face me. I did the same thing. He began playing with my hair.

"I want to be with you."

"Ritchie, I thought we said—"

"I'm tired of pretending I don't care about you. It's so hard keeping my feelings locked away. Look me in the eyes and tell me you don't want me and then I'll never mention it again."

The room was so silent, yet the silence seemed loud somehow. I could hear the clock ticking. It was like that show *Countdown*. I only had thirty seconds to answer.

"I can't." Damn me and my honesty. Honesty always got me into trouble. I gave myself up to my feelings and I let them take me to unknown territory.

I let myself feel every moment with all my senses. I could hear his breath quicken, and I swear I could hear his heart thump louder and faster. I looked deep into his eyes and saw a never-ending sea of green. There was a pure passion for me. He could see into my soul the way I saw into his.

I did what I'd always longed to do. I ran my fingers through his hair. It was getting quite long now, past his ears. I loved it long. Yes, I thought. He *was* beautiful.

He guided my chin sideways and kissed my neck over and over again. I turned and raised my hand. I stroked his beautiful face, grabbed his neck and pulled him down towards me. I kissed him slowly and passionately on the lips, as he pressed his thigh into my groin, and then I felt just how much he really liked me.

He moaned slightly as I started breathing heavily. We got the shock of our lives when there was a knock on his bedroom door. I jumped up as fast I ever had in my whole life. I quickly ran into the en-suite bathroom while Ritchie spoke to the housekeeper. They seemed to be talking for what seemed like hours.

I freshened myself up when the talking seemed to have stopped. I walked out of the bathroom and realised that Ritchie must have stepped out. I sat on the bed and thought about what had just happened. We were walking a dangerous path now. Was it a path I was willing to take? I then remembered that I was meant to meet my boyfriend at the cinema that evening.

When Ritchie returned, I explained that I had plans. He looked a bit disappointed, but he was resigned to the fact that I had to leave. I think we both knew that we needed to stop before we did something we regretted. Perhaps it was a blessing in disguise. We reluctantly parted ways.

***

Even though I was in a world of my own, I actually enjoyed watching the movie. For a moment, it was like I'd dreamt the whole thing with Ritchie. Was this really happening? I'd always been so sensible, even as a child. I mean, I said I would never cheat on my boyfriend, but I'd betrayed him without a second thought. What kind of person was I? Would he sense what I'd done? I used to be a decent person. I never knew that I was capable of doing these things. What happened to me? I guess Richard Cunningham happened to me.

How I managed to act normal around John, I had no idea. We'd always had an okay relationship. He was twelve years older than me, but I'd always liked the fact that he was an intelligent, honest and worldly man. We had similar ideals and I trusted him completely. Oh, I hoped he'd never find out, and obviously I could never tell him. He'd had bad experiences in the past with his exes. I wasn't sure if he could handle something like this. He also had a bit of a drinking problem and suffered from depression occasionally. I knew this would push him over the edge. And after all those years together, I did care for him, but I could feel myself falling for Ritchie. I used to laugh at women who said that they loved two men at the same time. I thought they were stupid bimbos, but maybe they were right after all.

No, Ritchie would be my secret and, funnily enough, I trusted him to keep our secret. I had always been a good judge of character, but not of my own, apparently. I knew Ritchie. Since the day I had first looked into his eyes, I think I knew him. It was like I'd left my body, entered his, and walked the corridors of his mind. Like a wonderland, there were so many things waiting to be discovered. He'd bared his soul to me, and he'd seen mine. No matter what happened to us in the future, he'd always be under my skin.

How silly this must sound to people. Oh, believe me, I knew that one day he might very well tire of me, get married and have children. Once he got his inheritance at age twenty-one, I might just be a distant, almost non-existent memory. I chose not to think of that day. I would cross that bridge when it came. For now, I would indulge. Breathe in the very essence of him, submerge myself in his world and his very being.

First thing on Monday, Ritchie was sitting at his bench in science class. He stared at me so intently as I walked into that class that I was a bit paranoid people would notice.

"Hi, Francesca."

I don't know how two words conveyed such suppressed emotion. The tension was there, and the spark had been lit. I sat down and we grinned at each other.

"Hi, Ritchie. How are you?"

I impulsively gave his thigh a squeeze, and he put his hand on top of mine when he said, "Oh, I'm more than fine. I've been looking forward to seeing you all weekend, and I've never looked forward to Mondays!" His expression became serious when he added, "I really didn't want you to leave on Friday."

"I know."

I withdrew my hand as the science teacher approached the bench with a textbook and the day's task. I began reading out the details, and when I turned to look at him, he was staring hungrily at my lips.

"Stop. I can see what you're doing."

"Stop what? Am I that obvious?"

"Yes. And you haven't heard a word I said."

He looked at me sheepishly and replied, "Uh, sorry. Wrong place, wrong time?"

It was a bit of a surreal morning. The calm after the storm. The air was still electrically charged, but carefully controlled. From time to time, I would look into his eyes and we would communicate like that. They oozed veiled passion. Although it made me feel a little bit uncomfortable, no one seemed to notice, and the voice in the back of my head faded. Maybe we could do this. For now, I'd just enjoy the tantalising atmosphere. We'd save it all for later, when the time was right.

When home time came, we were sad to say goodbye. I had to go to a doctor's appointment to get x-ray results. I'd been having back problems for years. It meant I'd have to tutor Ritchie tomorrow. He insisted on walking me to the train station and we allowed ourselves a moment of brief physical contact – a goodbye hug and quick kiss on the cheek. We tried not to let it linger.

Chapter Six

As the students entered the church for morning mass, I tried to spot Ritchie in the crowd. We normally attended mass on Monday morning, but it had been rescheduled for some reason. It was probably some kind of important announcement. Staff normally sat at the back during the service. I just wanted to catch a glimpse of him to relieve the boredom. This time, I actually heard him before I saw him.

"Who said that? I am not gay!"

Oh shit, that didn't sound good. I saw Year Eleven emerging through the door and immediately raced towards the sound of Ritchie's voice. I had to make sure that Ritchie didn't involve himself in another incident. His mid-year review was coming up and I wanted them to see how much progress he was making.

For some reason, it gave me a little thrill when he lost his cool in this way. He was so strong and intense. Strangely, I knew he would never aim that towards me. I kind of liked it when it was aimed at idiots like Michael. One problem, though, was that it could land him in a whole lot of trouble.

Next minute, I saw two boys behind Ritchie laughing mischievously. One pushed the other one into Ritchie, and that was when I tried to prevent what happened next. When he lost his temper, he really lost it. He grabbed the boy's collar.

"Ritchie, please make the right decision. It's not worth it," I said, whilst firmly holding his arm. I could feel his bicep rigid with strength. It was like he suddenly realised I was there, and he came to. He let him go just like that. The two mischievous boys grinned at each other as they rushed to their seats. Luckily, the incident hadn't been witnessed by many.

"Come and sit with me during service."

I led him to where his class were sitting, and I gave him a minute to collect himself when he sat down.

"He started it. He said I was gay."

"I know. I heard. You did the right thing when you let him go." I couldn't help but elbow him affectionately, and I was rewarded with a half-smile. That got me. Every time he smiled, it got me. My soft spot. My weakness. If only he knew how much control he had over me. It occurred to me that I might just about do anything for him.

Next period was English. It was tough. There was a forty-five-minute reading test, which meant I couldn't read anything for him. We walked to the one-to-one room and I reassured him that I could scribe for him if need be. I got him to read the questions to me twice, hoping that it might help, and although he misread a couple of words, he seemed to be doing okay. At a very slow pace, though. I had to keep reminding him to move onto the next question if he got stuck. When he was on the last question, the long answer question, he became fidgety and nervous. I decided to scribe for him at this point, as his hands were visibly shaking. Unfortunately, when he'd finally formed an answer, he'd already used up the extra fifteen minutes he was entitled to due to his statement. The test was over.

"I'm sorry, Ritchie, but your time is up." He looked so stressed that I was concerned he might run off.

"I didn't even finish the test, Francesca," he complained, sadly.

"Don't worry. I think you did okay."

"But I needed to finish the long answer question; that's where the most marks are awarded."

"It's just a mock, and it looks like you did really well on the other questions. That might get you a pass."

"The real thing is coming up soon. If I can't do it now, I won't pass it."

"I know you don't want to hear this, but the important thing is that you've tried your hardest."

"What if my hardest isn't good enough?"

"It is, Ritchie," I replied, frustrated. It was like no matter what I said, he was going to feel like a failure anyway.

"Stop this now. I hate seeing you like this. You tried really hard and I'm proud of you. Put yourself down as much as you want, but I have nothing but admiration for you. Back in the days, I retook maths twice. Can you believe that? At least you passed some of your GCSEs last year and you only have to get a few more. You can't tell me that the support I've given has been a waste of time. I believe in you. I wish that you could see what I saw."

Rant over, I took a deep breath to calm myself down.

He seemed to take in what I'd said. The tension seemed to fall away from his shoulders, and he relaxed a little. His face returned to its normal colour and he faced me.

"No one has ever said that they were proud of me."

"Well, I bloody meant it."

"Sorry, I'm so depressing sometimes. I shouldn't feel sorry for myself, but I just can't cope with things sometimes and all I can see is the negative side. Thank you for doing so much for me. I don't know why you care about me, but I'm very lucky to have you."

"You don't need to apologise, and there's so many reasons why I care about you. If only you knew."

"Knew what?"

I so wanted to tell him that I was falling for him big time. Luckily, I was saved by the bell.

Ritchie was a little quiet during art, but he was quite a good artist and I decided to give him a bit of space. To be honest, he didn't particularly need support in art. So I roved, offering help to those who needed it more. I had often demonstrated shading or blending techniques, which meant that I had earned a bit of a reputation.

I ended up getting a bit of a fever towards the end of the day and had decided to go home early, which meant that tutoring was cancelled for that night. It turned out to be a nasty cold and I stayed off for the rest of the week. I told Ritchie he could call me between four and six if he needed to speak to me. He called me every day that I was ill, and we talked about random things. I think he was making an effort to be more positive. There were a few times when I got the feeling that he wanted to say more, but he didn't. He asked if I could tutor him on Saturday if I felt better. And so it was on this occasion that his mum and I had an awkward, but very interesting, chat.

***

I was a little surprised when I pressed the doorbell and Ritchie's mum opened the door. He usually opened the door when I came to his house.

"Hi, Beth. How are you?"

"Oh, good, thank you. Richard just stepped out to buy some shopping.

He said something about cooking steak. Your influence, no doubt."

"A good influence, hopefully."

"Of course. Would you like some tea while you wait?"

"Yes, that sounds good."

"So, I've been meaning to ask you something."

I wondered if she had planned this. I knew something like this was going to come up soon, but I waited until she continued.

"You're quite close to Richard, and you spend a lot of time with him. I'm sorry to ask this, but do you think he's gay?"

"No, he definitely likes girls. He told me all about his date with Casey and I got the impression that it went well."

"Oh, thank goodness. I was beginning to worry. I'm not homophobic, but you don't understand what it's like in our family. He's already an outcast as it is."

I kind of thought that was homophobic, but I didn't comment. I could see she had more to say.

"You've been really good to my son."

"Well, he's a good student."

"In some ways, you've been his mother over the last six months. Richard
always had nannies when he was young, as I travelled often to avoid his father. You see, we didn't marry for love. He was a cruel man. You may be shocked to hear that I'm glad he's gone now."

I was surprised at how candid and open she was, but it was good to finally know more about Ritchie's childhood.

"Ritchie has never really spoken about his dad."

"They had no relationship at all. I suppose Richard and I don't have much of one either. I've not told many people this, but I regret that."

"It's not too late."

"Maybe it is." Abruptly changing the subject, she added, "So, tell me, have you ever been to Bath?"

"Yes, once. Mainly to see Stonehenge."

"Would you like to come with us to a family get-together? It's Richard's grandmother's birthday – she's turning ninety."

I was surprised at this invitation. "Are you sure?"

"Yes, I'm sure. Richard needs to continue studying. He's far too behind. He can't stay at St. Paul's for another year."

"Sounds good. I'd be happy to come along."

"And you'll have a chance to meet Casey."

Oh, great.

Saturday went by quickly. His mum was in and out of his room making arrangements with me for the trip, so Ritchie and I didn't have any alone time. We were to leave for Bath during the February half term, which was in one week's time.

Later that night, I told John about me staying with Ritchie's family for the week, and because he'd be working the late shift at the hospital, he didn't seem to mind. Beth was still going to pay me and for John, that was a good enough reason to go.

The weekend went by so quickly, and before I knew it, I was back at work. I had a meeting with the counsellor after lunch. Apparently, Karen had been working with Ritchie for almost two years and I wasn't sure what to expect. I was hoping she wouldn't question my relationship with him, but I was certain that he wouldn't have said anything.

"Nice to officially meet you, Francesca. I've seen you around, but we've not had a chance to meet properly."

"Nice to meet you too."

"Okay, this meeting is about our friend, Richard Cunningham, with whom you work very closely." Talk about stating the obvious.

"Yes, that's right," I replied, not really knowing how to respond.

"I have to say that Richard has been one of my most difficult cases. He has so many underlying issues and he doesn't like to address them. I tried a few different strategies, but he never opens up."

"Oh, I was under the impression things were going well, due to him showing improvement recently. But then again, he doesn't really tell me about his sessions with you."

"That's not surprising at all. He doesn't want to communicate. A case of possible mutism."

"I'm not sure about that. He does speak to me fairly openly, but I don't tend to question him, especially when he's feeling uncomfortable."

"Really? That's hard to believe."

"Well, it's true."

"Maybe you can help then. What kind of strategies have you used with him?"

"I guess I'm fairly open. I have a good sense of humour and I try to put myself in his shoes. I've tried not to patronise him and I've managed to find some common ground."

She probably didn't agree with my approach, but it had always worked for me. I had studied psychology, but obviously I wasn't a qualified counsellor. I began to see why Ritchie might not like her. She was presumptuous.

"As a counsellor, I need to keep boundaries. Your relationship is a bit different, as you work with him every day." She paused briefly, then added, "I think I'm going to end the sessions."

"I could talk to him if you want?"

"No, I don't think there's any point." I was a little bit annoyed that she'd given up on Ritchie. On the other hand, maybe he'd be pleased.

Karen must have spoken to Sue, because just before I left to go home, Sue asked me to stay for a bit.

"It seems like the sessions aren't going well. I suggested that you do the sessions instead. I had a look at your timetable and maybe we could take you off art and one period of geography. That way you would still be supporting him for the required twenty hours."

Although I was disappointed about not being able to support him in art anymore, I was happy to run the one-to-one sessions. In the past, I had run mentoring sessions, which was a type of counselling with primary school aged children. It was pretty intense stuff but could also be enjoyable.

"Of course, you'll have training with the counsellor after the February holidays."

I didn't leave until about four. Nevertheless, there Ritchie was, waiting outside the school gates. I decided against telling him about the counselling until I'd found out why it hadn't gone so well. When questioned, he looked away shamefully.

"I don't like her or those sessions. She keeps asking questions, and I don't want to answer them, especially if she's the one asking them."

"What if someone else does them?"

"I still don't want to." This was going to be a difficult one, I thought.

"Apparently, I'm going to do your sessions now." I let that sink in a bit. "I might have to ask you uncomfortable questions from time to time," I added.

"For you, I'll try, Francesca. But I've got a lot of issues – you might not like what you find."

"We all have issues. Almost anything you tell me is confidential, and it's only to help you."

"I find opening up really hard. I'm afraid to go there."

"I'm going to get training for it and then maybe we'll go there together, Ritchie."

"You don't need training. You're the best."

"Thanks, but Karen has a lot more training and experience. Are you really sure you're okay with me doing the sessions?"

"Yes," he said, with a note of finality.

"I truly hope I can help you."

He reached out to put his arm around me in a sort of half-embrace. I felt his warm hand on my waist and I couldn't help but get just a little excited.

"You will," he said. "You already have."

Chapter Seven

We were on our way to Bath, and for some reason, I was so nervous. Firstly about meeting his family, and secondly about spending time with him. Nothing had happened since that time when we'd kissed. I thought about it every night, and I'm sure Ritchie thought about it sometimes. I wasn't really sure what was going on between us at the moment. Maybe it had been a mistake, or maybe it was just hiding under the surface. I was afraid of myself. I had almost lost control the last time, because I'd wanted more than a kiss. What would I do if it happened again?

Ritchie and I sat in the back while his mother drove. She'd collected me from my flat, so I didn't have to worry about transport with a suitcase.

"How are you feeling, Francesca?"

"I'm fine, Ritchie. I just get a bit travel sick." I was also aware of the fact that his mum was looking in her rear-view mirror at us. She was quite observant sometimes and I wondered if she could read my thoughts. Was I that transparent?

I was very aware of Ritchie beside me for that whole journey. I kept seeing his hand on the seat next to mine and feeling this strange tingly sensation along my side that was nearest to him. It was that electric charge resurfacing again. Each time we made eye contact, I quickly turned away. I hoped that Ritchie didn't think I was deliberately avoiding him.

***

I couldn't believe the size of the house. It was more like a mansion. An actual butler came to greet us and take our luggage. We were all shown to our rooms and told to meet in the conservatory for pre-dinner drinks. Beth went straight to her room, but Ritchie lingered in the doorway. I know he was itching to come in. I could tell because he looked restless.

"Come in if you want, Ritchie."

"Do you mind?"

"Not at all."

He shut the door slowly and quietly. He stood, as if he was unsure what to do, like he was trying to build up the courage to ask me something. Finally, he asked, "Do you wish it never happened?"

Obviously, I knew what he was referring to, and I'd been wondering when we would finally talk about it. Still, the timing was a bit random, and it did catch me off guard a little bit.

"Because I don't, Francesca."

I stood by the window, looking out at the stunning grounds, and I got lost in my own world for a minute.

"I like you, Ritchie, but you'll get fed up with me soon. What could you possibly want with me?"

"How can you say that?" I felt his hand on my back, as he stroked my hair gently. "What don't I like about you?"

"Look at me. Look at you. Big difference."

"Are you trying to say that you're not good enough for *me*? I think you're incredible. And you're smart. *And* you're talented. *I'm* the one who can't compete with that."

I shook my head disbelievingly.

"Oh my god, you don't believe me, do you? I wish you could see how much you mean to me. And the amazing thing is that you care about me too."

"I care about you too much, though," I whispered.

"That's why I need you." His voice was laced with emotion.

All I wanted to do was hold him. I turned around and held him tight. It was such a simple embrace, but I think we both needed to physically feel comforted by one another. He took in the scent of my hair as I lay my cheek against the curve of his neck. He wrapped his hands around my waist and held me closer for what seemed like hours. I almost said that I loved him then, but I held it back. Although, deep down inside, I knew that I did love him.

Afterwards, when we had managed to break the embrace, Ritchie went back to his room. I mindlessly unpacked and freshened up.

I opened the door and was about to step out, when I saw an attractive young lady walking towards Ritchie's room. I guessed that it was Casey. A stab of jealously hit me and I quickly went back into my room. I felt a bit silly because she was a seventeen-year-old girl. I was almost thirty and I was acting like a schoolgirl. I knew that this was going to happen, and I shouldn't have been surprised. I decided that I would play it cool.

Soon after, I heard a knock on the door. Ritchie knew I wouldn't know where the conservatory was and escorted me there.

It was enormous, bright and plush. What it must be like to have access to that type of money. Quite a few people were sitting there – Ritchie's relatives, of course. Good-looking bunch, but the air felt unfriendly and repressed. They looked at me almost disapprovingly, like I had dressed wrong.

Ritchie could sense how I felt and whispered, "So this is my weird family." We both laughed a bit, even though it seemed out of place at the time.

The next hour was spent introducing myself and being bombarded with questions. Then, I finally met Casey. Instead of saying hello, she said, "I've heard a lot about you."

"I've heard a lot about you too." She raised her eyebrows when I said this – as if she didn't believe Ritchie would tell me about her. She also looked up and down at me in a way I can only describe as scornful. I began to think it was a mistake coming, but I'd only agreed to do this for Ritchie.

Ritchie's grandmother seemed pleased that I was helping Ritchie improve and was apparently a lot softer in her older years than she had been in her youth. Ritchie told me that, back in the day, she had pressured his mum into marriage with Ritchie's dad, who was also named Richard, by threatening to disown her. Beth ultimately forced herself to do the deed for financial reasons and her mother's approval.

When the meet-and-greet was over, we all moved to the biggest dining room I had ever seen. I sat beside Ritchie, and unfortunately, Casey was sitting on the other side. I wasn't particularly looking forward to this. She obviously didn't want me there. I guess I could understand why. All three of us hardly said a thing. Occasionally, Beth would ask Casey a question from where she was sitting, opposite us. I think she was trying to lighten the mood. I could tell that Ritchie was as uncomfortable as I was.

As soon as I could, I returned to my room. I felt so tired for some reason, so I decided to try and have an early night.

Later that night, there was a light tap on the door. I got out of bed and opened the door. Ritchie put a finger to his lips indicating for me to be quiet. I stepped aside and let him in. I was a little self-conscious, as I was naked under my oversized T-shirt.

"Sorry about my family. They're so retarded."

"No, it's fine. I'm just so tired and I was going to have an early night."

"Oh, am I disturbing you? Do you want me to leave?"

I pondered this for a second. I could do the right thing and say yes, or I could ask him to stay.

"I want you to stay, but we might get into trouble."

"No one knows I'm here." He kicked his shoes off and lay down on the bed. I then joined him and, as I lay down, I noticed Ritchie making no secret of the fact that he was looking at my legs.

"I've never seen your legs before. You don't wear skirts, do you?"

"No, it's been a long time since I've worn a skirt."

"You should. You've got great legs."

"Thanks." Suddenly, I didn't feel as tired as I had before. I was enjoying this. As I gazed into his eyes, I had a sudden impulse to say something cheeky. I went there.

"I don't have anything on underneath." It was quite amusing the way his jaw literally dropped. "Do you want to touch me?"

"Do you want me to touch you?" His husky voice dripped with desire.

"I wouldn't say it if I didn't want you too," I responded demurely.

Guiding his hand to my thighs, I initiated what followed. His fingers shook slightly at first, but he quickly became more confident. He explored each curve of my leg, running his fingers past my calf, over my knee and along the outside of my thigh. He was barely touching me, yet I felt goosebumps all over me and a delightful shiver ran down my spine. He drew his gaze from my thighs to my breasts. I looked down and saw that my nipples were erect. I began stroking my hard nipples in a circular motion with my fingers, while I fixed my eyes on Ritchie.

"Touch me here."

He cupped my breasts softly, as he fondled my hard nipples with his thumb. I could hear his breath quicken when he squeezed a little harder. I got up onto my haunches to unbutton his shirt. He observed with fascination as I ran my fingers along his chest, which was naturally broad with some definition, but not too built. He didn't have much chest hair, which is just the way I liked it.

I caressed his chest with both hands. My hair fell across him as I kissed his chest. From his belly button to his neck, I licked him, savouring the taste of him. Then I found his lips and I felt his hands on me, pulling me closer until I was on top of him. I could taste the lust on his hot tongue. The taste of him, the smell of him and the pressure of his erection consumed me, and I lost awareness of space and time.

He somehow ended up on top of me and I wrapped my leg around him. I wanted him to penetrate me. I imagined him thrusting into me right then and there. Suddenly, a nagging thought entered my mind, reminding me where I was and what I was doing. It was like a bothersome voice bringing me back to reality. Despite what we both felt, we had to slow things down.

I stopped and gently pushed him back. Playing with a lock of his hair, I smiled at him and said, "We better stop."

He put his head down coyly. "Am I getting carried away?"

"We both are."

We both lay on our backs, just thinking about what had just happened for a while. Staring at the ceiling. Again. All we could hear was the sound of our breathing, in rhythm with one another. I found myself snuggling his chest, listening to his heartbeat slowing down. We lay like that for ages until we fell asleep.

***

I woke up to a bright, sunny room, feeling uplifted like I had the best sleep ever. I realised Ritchie was on the bed, lying beside me. All the things that had happened last night flooded me and a thrill of guilt and pleasure flowed through me. He was still asleep with his lips slightly parted and I thought about how beautiful he was.

Sensing my movements, he stretched out and rubbed his eyes. With his eyes still closed he asked, "Was it a dream?"

"No, it wasn't, Ritchie."

He breathed a sigh of relief. "Good. Have you been up for long?"

"Not long. I hope I didn't wake you. I didn't want to disturb you. You looked so lovely."

"Me?" He laughed as if I was joking and genuinely didn't believe that.

"And I was thinking that I would love to draw you some time."

"I thought you didn't like doing portraits?" He got into a sitting position, giving me his full attention.

"I've never had a desire to do one until this very moment. You're such a beautiful man."

He hung his head modestly. "I feel kind of embarrassed actually. That's a huge compliment."

I gently lifted his chin up, so that I could see his eyes. "The most beautiful man I've ever seen."

His face reddened. "Thank you. You're the beautiful one – inside and out. You've been so good to me. I wish I could repay you."

"You don't owe me a thing."

"I received a small portion of my inheritance when I turned eighteen. Is there anything you want me to get you?"

"No. All I want is your company."

***

When Ritchie went back to his room, I had a wash and managed to find my way down to the dining room. It was like a hotel. I chose two croissants and some tea and headed back up to my room. I assumed it was okay to do that as I saw others do the same. I found it quite funny, like I was staying in a bed and breakfast. It was all very surreal.

A while later, Ritchie came to see if I'd already had breakfast. He and his cousins were going to head down to the pool, and he asked if I'd like to join them. I declined and suggested that he spend some time with Casey before she started feeling neglected. I was going to hang out in my room, maybe explore the enormous library and maybe read or draw on the balcony. He reluctantly agreed to go without me but said he would return at around lunchtime to begin tutoring.

Later, I stood outside his door knocking, but there was no answer. I checked to see if it was unlocked. I wasn't really sure if I should because Casey might be in there with him, but I couldn't hear any noises, so I turned the knob.

There were clothes strewn on the bed, only Ritchie's, and I could hear running water coming from the bathroom. I cautiously stepped in and called out, "Ritchie?"

"Francesca, is that you?"

"Yes," I answered. He stepped out of the bathroom with nothing but his underwear on.

"I was about to step into the shower."

"Oh, I'll come back later," I answered, trying not to draw attention to the fact that I was gawking.

"I'll only be a few minutes. You can wait if you don't mind."

I suddenly felt an overwhelming urge. Plucking up my courage, I impulsively made an alternative suggestion.

"Or… I could join you?"

What followed was what sounded like a hitch in the throat. I guessed that had caught Ritchie right off guard. Unable to disguise the fact that I had surprised him, he blurted out, "What – in the shower?"

"Well, yeah. Only if you want me to."

"Oh my god, *of course* I want you too. I just can't believe this is happening."

Enough of this small talk, I thought to myself.

"Would you like to undress me?" I gave him my 'come hither' look.

"More than anything," he answered in a thick voice.

"Come here," I coaxed.

He slowly approached me, and as he came closer, I noticed how dilated his pupils were. I felt flattered by the longing in his eyes. I never thought of myself as being beautiful, but the way he looked at me made me feel like the only woman in the world.

He stroked my face softly and, stealing a small kiss, he began unbuttoning my shirt. There was a slight intake of breath when he saw my breasts in their black plunge bra, which gave me a thrill of satisfaction. He then unzipped my jeans and I quickly kicked them off. The blood pumping through our veins was intoxicating. The moment intensified indescribably as our faces became flushed from heat and pure desire. I looked deep into his eyes and placed my hand on his chest to feel his heart beating powerfully. Even attempting to remove my bra a few times didn't ruin the moment, and once he managed to get it off, he stood there as if transfixed by my breasts. I then guided his hands to my underwear, which he proceeded to remove. He ogled my body hungrily.

"Wow," was all he could say as his eyes lingered on my naked body.

He reached out and caressed my breasts. He seemed to realise that he still had his underwear on. I could tell he felt a little self-conscious about removing them, but he did, and he had a decent enough package. Not huge, but a good size. I gave him a cheeky smirk when he saw me looking, and he returned the smile red-faced. He took my hand and led me to the shower.

We let the warm water cascade down our bodies. I found his lips with mine, firmly grabbing his buttocks while I kissed him. I ran my hand along his back whilst entwining my leg around his thigh. I caressed his hip with my inner thigh and pressed my groin onto him. He gasped with pleasure as he felt me rubbing against his naked flesh. He held my thigh against him and licked my neck. Oh, how I wanted him inside me. Instead, I pushed him back and gripped his erection. I massaged it firmly in a circular motion, up and down, whilst kissing him deeply on the mouth.

A few moments later, his breath started to quicken and become heavier as he started to orgasm. He threw his head back and groaned. I watched with utter and complete enthralment. After a while, he opened his eyes and put his forehead against mine, as if breathing me in.

"Oh, Francesca." We stood like that for a while as we tried to comprehend what just happened.

"We better start your tutoring."

He laughed. I knew it was because what I'd said was so random and out of context.

"But what about you?"

Obviously, I knew what he meant. I so wanted more, but I almost wanted the tantalising torture, the anticipation of what might happen next.

"Next time."

We finally turned the shower off and I stepped out first. Dripping wet, he stepped out next. Tendrils of wet hair covered his eyes until he pushed his hair back with his hands, opened his eyes and stared right back at me. It was only a small thing, but it was the sexiest thing I'd ever seen. Maybe it was the way he was standing, or the hot water rolling down his face, or the intensity of his gaze, but I ogled him from head to toe with no shame.

Chapter Eight

I decided that we should study in the library. It may sound like I was contradicting myself, but I didn't want Ritchie distracted by me during his studies. I chose the library as it was more public, and I wasn't going to risk doing anything there, besides what I was getting paid for. Also, his studies were very important to me. He didn't have much time left, and I was concerned that he wouldn't pass English. He had to pass this year, even if it meant leaving school and moving away from me.

I wasn't looking forward to that day though, because that might be the day I lost Ritchie for good. He had to explore, have new experiences, and perhaps meet someone new. He was considering taking a year out to travel to America, as he had family there. Apparently, Casey was hoping to accompany him, as she also had relatives in California. Although the thought saddened me, I knew Casey was better for him than I was. She was younger, more attractive, and socially accepted by his family.

My partner and I would move to Canada eventually and join his family's business, which was my dream. Or had been a few years ago. A chance to get out of the education sector, move away from London, and use my creative skills, which were being wasted. There would be no place for Ritchie in my life, would there? I kept telling myself this in the hope that we would be able to part ways and lead decent lives, and hope that nobody ever found out what we had done or what undoubtedly was going to happen. Why couldn't I just walk away now? It was because I loved him. Loved him with a desperate, obsessive need and a deep and dark desire.

Despite how I might feel, I had nothing to offer him. How could I stand in the way of him getting married someday, having a family and falling in love with the right person? Only distance and time apart might be able to break our destructive bond. I didn't have the strength to give

him up, yet if he no longer wanted me, that would be reason enough
for me to leave him alone.

We studied science until around six, and then he abruptly stood up
and said that he needed to go into town and that he would be back for
dinner at seven. He was a little evasive about why he needed to go so
suddenly, but I just hoped that he would be back by dinner time.

***

As dinner was being served, Ritchie arrived with a rucksack, looking
flushed in the cheeks. He sat between Casey and his mum. I was sitting
on the other side of his mum. He apologised for being late and tried to
make eye contact with me as if to say *Are you okay?* I gave him a slight
smile to reassure him that I was alright and had survived a whole
twenty minutes of uncomfortable conversation with his mum and Casey.
Knowing that Casey didn't particularly like me had made it worse.

Sensing the atmosphere between all of us, Beth tried to lighten the
mood by asking, "What did you need in town, Richard?"

"A book – *The History of Racism in Britain.*" Ritchie gave me a look,
communicating to me that I should play along.

"Oh, that book," I commented. I had no idea what book he was
talking about.

"Oh, I didn't realise you were studying that. Sounds interesting.
Luckily, you're just in time for dinner."

Beth hardly ate a thing and got up to talk to another lady who looked
a lot like her. I sat twiddling my thumbs for a while, extremely aware of
Ritchie's and Casey's awkward conversation. I could see that although
he was trying to make an effort to pay attention to her, he didn't look
all that interested in what she was saying. From what I could hear, she
was talking about what dress to wear to his grandmother's birthday
party the following day. His responses sounded wooden, like he didn't
really care what she wore. I bet she would look great though, whatever
she decided to wear. I wasn't even going to try to compete with her. I
knew the outfit I'd brought wasn't particularly flattering or expensive. It
was all I had, and I wasn't keen on spending money on something fancy.

After a while, I slipped away and back up to my room, leaving Ritchie
with Casey. I still didn't know why he'd gone into town. It was obvious
that he hadn't really bought a book, and he hadn't mentioned anything
earlier.

I decided to sit out on the balcony for a while to look at the moon. I usually loved looking at the moon and other celestial bodies. However, that night the moon seemed to be smiling mockingly, as if to say, *You're falling for him. He doesn't want you, he wants Casey, and he's not coming to see you tonight.*

I went back inside, as it suddenly felt a lot colder than it had a minute before, and got into bed. I left the door unlocked in the hope that Ritchie would come and see me later on that night, and eventually I fell into a restless sleep.

I woke up to a strange knocking sound. I reached over to put the lamp on and nearly got the fright of my life when I saw Ritchie opening the door. I half expected to see a ghost, because I was still half asleep. Feeling a little conscious of the fact that I probably looked a bit rough, I rubbed my eyes in an attempt to un-blur my vision.

"Sorry. I woke you, didn't I?" He approached gingerly.

"You did, but I wasn't sleeping very well anyway. I thought you weren't coming tonight."

"Casey was in my room for ages. I couldn't get rid of her."

"Maybe you should try to get to know her. Don't worry about me," I said, almost bitterly. I hadn't meant the comment to be negative, but it was laced with sarcasm. I felt annoyed with myself for being like that with him.

"We've got nothing in common, Francesca," he replied.

"What about tennis? You both like tennis. You have to give her a chance."

He obviously didn't like what I was saying. It was like he was having an internal battle.

"Please let's not talk about her now," he pleaded.

"Look, I'm not trying to tell you what to do. I just think she's better for you," I pushed.

"Please don't say that," he muttered resignedly.

Feeling a bit guilty for making him feel uncomfortable, I added, "I'm glad you came to see me tonight, though." I realised then that he had a box in his hand.

"I've got something for you."

He handed me a jewellery box. I wasn't expecting any gifts. I opened it, and inside was one of the most beautiful pendants that I had ever seen. It was an ammonite pendant – like mother-of-pearl, but with vibrant red, blue and green hues. I had wanted one of these for a long time, but had never bought one because they were too expensive for me.

"Oh, my gosh! How much did you spend on this, Ritchie?"

"It doesn't matter. Do you like it?" he asked anxiously.

I suddenly felt really bad for being sharp with him before. I'm not a very emotional person, but I felt a tear about to run down my cheek that I quickly wiped away. I sat down heavily on the bed and responded, "I love it."

"Are you okay, Francesca?" He sat beside me and rubbed my back affectionately.

"Yes, I'm fine. You didn't have to buy this for me."

"I know. That's why I want to buy you things. You don't seem to care about my money. I love that this small gift means something to you." I felt an overwhelming sense of gratitude and love for him just then. I stared straight into his eyes and he stared right back.

"Thank you so much, Ritchie." I felt like what I was really saying was *I love you.* Sometimes I got the feeling that he could read my mind just from a look. He knew because I saw a shine in his eyes.

"It was the least I could do. I owe you so much already." Before I could respond, he unexpectedly added, "I would do anything for you, Francesca."

I had the strangest feeling that he was saying, *I love you too.*

***

The next morning, I woke up alone. I didn't remember falling asleep or Ritchie leaving, but the jewellery box beside me reassured me that the previous night hadn't been a dream. I wasn't sure if we'd be studying that day, as it was his grandmother's birthday and I'd heard that relatives and friends would be arriving from all over. I was planning to check with Ritchie soon. However, when I came out of the shower, I saw a large box on my bed and a note:

Francesca
I really really hope you like this...
Meet me in the library at 11
-R-

I realised Ritchie had bought me another present. This was too much! The pendant was more than enough.

I opened the box and inside was a red dress – a beautiful one and exactly the right size. I guess you could call it a wraparound dress, tailored for a big bust. Although it wasn't too tight, it was quite low cut and there was a long slit from the thigh area down the side. There was also a pair of stockings and black, suede mid-heeled shoes. He knew I couldn't walk in high heels. I swallowed nervously, unsure of whether or not I'd ever have the guts to wear it.

Maybe I should just give it back. I wasn't sure what to do, so I put it inside the large chest of drawers and left it there. Then I headed down to the library at eleven.

He was already in the library waiting for me, sort of wringing his hands anxiously. I blurted out, "It's too much. You're giving me too much."

"Don't you like it?"

"Yes, it's stunning. Thank you, but…" I just wasn't sure how to respond.

"I was hoping you would want to wear it tonight."

Panic flooded me at the thought of wearing it tonight and at the same time. I didn't want to disappoint him.

"Oh, I don't know Ritchie," I finally managed to say.

"You have a lovely figure and you're always hiding it."

I stood there frozen, trying to decide what to do. It was silly how a dress made me feel this anxious. How could I give it back to him without hurting his feelings? I just couldn't bring myself to say no to him.

"Even John couldn't get me to wear a dress. Ever."

"Sorry, I didn't mean to force you. You don't have to wear it," he remarked sadly.

"Okay, I will. For you."

Suddenly, he had a huge smile. He got up excitedly and gave me a hug.

***

Time seemed to fly by whilst we studied science, and before we knew it, it was time to get ready for the party. I'd kept my hair in a bun for the day, so that it would be wavy. I knew my hair looked good, unlike my skin which always had blemishes. I managed to put on the thin, fine stockings without ripping them. Admittedly, my legs did look quite nice in them. Next, I reluctantly put the dress on, unsure of how it would look on me. Surprisingly, it did look good on, although I couldn't help feeling embarrassed about showing cleavage. It emphasised my waist and what Ritchie had once described as flaring hips. Okay, I had to give it to him – the dress suited me well.

I put on the ammonite pendant, the dress making the red lustre stand out, and painted my nails red. I was never competitive with other women, but tonight I was determined to look good for Ritchie. Casey would be there, and for some weird reason, I needed to prove to myself that he found me attractive. So I wore some tinted lip gloss. Fairly minimal, but enough for me. I let my hair loose. Dark waves cascaded down to my tailbone. When I looked in the mirror, the woman I saw was me, yet it wasn't me. I had to admit that I felt damn sexy, and it was empowering. I had said that I would meet Ritchie in the ballroom at eight, so down I went.

I had never got so many stares in my life. It felt weird and a bit creepy in some ways, especially the way some of the men stared. After a while, some people introduced themselves to me, and I just explained that I was Ritchie's tutor. I overheard one elderly man saying that he would have done much better at school if his tutor had looked like me. Luckily, I spotted Ritchie entering the room at that moment, as the conversation was going in the wrong direction.

I had never considered how Ritchie might react when he saw me in a dress. He was standing with Casey and his mum. Casey did look great, as I suspected she would, in a sparkly blue dress and curly blond locks. Not an ounce of fat on her and perfectly applied make-up. Beth spotted me first and tapped Ritchie on the shoulder. He turned toward me and stared. Just blatantly stared. His eyes grew larger, as if he couldn't believe what he was seeing, and his mouth opened. Beth must have seen it. He quickly recovered, though, and his expression became a bit more normal.

"You all look very nice." I really wanted to tell Ritchie how sexy he looked. He wore a navy-blue suit, fitting him to perfection. He didn't look like a teenager. More like a twenty-something-year-old. It made me feel slightly better about having a thing for an eighteen-year-old.

"Thank you, Francesca," Beth replied.

Casey remained silent, but Ritchie added, "You look fantastic." He wasn't being particularly discreet when he said this. I noticed that Beth looked back and forth between us, and I felt a bit worried that she saw too much. Hopefully, she would just put it down to Ritchie just being a normal young man who noticed these kinds of things.

After a while, Beth went to speak to her mother, who was surrounded by lots of people wishing her a happy birthday. Ritchie, Casey and I stood there awkwardly, not saying a word to each other, until the moment was broken by the arrival of some of Ritchie's cousins and Casey's friends. She seemed relieved by the distraction and took the opportunity to talk dresses with some of the girls.

As soon as there was a moment to talk privately, Ritchie quietly said, "You look so beautiful." I felt my cheeks heat up, as I still couldn't get over the fact that someone as handsome as Ritchie thought I was beautiful.

"Me? You look great. You could easily pull it off for a twenty-one-year-old."

He actually looked down at himself, as if judging whether or not he looked like a man. "Really?"

I nodded in response and he seemed very pleased that he looked older.

"Do you think your mum noticed the way we looked at each other?"

"I don't care if she saw us. What normal red-blooded male wouldn't stare?"

I giggled a bit, like a silly schoolgirl, at the flattery. I wasn't used to this kind of attention. I was almost embarrassed by it, and that was partly why I'd never really been into wearing dresses. I didn't like unwanted attention, but tonight I wanted his attention.

Unfortunately, other people had started gathering around, so the conversation ended there. We sort of hung around each other but didn't really speak. Some of his cousins chatted with him, mostly about sport, and I kind of joined a conversation about the food at the party. Every now and then I would feel his eyes on me, and I wondered if we would have time alone later.

The evening went fairly well, despite my social inadequacies, and the buffet was nice. I managed to wish his grandmother a happy birthday through the throng of people and thanked her for welcoming me. She seemed very popular with the family, but I suspected that it might have something to do with the will. Although, after meeting much of his family, I did feel that she was one of the nicer relatives he had. She didn't seem to mind having me around and seemed to care about Ritchie's education.

Music played softly in the background as some couples danced. I thought it was sweet when his grandmother asked him for a dance. She then got Casey to swap places with her, obviously trying to encourage some kind of relationship. After a while, I found myself unable to watch.

Luckily, a middle-aged gentleman asked me for a dance, and I almost turned him down, as I wasn't really into strangers groping me. I accepted to distract myself. He turned out to be quite the gentleman and he told me that his name was William. Bill for short. He asked me my name and I explained that I was Ritchie's tutor. He seemed a bit surprised at this. Maybe people didn't normally bring their tutors along to family occasions. From the corner of my eye, I saw Ritchie staring at us, even though he was dancing with Casey. Next minute, Ritchie asked to cut in.

"May I have this dance?"

Bill stepped back and said, "Well, it was nice to meet you, Francesca. See you around."

When he was no longer in earshot, I commented, "Maybe we shouldn't, Ritchie. What if someone suspects something?"

"It's only a dance, Francesca. Mum brought you here to babysit me, so she asked for it."

Feeling daring, I replied, "Okay, let's dance."

We both weren't particularly good slow dancers, so we fumbled along. The mood lightened when I stepped on his foot and we chuckled at ourselves. When we managed to regain our composure, the mood changed.

Leaning in more closely, he whispered in my ear, "You smell great." His breath on my neck gave me a thrill and I exhaled heavily whilst tilting my head back. He pulled my waist a bit closer.

Worried that we were revealing a bit too much, I pulled away, loosening my grip. Just then, Casey cut in, and I immediately moved aside, not wanting to draw extra attention.

After that dance, I lost interest in trying to be sociable. I tried to catch a glimpse of Ritchie, but I couldn't see him. I was also quite tired. I was an early riser and usually couldn't stay up very late anyway. I decided to slip away quietly.

When I opened my bedroom door, there he was, standing in front of me. I wasn't wholly surprised, but I wasn't expecting him to be standing there. He didn't say a word. His expression said it all. I was almost afraid of the look in his eyes, which were overflowing with such a powerful fervour. A smouldering fire burned deep within those eyes.

"How long have you been here?" I asked curiously. I hadn't seen him leave.

"Not long." I got the feeling that he wasn't here to talk.

He strode toward me, pulled my pelvis toward him and passionately kissed me. His grip was strong, like he didn't want to let me go, and his lips stayed on mine as if to savour the taste. He ran his fingers through my hair and kissed me harder. There was a want and a need in every movement, and it got my blood flowing. Losing my composure, I tugged his hair forcefully while he kissed me. He shuddered with stimulation, maybe slight pain, but he didn't tell me to stop. All I could feel were his hands on my body, touching almost every part. I grabbed his buttocks and hungrily pressed his hard-on against me. Feverish with raw sexual desire, I enjoyed the tantalising torture. I had to bite my lip to keep myself from saying, 'fuck me'.

He lifted up my dress. He traced my knicker line with his fingers and brushed my mound with the back of his hand. I whimpered breathily, unable to control myself anymore. I had been holding this in for so long, I thought I was going to combust when he started to take my dress off.

Running his hands along my body from my calves to my breasts, he slid the dress off over my head. He led me by the hand to the bed and lay me down, and he whispered in my ear, "Do you trust me?"

"Yes," I answered.

"Close your eyes."

I wasn't the submissive type, but I would have done whatever he asked of me then. So I forced myself to close my eyes. He knew I wasn't too keen on doing that, so I think he meant to reassure me by gently tracing the outline of my eyebrows, my cheeks and my lips and kissing me softly. There was a pause, and the weight on the bed changed as he changed position. Next minute I felt my suspenders being unhooked and my knickers sliding off. I felt a bit vulnerable, because now he was in control and I'd given him permission. I involuntarily squirmed in response and he obviously saw that. I felt him move closer and his breath on my ear.

"Do you trust me, Francesca?" he asked again.

"Yes, I do."

I then felt his hand on my inner thigh and between my legs. His fingers slid between my labia easily, as I was so moist. Finding my clit, he stroked me up and down. His heavy breath on my neck sent shivers down my spine.

"Kiss me," I demanded breathily, and then I felt his soft hot lips on mine. His fingers slid inside me. He repositioned himself slightly, as he pushed deeper inside, simultaneously fondling my clit with his thumb, and my G-spot with his two fingers. They slid in and out, over and over again. My heartbeat raced faster, building up until finally my toes began to curl and I had one of the strongest orgasms I'd ever had. I moaned with pleasure. I had been so het up with veiled desire since the beginning of the evening. It was a delicious release.

I opened my eyes and saw him staring down at me, totally focused. Unspoken communication passed between us.

What he did next was so sexy and a bit dirty, but I loved it. He ran those fingers along his own lips and nose, both inhaling and tasting my aroma whilst maintaining that intense gaze of his. I watched with a kind of intriguing fascination. I had just seen the dark side of Richard Cunningham.

He went into the bathroom for quite a while, and by the time he returned I had started to drift off, the tiredness from earlier hitting me. A comedown from the endorphin rush I had just experienced. He emerged rosy cheeked with a few beads of perspiration on his forehead and a satisfied expression.

"I've got to get back, my love."

"Good night, Ritchie," I answered sleepily.

Leaning down to give me a kiss, he said, "Sweet dreams, Francesca."

Chapter Nine

It's funny how I understood why we parted that night rather than continue. We both craved that sadistic torture of being so near, yet so far. Perhaps it was because it was *forbidden*. Perhaps it wouldn't be so intense otherwise. For now, I would indulge in his fragrance, his heat, his aura. I couldn't get enough of it. So what followed was a rather restless sleep filled with dark dreams and hidden desires. I kept wishing that he was beside me, yet I was glad that he hadn't spent the night. I just didn't trust myself. He had left his essence behind like a residue, and strangely I didn't feel alone.

The next morning, I woke up feeling paradoxically both ashamed and contented. I was guilty about what I'd done to John, as he had never been unfaithful. The other part of me was glad. I would have regretted it if I hadn't done anything with Ritchie. Why I seemed to enjoy this destructive need, this obsession, I didn't know. Maybe we all had it inside of us.

I went down to breakfast, feeling invigorated after having a shower and ready to face Ritchie's family. They seemed unusually nice, but that could have been due to me being in such a good mood. But for some reason, Ritchie was sitting alone, staring down at his coffee. I silently sat beside him. He quickly looked up, as if I had jerked him out of his thoughts and smiled at me sweetly.

"Good morning," I declared cheerfully.

"Good morning, beautiful woman."

"I have to ask. Where did you learn how to do that?"

His face blushed with the memories of last night. "Promise you won't laugh, but I looked it up online."

We both laughed.

"No shame in that at all." Feeling a bit cheeky, I added, "Guess what I did this morning?"

"What?"

"When I was having my shower, I lost control, and I thought about you while I did it." I was pretty sure that was the first time he'd been told that.

His eyebrows rose with disbelief. "Are you serious?" he asked in astonishment.

"Oh yeah," I answered seedily.

"You're so damn hot," he said, while partly covering his mouth.

"And you're so damn sexy," I murmured softly. He grinned at the compliment, clearly enjoying our flirty banter. Before he could respond, we were jolted back to reality when Casey interrupted our moment.

***

We met in the library and decided to refocus on English. He'd promised to spend time with Casey, so he was going to cut our study time short and regretfully probably wouldn't see me later on that evening. Apparently, she was returning to Oxford the following morning. Even though this annoyed me, it made me appreciate the time we had together more.

Throughout our session, I noticed that we were much more touchy-feely than we used to be. Every time we spoke or made a joke, I had to touch his arm or his thigh, and he would stroke my hand from time to time. He seemed very relaxed, chatty and cheerful. We got the work done as well as saying lots of silly things and getting into fits of giggles. He never used to laugh like that, and I was pleased that he was no longer so quiet and shy. Then again, he never really was when he was with me. He was only like that with other people. I wondered what it would be like once we returned to school. How would we hide our chemistry?

Sooner than expected, the time passed and he left to take Casey to dinner in town. Before he left, he walked me back to my room and placed a lingering kiss on my lips. It was a kiss full of promises, suggesting that it wasn't over yet. I could still taste him when he left.

I went down to dinner alone and happened to end up sitting next to Beth, who asked how Ritchie's studies were going. I said they were going well, as long as he kept up with his revision. He really did seem to be doing well in English now. We had worked on timings, spelling, punctuation and grammar. I truly hoped that he would at least get that 'C' grade, as that would be all he needed to get into university. The problem was that when he got stressed, it affected his concentration, and he might end up getting a lower grade than he was capable of. His anxiety levels seemed to have lowered somewhat, but only time would tell. I really had to make an effort not to distract him. He deserved only the best.

That night, I lay in bed imagining that Ritchie lay beside me. I pretended that I was him and fantasised about him penetrating me. My own hands slid between my thighs as I tried to relive what happened the night before. He'd left his vest here and I had kept it specifically so that I could smell him. Even though I wasn't physically with him, his essence consumed me yet again. Sometimes I felt like I was no longer my own person. I existed to be with him. How I envied Casey, who might have a future with him. On the other hand, if we were together as an item, I doubted that I could go about my daily life. Every day I would experience a self-destructive never-ending obsessive cycle. I wouldn't be able to function normally. I hoped that he was thinking about me while I was thinking about him. A niggling thought crept into my head. *What if they were having sex right now?* I clutched his vest tightly and fell into a fitful sleep.

***

The last day had arrived and Casey would be going home this morning. I would have the day with Ritchie; I doubted he would want to spend it studying. Disappointingly, when I got to his room, I could hear noises. The anxieties from the previous night resurfaced. Casey hadn't left yet. It made me feel bad that while I had been obsessing about him, he had probably been with Casey that whole time. I know it sounds ironic, but the thought of him making love to her was almost unbearable. Yet, I had a boyfriend, and I couldn't expect a teenage boy with raging hormones to sit around waiting for me.

I went back to my room and waited, and a little while later, Ritchie knocked at the door. I wanted to ask him about what had happened with Casey but decided against it for the moment. Instead, he suggested a day out in town, as we had never really had a first date before. He wanted me to see the glass-blowing workshop and to take me to a restaurant that had great reviews. It sounded nice. Maybe we should hang out, rather than just trying to find secret opportunities. I could make believe that we were an actual couple for a day.

We had a great time exploring. We tried glass-blowing, went to all sorts of shops, and had a lovely meal at an award-winning Indian restaurant. We even went into a random Dungeons and Dragons type store, which had us in fits of laughter because it reminded us of an episode of *The Big Bang Theory*. We were so full that we decided to walk some of the way back, even though we'd had a couple of drinks and the walk was over an hour long.

Throughout the whole walk back, we talked. People who knew Ritchie would have been so shocked to hear him chatting away so comfortably. It was such a breath of fresh air seeing him like this. I so wanted to ask what had happened with him and Casey, but I didn't want to ruin the mood. The sun had set some time ago, and despite the darkness and the cold, we continued on. The darkness was a welcome camouflage, hiding us from straying eyes. Only one vehicle passed us. The rest of the time we were alone in our dark bliss.

Inevitably, we stole a kiss here and there. We whispered secret promises to one another, so that only the shadows might hear. Once the lights of the manor appeared, we exchanged one final sweet kiss.

"I had a great time, Ritchie."

"I had a good time too."

"I'm going to miss you when we get back. I know I'll see you often, but it's not the same."

He became very still, and his expression became sad, as we remembered the reality of our situation. I swept a strand of his hair away from his eyes tenderly and he gently clasped my hand. It was heart-rending. We stood like that for a long time until we heard a car approach. We briskly made our way inside. I just hoped that his mum wouldn't be upset that we hadn't studied today.

Once I returned to my room, I had a long hot shower. The hot water mingled with sudden and unwanted tears as I thought about how much I wanted to spend more time with Ritchie. I had to return to my normal life, constantly fantasising about what could be rather than what was. I wondered what John had got up to while I was away – he'd probably got drunk most nights. For a brief moment, I felt concerned for him and I had to accept the fact that I still cared for him. Maybe it was okay that Ritchie had Casey, because I had to be there for John. We would just have to lead double lives and hope for the best. That way I wouldn't get sacked disgracefully and Ritchie's family would be satisfied. I firmly told myself that, no matter what, we would continue to see each other. My feelings for Ritchie were on another level, so maybe we needed that boring, mentally healthy routine to keep us grounded. But while our fires burned for one another, I couldn't leave him alone. Not yet, anyway.

***

I headed downstairs to get a quick bite to eat. Beth was already sitting there, sipping a coffee. I guessed that she probably hadn't eaten breakfast, as usual.

"Good morning, Beth," I said as I approached the table.

"Good morning, Francesca. Did you sleep well?"

"Yes. Actually, I just wanted to say thank you for inviting me."

"Oh, there's no need to thank me. In fact, I'd like to thank you for looking after Richard. He really looks up to you." If only she knew the full story.

"He's a good person, and I hope I'm helping him."

"You are. His studies seem to be going well, and he's been a bit more sociable than before. I've tried to set him up with Casey for years, and all of a sudden he's showing an interest."

"Yes, we had a chat about it and I told him to give her a chance."

"So, it was you who convinced him to go on that date. I suspected that was the case."

"I thought it would be good for him."

"You have a lot of influence over him. It's been hard trying to find the right support for him. I wish I'd hired you as a nanny years ago." As Ritchie joined us at the table, she added, "Speaking of the devil."

"Nothing bad, I hope?" he joked. For the first time, I saw Ritchie share a joke with his mum. It was a small thing, but a big step in possibly repairing a damaged relationship.

After he had eaten, we said our goodbyes and left for London. The journey started off okay, but gradually the thought of returning weighed heavily on my mind. I wished I could put him in my pocket to keep him close to me, always.

***

I couldn't tell whether or not John was happy to see me when I got back. However, he had cleaned the house and cooked a meal. He was normally lazy, so that was a pleasant surprise.

He asked, "How was it?" He seemed interested and disinterested at the same time.

"It was good. We got a lot done and I got to see some of the sights too."

"How was the family?"

"Okay, I guess. A little weird maybe."

He gave me a brief hug and ironically, that comforted me because I was away from Ritchie. I still felt safe and secure with John, but whenever Ritchie held me, I experienced electric sparks. I had never felt this with John. Come to think of it, John and I rarely had sex nowadays; though, the last time we had been intimate, it was Ritchie's face I saw.

Chapter Ten

It was Monday already, and as it was an inset day, there was no Ritchie. After getting our cups of tea and coffee, we headed straight to the hall to begin staff training. During the SEN training, where we had to discuss our thoughts in small groups, it seemed that gossip was what they were more interested in. They gossiped about Ritchie and his family like they knew what they talking about. They discussed their spoilt rich kid theories and asked me about the family's wealth. I had honestly never really asked Ritchie about that and it was pretty obvious to see that they were loaded.

What I did know was that Ritchie would inherit money at the age of twenty-one, but I had heard that there was more to it – a clause in the will. It was by chance that I had come across this information when I had overheard a conversation at his grandmother's birthday do. I would have to leave that to Ritchie to tell me if he wanted to, and it certainly wasn't for the staff to know about. I got the impression that the staff thought he was a spoilt rich boy who got what he wanted. Perhaps his classmates thought the same, or maybe there was an element of jealousy. One thing was certain: the conversation had left a sour taste in my mouth, but I bit my tongue. I wanted to say that it was unprofessional to talk that way, but who was I to say that?

I spent the afternoon receiving intense training from the counsellor and I was to start the sessions the following day.

***

"So, tell me, what makes you feel happy?"

I was attempting to run the first counselling session in the one-to-one room. I had no idea how this was going to go, and I felt like they had asked me to run the sessions just to tick a box. It didn't seem to matter to them that I wasn't qualified. In their eyes, they were providing what was required in his education plan. I wondered why they hadn't just got him another counsellor, but Karen was the buy-in counsellor assigned to the school.

I smiled warmly to put him at ease. I could tell that he was feeling a little uncomfortable by the way he was wringing his hands.

"Sometimes music makes me feel good."

"You passed music last year, didn't you? What instrument did you play?"

"Guitar - but I don't play anymore."

"Why not?"

His expression darkened as he grew even more uncomfortable.

"That's what made me fail my other GCSEs. I was so angry with myself for being way too focused on music. I got rid of it all."

I couldn't believe he had given up something he loved because he was angry with himself. "That's a shame; I would have loved to hear you play. I used to write songs, but I can't actually play an instrument."

He seemed to perk up at a possible change of subject and said, "I didn't know you wrote songs, Francesca?"

"Well, it was a long time ago."

"Maybe you can sing them to me one day. Can I ask you a question? What makes you feel happy?"

"Lots of things. Art, music, stargazing. The list goes on."

Realising that we'd gone off topic, I continued. "Okay, let's move on. Can you tell me all the things you like about yourself?"

He shifted uncomfortably and shook his head dejectedly. "I don't know, Francesca," he muttered.

"Anything you like about yourself Ritchie," I said, trying to goad him on. I waited. It seemed like it was so much effort for him to identify something positive. After some time, I said, "Come on, there must be something?"

He startled me, as he abruptly stood up, walked to the window and pushed his hair back with frustration. It was the strangest reaction that I had ever seen to such a simple question. I think I had inadvertently found his Achilles heel. I suddenly found myself not sure how much to push him. I wish he didn't get so frustrated sometimes. We'd had a really good time in Bath; it was awful seeing him like this now.

I cautiously went up to him and sort of rubbed his arm in an attempt to comfort him. "There are so many things you could like about yourself," I said.

I was hoping that he wouldn't shrug me off. He didn't, but he remained unresponsive. I guess that was the side of him that the other members of staff were referring to. I must admit, it was a bit bizarre, but I had this overwhelming need to help him. Wondering how to approach this, I put my arm around him and continued.

"Let me tell you what I like about you. You're caring, kind and considerate. You're intelligent, hard-working and creative. The list goes on forever, Ritchie."

I waited for what seemed like forever, then all of a sudden, he turned away from me and put his face in his hands. I heard a hitch in his throat – the unmistakable sound of crying. I felt awful. I had no idea that such a small question would have pushed him so far and I certainly hadn't meant to upset him. What happened to make him hate himself so much?

"I'm so sorry, Ritchie. I didn't mean to upset you."

Admittedly, it wasn't the first time I had reduced a student to tears during a one-to-one session, but this was only the first session! Surely this wasn't meant to happen. I scolded myself, though I wasn't clear what I had done wrong. I dreaded what future sessions would be like. Maybe I wasn't cut out for this after all. I really shouldn't have been asked to do this.

Slowly but surely, the sniffles eventually died down. I didn't ask any more questions, as I was aware that the bell was about to sound. I told him to go to the bathroom and freshen himself up. Without saying a word, he got his rucksack and left the room. It was home time now anyway. I doubted he would be going to tennis club. I knew that he probably wouldn't want to see me there, as I'd done enough damage. I just hoped he didn't hate me. I feared that I had severed our bond for good.

As I expected, he was not at tennis club. He must have left as soon as the bell went. I walked slowly to the train station, hoping that he was still around. I felt guilty and scared that I might lose him. I know that I shouldn't have felt this way, as I had only been doing my job. I desperately wanted to make him happy and I couldn't stand the thought of him being annoyed or disappointed with me.

I went home, feeling more and more worried as the evening went on. I wanted to call him, but I wasn't sure if it was the right thing to do. Would he even talk to me? I had to give him space. We usually weren't very good at giving each other space. I tried to force myself to leave things alone until later, but when I couldn't wait any longer, I sent a text message saying that I was sorry and that I hoped that he was alright.

A few minutes later, my mobile started ringing and I practically jumped out of my skin, both with anticipation and trepidation.

"Hi, Ritchie," I forced myself to say.

"Hi, Francesca," he replied in a strained voice.

"I'm so sorry. Please don't be angry with me," I said quickly in a single breath.

"You don't need to apologise."

Relief flooded me. "I just can't stand the thought that I hurt you."

"No, I needed it. I have to stop being like this," he said almost angrily, more to himself than to me.

"I thought that you'd want nothing to do with me."

"I would never do that to you. I'm messed up, but my feelings for you won't change."

"I'm so glad to hear you say that." Then I finally dared to ask, "Ritchie, why do you hate yourself so much?"

"Maybe I'm damaged goods."

I knew there was more to it, but I didn't push anymore. His answer hinted that he knew why. One day he might tell me, but he might never tell me.

"You're too young to be damaged goods." I wished I could have held him then, to reassure him somehow.

He didn't respond and instead asked, "Can I see you before school?"

I was relieved that he didn't blame me for it all, even if it was an absurd thought.

"I'll come to your house."

***

The front door opened, I stepped in, and we stood facing each other. He looked a bit morose from the day before, so I automatically reached out to stroke his cheek. I wanted to say something, but I didn't know what. Finally, I found the words.

"I care about you so much," I said before I could stop myself. I conveyed a lot more than I meant to, making me seem even more desperate. I just hoped he would respond to me.

My doubts were washed away when he closed his eyes to feel my hand on his skin and visibly inhaled the touch. It was like he was breathing in the scent of me. Laying his hands on my waist, he pulled me close in a loving embrace. My breasts pressed against his chest and the warmth of his body flowed through mine. I pulled back slightly, and longing consumed me as I drowned in his eyes.

We kissed, I tasted his forgiveness, and his need for me spilled over. My eyes began to sting like we had been apart for years, and I lost myself in the moment. Those few minutes were pure bliss. It was meant to be. How could it not be? Fate had intended for us to cross one another's path. If it was so wrong, then why was this happening?

It was wrong, because I already had someone, and because I was abusing my position. I had a duty of care to uphold, and he had a future to live. I wasn't going to deprive him of that, but I decided that we had to continue to be together. It felt so right that it shouldn't be wrong. I loved him, and I would keep him for as long as I could.

Ritchie was fairly quiet for the rest of the day. It seemed to take him a while to recover from that session, but I think we had crossed a difficult hurdle. And he was more aware of the self-hatred he had for himself. I still had the feeling that something had happened in the past which had triggered it. Only time would tell. We had already built up trust, so he would have to tell me in his own time. I just hoped it was something repairable. Is it ever repairable, though?

***

Ritchie's mood perked up considerably over the next few weeks. He'd had a few assignments, so I had purposely arranged our tutoring sessions in the living room within earshot of his mother. She had been around a lot more. Plus, it was good to keep up an appearance of normalcy.

The only time we were truly alone was during our counselling sessions, which had surprisingly gone fairly well. He actually managed to identify two things he liked about himself: the ability to play an instrument and determination. I have to admit, I wondered if he said those things only to please me. Did he really believe it? I really did hope so. He did seem to genuinely want to improve his outlook.

Sooner or later, that dreaded day came. Casey and Ritchie date night. Beth felt she needed to push things along and had asked me to persuade him to agree. She had assumed that he was shy and that was why he hadn't really been in contact with Casey. Apparently, I had a lot of influence over him. He agreed to it after I explained that it would keep his mum off his back for a while and that it was important not to raise suspicions.

Casey seemed quite keen, probably due to the thought of sharing

Ritchie's fortune. I had to accept that he might lose his virginity with her, as she struck me as the sort who would use sex as a form of persuasion. Then again, many women did that, and he could do a whole lot worse. Maybe underneath it all, she was a decent person. She was only seventeen years old, after all. It weighed heavily on my mind, though, as it seemed that people do tend to bond with the person they first have sex with.

The days leading up to the date were filled with anxiety for me and for Ritchie. It was obvious that he felt quite nervous. Whether it was due to being socially awkward or being fully intimate, I wasn't sure. Maybe it was a bit of both. The day before the date, he finally opened up and spoke about it with me.

"What should I do if she wants to go all the way?"

I visibly cringed and I bet that he saw that. I kept my wits about me and came up with a sensible answer.

"If you're ready, then why not?" I managed to get out, without really meaning it.

"You know what I mean," he said. He waited for me to respond. When I didn't, he added, "What if I want my first time to be… with you?"

That really threw me, and I actually stopped breathing for a minute. Although I had often thought about it, we'd never actually spoken about it. I guess I had deliberately avoided the subject.

Since the counselling incident, things had cooled down between us for various reasons. One reason was that my grandmother was suffering with dementia and seemed to be getting progressively worse. Recently she'd had a bad fall and I'd been to see her at the hospital a few times after school.

Not only that, but my mother's multiple sclerosis had worsened, and it was seriously affecting her mobility. My father was overloaded with the burden he had to bear. I'd cancelled some of our tutoring sessions, but Ritchie had understood. He knew I was worried about them and he was very supportive, showing a maturity beyond his years.

In some ways, it had been nice building up more of a friendship with him. Just chatting on the phone and eating lunch together. I enjoyed having someone to talk to, as John often wasn't very talkative and was easily distracted. It might have surprised people if they knew how articulate Ritchie really was. For me, it made him all the more intriguing.

Despite my good intentions towards my family, I looked forward to seeing the side of Ritchie I had seen in Bath again. What frightened me was that I knew I would be prepared to cheat on John completely. Yet I couldn't let John go, because Ritchie and I could never be a couple, and so I would continue to deceive him.

***

I know I shouldn't have, but I felt really glad when Ritchie called after his date with Casey, until he explained what caused it. According to Casey, Ritchie was too attached to me. Basically, I was a creepy old woman with ulterior motives. Unfortunately, that was spot on. I'm sure others felt the same, and that was why it was so important to keep things under control.

"She said things about you, Francesca," he said in a distressed tone.

"It's okay. I understand where she's coming from. I would feel the same way if I was her."

"No, I can't be with her if she doesn't respect you," he said stubbornly.

"She doesn't have to respect me, Ritchie," I pointed out.

"How can I show any kind of love towards someone who sees you like that?"

"It doesn't matter about me, though."

"What? How can you say that? You matter to *me*," he said vehemently.

"You can't put your life on hold for me."

And that statement hung like an unwanted smell in the room and lingered. He knew it was true.

"Look, can we stop talking about this? I don't like arguing with you."

He did seem quite highly strung. He could be neurotic at times. Not wanting to create further tension, I did what he asked. I wasn't sure why I was sticking up for Casey anyway, especially if I could have more of Ritchie for myself. I guess there was still a part of me that didn't quite believe that he felt the same way that I did. I often thought that he was too young, too good-looking and too naive to really love me. I had been let down by so many people in the past that I was often quite suspicious of people. Although when I was with him, I felt that his feelings were genuine.

"Okay, let's drop the subject."

The stress seemed to evaporate into thin air, and he immediately looked a lot more relaxed. And for some reason, I found it quite amusing and laughed, like he needed my permission to relax.

His face softened, a smile forming at the corners of his lips, and he said, "I'm hard work, aren't I?"

***

Coincidently, after being called a creepy old woman with ulterior motives, Ritchie's attachment to me was brought up at the last place I wanted it to be.

On Monday morning, when history was in full swing, Rosie – an assistant SENCO from the LSU – walked in. She made her way towards me. Bending down to whisper in my ear, she announced, "Sue would like to see you in her office at the start of second period."

"But I'm supporting Richard next period," I protested, unable to hide my disappointment.

"I'm sure it won't take too long," she replied as she turned away, obviously not interested in discussing it further.

Ritchie watched the whole thing with interest and commented, "What's that all about then?"

"I don't know, but apparently I have to meet Mrs. Callaghan in about twenty minutes."

Prickles of anxiety clawed at my stomach. I had a really bad feeling about this so-called meeting.

Sensing my apprehension, Ritchie quietly said, "Do you think it might be about you know?" I nodded. "Don't worry, I'll back you up. They won't get a thing out of me."

I knew he was trying to comfort me, as we had discussed this scenario before, but the prickles became barbarous thorns stabbing at my insides, so much so that I had to leave the classroom.

I stood outside Sue's office like a naughty child who had been sent to the principal. She caught sight of me through the small window in the door and waved me inside. I cautiously stepped in with a heavy head. She motioned to an empty seat and I sat down, not quite ready to face the music.

"Well, you're probably wondering what this is about. This meeting is about Richard Cunningham. I have some concerns regarding your relationship with him."

My worst fears had just come true. Trying not to give anything away, I innocently stated, "Okay. I'm not sure why. I guess I'm quite friendly, and maybe he does see me as a friend as well as his LSA"

"You seem to spend a lot of time with him, in lessons and during lunchtimes." She paused, expecting me to say something. "You were also seen walking with him outside the school premises," she added slowly and deliberately.

So, they didn't know about the tutoring. His mum must have kept that quiet. It wasn't illegal or anything, but it was frowned upon. I thought it best not to mention it. It was a miracle that no one had seen me entering his house.

"Oh, I believe we were going in the same direction that afternoon. He seems to get along very well with me, and if he has something on his mind, it's good if he talks to someone about it before it manifests into a violent outburst. You've probably noticed the frequency decreasing."

Nodding, she agreed. "Yes, both his temperament and levels have improved, so that does indicate successful strategies."

"I only want to help him, Sue, and I feel that I have. I'm not really sure what the big problem is," I said, playing dumb.

"I realise that this is uncomfortable, but it's my job to address issues that could arise concerning a member of this department. I don't want to question your motives, and to be frank, I'm more concerned about Richard."

"I understand that. Look, maybe he does rely on me too much, but I think he needs that right now."

"That's not what I mean. Has he ever made any inappropriate comments or actions towards you?"

I put on the best performance of my life feigning indignation, which wasn't too hard.

"Oh my god. No. He has *never* done anything like that! He may have trouble making friends, but he is *not* some degenerate."

I paused for breath then continued my little rant.

"And the counselling sessions – that was the school's decision. It wasn't my idea. Why ask me to do them if he spends too much time with me? It just doesn't make sense."

I was careful not to mention lunchtime, as that had been my idea. Knowing that she had no comeback, she tried to change the subject slightly.

"Are you happy to continue with the counselling sessions?"

"I don't mind doing them, but whether or not I should run them is a different matter. He doesn't enjoy them, but he's trying hard, and I don't think he would respond well if there were any changes at this point."

"Can you give me a written report on some of the things you've covered and how he responded?"

"I thought that was supposed to be confidential?"

As if right on cue, Richard knocked on the door.

"I also need to speak to Richard," she said as she motioned him inside.

I didn't dare glance in his direction, and I didn't need to. I knew he would do his utmost to protect me, and even though he must have felt extremely uncomfortable, he obediently sat down, understanding what was at stake.

***

I purposely headed on my own to Ritchie's house for tutoring, though I sent a text to explain why. We couldn't arouse any more suspicions, and obviously someone had seen us walking together before.

Just after I arrived, he told me what had been said when he was called into Sue's office. She had asked him some similar questions, and it sounded like Ritchie's responses corroborated with mine.

Beth was in when we got there, so I followed her into the kitchen. I went straight up to her and asked, "Did you receive a call from the school today?"

"No, should I have?" She immediately gave me her full attention. I heard Ritchie moving around in the background, deliberately avoiding the kitchen, but probably listening to every word.

I explained everything that had happened, because I knew she would be appalled. If I could get someone on my side, Beth was the perfect person. As I thought, she couldn't believe what we had been accused of and she had no idea who would make such an accusation.

"This is exactly why we kept the tutoring private. I'll call Sue tomorrow morning and straighten it all out."

"Thank you, Beth. It was a horrible thing to go through."

Oddly, she leaned to her right to look into the hallway, and I realised that she was trying to check if Ritchie was in earshot. Satisfied that he couldn't hear, she turned back to me and asked quietly, "Has Richard done anything that would cause people to make assumptions? I have noticed how close you are. Did he ever misunderstand your intentions?"

"No, he's always been decent towards me," I stated firmly.

"Please don't tell the school if he does anything strange. Promise me. At least tell me first."

"Of course, but he won't though, Beth. I'm an old lady. Nearly thirty years old!"

"You're not that old, Francesca, and you're a young-looking thirty-year-old who is extremely kind towards him. I suspect that he may have had a crush on you, but he seems a lot more interested in Casey now."

Ritchie, having changed his clothes, cleared his throat and walked in on that awkward moment. "It's all set up now," he announced.

I looked up gratefully and replied, "I'll be there in a minute." I turned back to Beth.

"Francesca," she said, "keep supporting him the way you do, because it's working. I need him out of that school at the end of the year with some decent grades."

I deliberately complained. "I just feel really annoyed with the school. I don't think I'll stay after this academic year. Oh yes – and I've been asked to report everything that has been covered during counselling sessions."

"Really? Well, I don't want them knowing my business. I'll give them one hell of an earful for this. Thank you for informing me."

My plan had worked. She was the most valuable ally I could have, yet the most dangerous in that she could find out the truth and put an end to everything.

Ritchie looked at me expectantly as I sauntered into the dining room, feeling satisfied.

"Wow, you're good," he commented, in a tone that was barely audible.

"Oh, did you hear all of that?" He nodded in response and I added, "Looks like she's on our side. She was really supportive actually."

"It's because she knows that as long as you're around, I'll be a good boy. You make her life easier."

"Well, whatever the reason, we need her on our side. We've got to be more careful from now on, Ritchie," I warned quietly.

"We have been, haven't we?

"You know what I mean, though."

***

The next morning, Sue was unusually nice when she explained that Beth had called her and dispelled any rumours. She apologised and reiterated the fact that she had only been doing her job. I thanked her politely and wondered what Beth had said. I bet it was the kind of conversation where you would want to be a fly on the wall.

It had been a close one, and I was almost proud of the way I'd managed to avoid trouble. I had never been this devious, but part of me began to relish what had happened. Living on the edge was kind of exciting, and I was beginning to get a taste for it.

Ritchie had been great too. He knew the importance of secrecy, and he had known exactly what to say. He'd been written off as some mumbling special needs case, but he was intelligent. He'd spent years on the edge, just looking in from the outside. He understood people. I still couldn't believe he was only eighteen. I also had the feeling that I wouldn't be having too many problems from the staff at St. Paul's while Ritchie still attended. That was another reason why I had to leave at the end of the academic year. My life would probably become a living hell if I stayed on after he left. They wouldn't forgive me for sticking up for Ritchie or for gaining his mother's support. And after all, I was only a lowly LSA. I'd been lucky so far, but my luck could run out. We had to be extra careful now around the staff, but especially around Beth. She noticed things, and I bet she knew more than what she had revealed from the way Ritchie behaved around me. That was why she'd asked that question about him. The old adage popped into my head: *keep your friends close and your enemies closer.*

Chapter Eleven

After our close shave, Ritchie and I didn't do anything to compromise ourselves. We made sure that we appeared to be seriously engrossed with the work in class. We still sat together at lunchtimes but spoke about things that were strictly school related. When we noticed staff walking by we were sure to raise our voices, so that they would hear how mundane our conversation was. Ritchie stopped bringing me fruit and no longer waited for me after school.

One particular weekend, I threw caution to the wind. I knew Beth was away for the weekend, so when John decided that he'd like to have a barbeque, I suggested that I invite Ritchie. I didn't live in the same area as the school, and we wouldn't be seen together publicly. I also felt guilty about having a good time at the barbecue while he was at home alone. I often worried about his thought processes when he was alone. I suspected that he may have self-harmed in the past. I had seen some strange looking scars on his arms and in other places. They were barely visible now, but I wondered about them still. I hadn't brought it up, afraid to reopen old wounds. Literally.

John was a bit apprehensive at first, but when I explained that Ritchie didn't have any friends and that he was always alone, he seemed to warm up to the idea. He could relate to him in many ways, and it appealed to John's good nature. He said that he'd gone through similar social issues when he was younger and would have appreciated someone offering a supportive hand. John suggested that Ritchie might enjoy meeting my sister, who was seventeen and probably had lots in common with him. He seemed to think that was very funny. I actually hadn't thought of that. She was also yet another social misfit, but would often get easily led astray in an attempt to be liked. Ritchie was way too stubborn to get involved in things purely for the sake of popularity.

For a brief instant, I almost changed my mind about inviting him. In the end I decided that I had to invite him. I wanted him to experience my family's carefree banter and their acceptance of anyone, no matter how odd. The possibility of him liking my sister was a risk I would be willing to take, as a sort of experiment. Yet another one. Examining his response to stimuli: namely, other women. My sister would be an interesting temptation – a younger, slimmer version of me.

During a geography lesson, I asked Ritchie, "So, do you want to come to a family barbeque?"

"Will John be there?"

"Yes, but he doesn't mind if I invite you," I reassured him.

"You might think I'm strange, but I'd like to meet him. The man who has kept you for ten years. And my competition."

"You'll meet him, and you'll like my family, Ritchie. They welcome everybody."

"I'm there, Francesca. When is it?"

"This Saturday."

I then realised that the teacher had called Ritchie's name, but he hadn't heard because we'd been talking. It didn't look good for us as we were supposed to be laying low, especially during school hours. I quickly nudged him and Ritchie cleared his throat to respond.

It was hard trying not to get lost in our own world. Even when we spoke about mundane or trivial things, it seemed to drown out the rest of the world. All I could see were his eyes, and all I could hear was his voice. His soft timbre was mesmerising to me.

Afterwards, we exchanged a look which meant *oops*, and I dearly hoped that no one had noticed.

Later on that day, we sat down to begin the counselling session. We'd had a breakthrough that time when he'd broken down. Since then, he had been less negative and more open. His sore spots were his music and his feelings towards his deceased father. His previous counsellor had pinpointed the father issue already, but the music issue was an odd one. I'd kept things simple for the last few weeks, not wanting to push him so much, and he'd opened up on his own, broaching some tricky issues. I was in no way an expert, but I'd always had a knack for getting students to talk about things that made them feel uncomfortable. There had been a few instances in the past where students had revealed experiences of abuse by parents.

For this session, I wanted to bring up his father somehow. We began talking about his music. I casually asked, "So, have you bought that music gear yet?"

"Not yet. I just don't want to be distracted by it."

"Okay, fair enough. As you know, I can't play an instrument to save my life, but I enjoy songwriting. Last year, I recorded one of my own songs and I was wondering if you'd like to hear it." I figured that I would give a little to get a little, and that me sharing might encourage him to play for me some time.

"I'd love to hear it."

I nervously handed the earphones to Ritchie with the song ready to go. Once the song had started, I had to turn away. I was embarrassed, because although I enjoyed writing songs and singing, I couldn't really sing. And it was personal, as the lyrics meant something to me. Apparently, my lyrics were dark and obsessive, according to the few who had listened to them. I sat like that for a few minutes until I felt a tap on my back.

"That song was beautiful. You have a sweet voice too."

"Thank you. I just wanted you to hear it."

"I know that wasn't easy for you to do. Thank you for sharing it with me."

"Now that you've heard one of mine, would you share some of your music with me? It's my birthday next month."

He smiled knowingly, realising that I'd planned that. "You know I can't say no to you, Francesca."

"Well, on that note, you might not like what I ask you next."

"It's about my father, isn't it?"

"I was hoping that we could talk about it, but you don't have to if you really don't want to."

He put his head into his hands and began massaging his temples. I was worried that he was shutting down again like last time. I hoped that I hadn't ruined everything. He took a deep breath and answered, "Okay, what do you want to know?"

"What do you remember about him?" I asked.

He kept one hand half covering his face, and without making eye contact, he replied, "Not much."

"How old were you when he died?" I could have easily got this information from his file, but I asked anyway.

"Ten years old."

"How did you feel?"

"I don't know. I didn't know how to feel. I felt numb more than anything else. It just didn't make sense to me. Every child should have a dad."

He became silent for a while, but just as I was about to prompt him further, he continued.

"My mum didn't cry, so I didn't either. He was a stranger to us. The only memories I have of him are vague – smoking cigars in his study, shouting at me and…"

I waited a moment, then asked, "And what, Ritchie?"

Just then, the bell rang.

***

Everybody arrived in dribs and drabs to the barbecue, and I found myself preoccupied with the anticipation of Ritchie's arrival. Sooner or later, after opening the door a dozen times, it was Ritchie's face I greeted. His hair hung sexily over his eyes. He swept it back and said, "Hi Francesca." He wore a light brown jacket, black jeans and a blue T-shirt.

I leaned over to give him a quick hug and whispered into his ear, "Hello handsome."

He smiled coyly in response and his eyes oozed sexual intensity.

"I brought some stuff," he said softly, as he handed me a Waitrose carrier bag.

"Thank you, Ritchie. Come and meet the family."

He cautiously stepped through and I introduced him to the family.

"I've heard a lot about you," John said as he shook Ritchie's hand.

"I've heard a lot about you too," Ritchie replied politely.

"Only good stuff I hope," joked John. Ritchie chuckled softly in response. "What's your poison?"

"Anything will be fine."

"Okay. Well, help yourself," John replied, pointing to buckets of ice filled with bottled and canned drinks. Ritchie chose a Corona and sat by me in the garden. My dad, uncles and John sat with us. I noticed how all the women had gravitated indoors to gossip as usual. My mum, aunt and grandmother just stared at Ritchie when they met him, probably because he was so good-looking, but it was a bit odd. It was obvious that they didn't get out much. I often sat with the men when the family got together, as I enjoyed the banter. My dad decided to embarrass Ritchie at the first available opportunity he had.

"So, where's your girlfriend?"

As Ritchie wasn't used to my dad's inappropriate ways and abrasiveness, I could see that he was slightly taken aback.

"Don't worry, he's only joking," I reassured.

"We had an argument," he piped up. I was surprised at how easily it seemed to slip out. Glad that he was already quite relaxed, I sat back curious to hear the verbal play.

"Bloody women," my dad responded.

"Can't live with them, can't kill them," I added. One of my favourite lines from the movie *True Lies*.

It was around that moment when my sister arrived. She sometimes sat with me, depending on what mood she was in. I couldn't help but watch Ritchie's reaction to her. He definitely looked with curiosity, and when I finally snapped out of my little trance, I introduced them to one another. The banter went on whilst John sorted out the food.

When the moment was right, I asked, "So, what do you think of my sister?"

"She looks like you. It's weird seeing someone else who looks like you."

"We do look similar."

"She's different from you, though."

My interest suddenly piqued, I asked a little too sharply, "How? In what way?"

"She looks kind of angry and unfriendly."

"She's not angry – maybe just a little depressed," I explained.

"You mean socially awkward, like me?"

I didn't intend on making negative comparisons between them. Luckily that particular conversation ended with an abrupt halt when a random overweight cat decided to join our barbecue. It flirted shamelessly in an attempt to get some food and made us all laugh.

Despite the awkwardness of the situation, I had a good time. As the evening went on, we ate, we drank, we danced and sang badly. My potato salad went down well, and John's barbecue skills were praised.

After the food, we started on the rum, which was a sort of family tradition. Ritchie really loosened up – he even got up to dance with us. It must have had something to do with the drink. Inhibitions fell away and conversation opened up. The topic turned to relationships.

"Soon I'll be bringing the old ball and chain home to Canada with me," slurred John.

"Hey, what did you just call me?" I responded playfully.

"Maybe I'll just trade you in for younger model," he joked.

"You'll never find anyone better than Francesca," added Ritchie, unexpectedly. Luckily the comment was misinterpreted as a joke, and my dad laughed, thinking it was really funny for some reason.

"Hey, what's that supposed to mean?" responded John.

"It means that the only thing you could get is an old hag," I interrupted, making everyone laugh. John and I often joked like this, but I doubted that Ritchie had ever experienced this kind of banter before in his family.

The night continued, until it was just me, John and Ritchie. They had both had a few and were just talking absolute nonsense. I almost found it sweet, the way they seemed to get along – John's acceptance of him and Ritchie's openness towards John. It may have been drink-fuelled, but they were both awkward in their own ways and had heard a lot about each other from me. I thought it ironic yet watched in fascination.

I couldn't believe my ears when John asked Ritchie to stay the night. Apparently, he was welcome to sleep on the couch, and to my surprise Ritchie accepted. John had inadvertently made my secret relationship easier by increasing our access to each other. Let John fall into that false sense of security. What he didn't know couldn't hurt him.

Whilst John slept soundly, Ritchie and I caught our moment. I walked through the living room, and in the shadows Ritchie lay dozing on the couch. The pale moonlight bathed him in an eerie glow. His leg was exposed from the sheet having slipped off, and I found myself drawn to his well-defined muscular thigh. Before I knew it, I was stroking his thigh and I just couldn't resist touching him between his legs.

He began to stir as his awareness increased. In the darkness, I found his lips – the alcohol making us braver. He lifted my nightie up, grabbed my buttocks and pulled me, almost lifting me on top of him. Knowing that John was sleeping in the other room fuelled our feverish frenzy. I grabbed his engorged member and gasped. It was so hard. Impulsively, I dropped to my knees, pulled his boxer shorts down and licked his hard erection. He breathed heavily, shuddering with anticipation.

"Shhh," I whispered in his ear and made my way downwards. I slid my mouth on it and sucked, softly at first, gradually increasing the strength of my pull. I ran my tongue around the ridge of the head. I sucked harder and harder, whilst massaging the base with my hand. At this point, he couldn't help but breathe fast and hard. Then finally, I felt warm liquid gush out of him.

Unfortunately, I heard a noise from the bedroom, so I quickly headed to the bathroom to freshen up, flushed the toilet and returned to bed. John put his arm around me in a sleepy embrace, and all the while, I thought of Ritchie. Knowing that he was just next door filled me with sexual frustration and I fell into a restless sleep full of lustful dreams.

In the morning, while John slept, I checked to see if Ritchie was awake. He wasn't, but he must have heard me making tea, because he stepped tentatively into the kitchen behind me. We just stood still drinking in one another. I put my arms around his neck, pulling him close and gave him a long kiss, which meant it wasn't over yet.

"I got a bit carried away last night, didn't I?"

"Well, I'm not complaining. That was one of the best things I've ever experienced," he replied.

I giggled ridiculously in response, feeling good that I had made him feel that good. The kettle finished boiling and he squeezed my bum as I turned to pour the tea. We sat together silently, watching mindless television, aware that John was next door. We looked at each other longingly, wishing that we could reach out and touch.

When I heard the familiar sounds of John rousing from sleep, I went into the bedroom.

"Where's my woman?" He sounded like he was still drunk.

"Be quiet, Ritchie is in the other room."

"What's he doing here?" he asked, suddenly sounding a lot more sober.

"You invited him to stay the night," I replied frustrated. He often didn't remember things when he drank too much, and I constantly had to repeat myself.

"Did I?"

"Yes, John," I barked.

"Oh," was all he said. He drifted back off to sleep and I had a shower.

When I came out, it looked like Ritchie had drifted off back to sleep as well. I watched him as he slept and I thought about how much I would like to draw him. I couldn't help myself, and I reached out to stroke his cheek, inevitably disturbing him.

A short while later, Ritchie woke up, showered, and announced that he would be going home. He lingered in the doorway as we said goodbye. We quickly embraced, and with his cheek against my head, he whispered in my ear, "I miss you already."

I breathed in almost painfully, trying to keep my composure. I just didn't want to let him go, but I did. I knew that it was going to be the longest Sunday.

I don't know how I managed to mask my feelings from John that day. I was but a shell of myself as I lurked around the place, biding my time. I knew I was just making things worse for myself, but I let the clawing shadows devour me. They pulled and tugged at me, sucking my breath away and exposing my soul to a world of pleasure and pain.

Chapter Twelve

It was the start of second period, and we were standing outside science class waiting for the teacher to arrive. Despite the turmoil my mind had gone through over the weekend, I greeted Ritchie robotically. Luckily, he broke the awkward silence that followed.

"I'm going to a swimming tournament on Wednesday after school."

"Really? Who are you competing against?"

"St. Aloysius and St. Barnabas."

"You didn't mention it before," I said, wondering if I'd be able to attend. I had promised to meet a friend who desperately needed some relationship advice that evening. I would have to reschedule or cancel. To be honest, I had spent years being a good friend, but I felt like I was constantly being let down by her anyway. She could wait.

"Please come and watch me, Francesca," he pleaded, as if he knew that I might not be able to make it.

I just couldn't say no to that face, and so I replied, "Of course I will."

He beamed at me and I just smiled goofily back. Ritchie seemed to be in such a good mood. He smiled much more often now and it was infectious. He was so beautiful. If the devil looked like that, we would all be in trouble, big time.

The morning went by uneventfully, and I couldn't wait to see him that evening for tutoring. Imagine my disappointment when Ritchie informed me during lunch that he'd be doing extra swimming practice for the next two evenings.

"When the hell am I supposed to see you then?" I complained. I could feel my stress levels rising at the thought of having no alone time with him.

"I just found out, Francesca," he mumbled. He looked down at his hands and began to fidget uncomfortably.

Realising that I was causing his anxiety, I quickly said, "Look, I'm sorry. I didn't mean to snap at you. Of course, you have to practise. I want you to do well. I'm your biggest supporter." I had no right to expect him to make time for me. I was already in a relationship, and he never complained when he had to make allowances for that.

He remained fairly quiet for the rest of the day, and I just felt more and more guilty knowing that I had made him feel that way.

The next day, there was a departmental meeting in the morning, which meant I was slightly late to English. I slipped in beside Ritchie silently and, when there was a moment, I turned and said, "Good morning, Ritchie."

"Morning, Francesca," he answered.

Well, at least he's talking to me I thought.

"How was swimming practice?"

"Not too bad. How was your evening?"

"Not too bad," I mimicked in an attempt to lighten the mood, and it seemed to work. His expression softened and I found myself feeling so relieved.

"Right, that's it. I'm requesting a new LSA," he teased back.

We both laughed, but then realised that people were looking at us. Group discussion was over and I didn't have a clue what they had been talking about! Thankfully, the teacher didn't ask for too much feedback.

***

I cheered as loudly as I could when Ritchie walked out onto the platform. His body looked strong and sexy, not in the least bit boyish. He didn't look up. I guessed he was in the zone. He definitely had his game face on, and I was proud of how calm and composed he seemed, despite the pressure to perform well. He dived in gracefully and swam steadily, in about fourth place during the first lap. In the midst of my frenzied cheering, I caught sight of Casey. Thinking I was mistaken, I looked again, and yes, there she was. Disappointment flooded me. Ritchie hadn't said anything about her being there. Determined to support Ritchie, I forced my eyes back to the competition. He remained in fourth until the final fifty metres, when he moved up to third place.

St. Aloysius won the tournament, much to everyone's dismay. They were St. Paul's greatest competition, as there was a bitter rivalry between the two that went back years. I never did find out why.

I waited outside the building, hoping to give Ritchie some comforting parting words before I left. Obviously, he would be feeling down after losing the competition, even though he would be receiving a bronze medal in Monday's assembly. Unfortunately, I bumped straight into Casey, who just looked at me. A moment later, Ritchie walked out. Then we all stood just stood there awkwardly.

"What are you doing here, Casey?" asked an annoyed Ritchie.

"Your mum invited me, and I wanted to see you."

I felt so uncomfortable, so I said "Ritchie, I'll see you at school tomorrow."

"No, you don't have to go," he replied in a tense voice.

"We have to talk, Richard," Casey said, in an attempt to persuade him to let me leave.

I could almost see the bubbles rising. I hoped I would never get on the wrong side of him. He looked angry. This was not good.

"Ritchie, it's alright. I'll go," I said quietly, trying to defuse the situation.

"Listen to her, Ritchie," agreed Casey.

"Don't you call me that," he responded heatedly. I wasn't sure what he meant until I realised that only I had ever called him by that nickname.

As much as I disliked Casey, I didn't want to witness a huge argument between the two, which I would undoubtedly get drawn into, whether I liked it or not. She was also his sort of girlfriend. Understandably, she didn't like me, but that was beside the point. Ritchie needed someone when I was with John, and he needed someone to love when I was gone. I could tell that she was interested in him, even if it was for money or status. I just hoped that I wouldn't regret what I was about to do.

"Ritchie, come here," I murmured softly, whilst putting my arm around him. Whispering in his ear, I said, "Calm down. She's made the first move to put things right — please give her a chance."

His rigid body was filled with tension. Then he closed his eyes, took a few deep breaths, and nodded. I felt him loosen up slightly. I could see that he was trying to formulate some words, and in the end, he decided to go with his true feelings.

"Look, Casey, now is not a good time. We just lost to St. Aloysius."

Relieved, I finally breathed. It occurred to me that I had been holding my breath for some time.

"I really do need to go," I said as I walked briskly away, in the direction of the train station.

"Thank you for coming. I'll see you in the morning," he called after me mechanically.

***

Ritchie looked a bit tetchy, when I finally saw him in geography class during third period the next day.

"How did it go with Casey?"

"My mum shouldn't have invited her," he complained.

"Maybe not, but did you sort things out?"

"Sort of," was all he could muster.

Weirdly, a strange mixture of jealousy and relief coursed through my system. It was obvious that he really didn't want to talk about it anymore, but I kept pushing.

"She just needs to grow up a bit, and then I'm sure you'll like her more."

"I don't know."

"If she's not right for you, I bet you'll meet someone at university," I proposed in a feeble attempt to cheer him up.

"Maybe."

This conversation was going nowhere. He was shutting down. He was using fewer syllables with each sentence, so I decided to leave it at that. The more I got to know him, the more I saw his temperamental nature and tendency to swing between moods.

"All I know is I'm glad you've never lost your temper with me. You're pretty intense when you're angry."

"Well if I do, you have my permission to slap me." He looked so serious when he said this that I had to laugh.

"No, you might enjoy it!" I commented cheekily.

I loved the way his laugh rose from deep inside him. I also loved the way he set his fiery green eyes on mine and replied, "I probably would."

Later on that day, Ritchie told me that he had a multiple-choice questionnaire test for science on Friday, which included all the topics that had been covered in the spring term so far. I was a little annoyed with myself for not knowing that he had a test, and I wondered when it had been announced. He tried to reassure me by explaining that he had been studying for it all week, but I knew the swimming competition had taken a lot out of him. I was also worried because we had mostly focused on literacy during our tutoring sessions two weeks before the swimming tournament.

I asked him if he'd like to study during the counselling session instead and he eagerly agreed. How he must have hated counselling to choose studying as an alternative option. Ritchie decided not to attend swimming club that evening, and I agreed to combine our two tutoring sessions into an extra-long one. I warned him that I was there to help him revise and wouldn't be messing around.

We sat at his desk in his room with all his science notes spread out – some on the floor, some on his bed. I devised a mnemonics-based system and we practised orally. His knowledge was fairly good. He just needed to remember some specific vocabulary and processes. We sat there until it was dark outside, and that was when we realised that it was almost nine o'clock. I had completely forgotten to call John to let him know that I was tutoring. My phone had been on silent and there were a few missed calls from John, so I sent a quick text explaining that tutoring had gone on a bit longer than planned in preparation for a test. I said that I would be on my way home soon.

"I better go now," I said glumly.

"Sorry, it took so long, Francesca. Thank you for all your help – I couldn't do this without you."

I put my arms around him, kissing him on the cheek, and said, "You're welcome."

I turned to leave, but he grabbed my hand suddenly and pulled me almost roughly towards him. The kiss was deep, with a hint of desperation. His tongue hungrily caressed mine and heat coursed through my veins. I had actually been trying to avoid this to ensure that I wouldn't distract him. Well, to hell with that now. It had been a long bloody evening.

Just for a second, my animalistic self took over as I pulled his hair hard while we kissed. He moaned, and I quickly let go thinking I had hurt him, but he led my hand back to his hair. I guessed he liked it. I grabbed his hair for a second time and pulled really hard this time. He grimaced in pain and whimpered. I stopped immediately.

"Sorry, I didn't mean to hurt you."

"No, I want you to hurt me," he said in a pained voice. I stepped back in shock.

"But I don't want to."

Shaking my head, I hurriedly got my bag and marched to the door. He stood in front of me blocking my way.

"Don't leave me. Stay with me," he pleaded sadly.

"I can't. I have to go. It's late."

"Francesca, I—"

Stopping in mid-sentence, he stepped aside. Sensing that he needed to tell me something important, I asked, "What is it, Ritchie?"

"Never mind. See you tomorrow." He was closing himself down. He wouldn't tell me now.

"Okay, good night."

When I got home, I felt exhausted, but for some reason I couldn't sleep. I replayed the bizarre experience with Ritchie in my mind. I didn't fully understand what had happened. There was so much going on beneath the surface, and I felt like I was only just beginning to unwrap some of the layers. At times, I knew him better than anyone else, but at other times, maybe I was just as clueless as everyone else. Should I have stayed with him? What would I have said to John?

***

Ritchie avoided my eyes as we sat waiting for the science papers to be given out. He was probably just embarrassed about the night before. I hated when he was moody. Sometimes he would keep that mood for days. Having flaws made him seem all the more real though – not so untouchable, but still beautiful and interesting. It was the secret psychologist in me who relished the challenge, I thought. John was also quite moody at times. Why was I always attracted to the brooding type? It was as if Ritchie and I were turning into a real couple with problems. Maybe I should give him space, but knowing me, I wouldn't be able to. His magnetic pull was too strong, like gravity. I knew how to deal with him, though.

Once the test started, I walked over to the other side of the class, responding to someone who had raised their hand. I continued to walk around the classroom until Ritchie raised his hand. He had to give me eye contact as he asked me to read a question for him.

When the test was over, he quietly said, "Sorry."

"Sorry for what?"

"Last night."

"You really didn't do anything wrong. I was just… Let's talk about it later."

I ate my quiche while he ate his sandwich in the lunch hall. Oh god, he was so handsome, just sitting there. It was all so effortless. Maybe that was why people thought he was gay. Everything looked perfectly coordinated, apart from his hair, which was wild and sexy.

I caught myself just staring at him unabashedly. He knew I was drinking him in like a delicious cocktail. And he stared right back. Neither of us broke eye contact. A small faraway voice reminded me that people might see us, and I wondered if anyone would notice how we sent non-verbal messages to one another. We continued anyhow. I unconsciously reached out to him but stopped short. Our hands lay inches apart. I yearned for his touch. If he wanted me to pull his hair, then I would do it. Anything he asked me to do, I would do it. He was going through a sexual awakening. It was part of his journey of discovery. Different things turned on different people. Maybe he liked it rough.

A tannoy announcement snapped me out of my reverie.

Ritchie was looking at me. "It's your birthday tomorrow, Francesca," he said.

"Yes, I'll be hitting the big three zero."

"Still can't believe that you're going to be thirty."

"Yep, I'm getting old now."

"You're not old. Not to me anyway."

Chapter Thirteen

Ritchie asked me to head to his house after school. Apparently, he had a surprise for me. I hoped he hadn't gone and spent a load of money. I pressed the doorbell and waited, but there was no answer. I assumed that he was either on his way or hadn't heard the bell, so I called his mobile. When he answered, I heard running water. He was in the shower and he would be down shortly.

I waited with anticipation until I heard footsteps running down the stairs and a wet Ritchie opened the door, but only slightly.

"Sorry, I didn't realise that you would get here that fast."

"Maybe you're just a slowcoach," I teased.

"Hey, I have a very good reason for my lateness, I'll have you know."

"Okay. Now I'm really curious."

Careful to remain mostly hidden, so that only his face was visible, he waited for me to step inside. He took my hand, brought it to his lips and kissed it softly.

"Happy birthday, Francesca."

I was about to reply, but before I had the chance, his lips were on mine. I responded immediately to his soft, warm, caressing lips. He smelled good, too. His body was hot from the shower, and steam rose from his skin. As if an enchantment spell had been cast upon me, I lost track of time and space. I had no idea how long we stood there, until we finally needed to stop for air. Suddenly, there I was, back on Earth, back to reality.

Still dizzy from the long kiss, I said, "Well, that's the nicest happy birthday I've ever received."

"It's not over yet," he said mysteriously as he led me by the hand up the stairs and to his bedroom. "Do you remember the night I spent at yours?"

"Of course I do, how could I ever forget?"

"Tell me about it. I've been waiting to get you alone for ages."

"We're alone when I tutor you, aren't we?" I pointed out playfully.

"That's not the same. You wouldn't let me do this during tutoring." He raised his eyebrows teasingly.

My interest was piqued, and I asked, "Do what?"

"Let's just say I want to return the favour," he replied huskily.

What he was planning to do finally dawned on me, and seeing the realisation on my face, he asked, "Can I?"

My body temperature rose at the mere thought of it. Then I felt a little self-conscious. "I'll need to have a quick wash though."

Smiling like the cat that had the cream, he eagerly asked, "So that's a yes, then?"

"Yes it is..." I replied as I made my way towards the stairs.

When I finished washing, I was greeted by a nervous looking young man.

"Are you okay?" I asked, slightly concerned.

"Yes. No. Maybe. I'm just – I've never done this before. What if I do it wrong?"

Standing very close to him, I demurely reminded, "You weren't nervous when you fingered me."

His face became flushed with the memories of that night. "I was actually. This is a lot harder to get right."

"It doesn't matter. I don't mind being your guinea pig," I joked.

Shoulders shaking as he chuckled with laughter, the tension seemed to disappear.

"I just thought of you as an actual guinea pig – the least sexy thing ever."

"Hey, don't ruin my attempt at dirty talk." At this point, we were both laughing. "That's more like it, Ritchie. It's supposed to be fun."

I dropped my towel on the floor and he put his arms around my waist, pulling me close. He stared into my eyes. It felt as if he was dissecting my thoughts and all barriers disintegrated. He must have felt my need, my desperation for him, as he read my thoughts. I was immersed in a world of green, gold and amber. And I surrendered.

He ran his hands through my hair, tugging softly, exposing my neck. Inhaling deeply, he took in my aroma as he nuzzled my neck. While he rubbed his smooth cheek against mine, I breathed the scent of him too.

He smelled as fresh as a winter morning and his kisses were as soft as cascading snowflakes, and I shivered, intoxicated. I was lost, so totally lost in his world. I'd never felt anything this intense, this real, yet so dreamlike.

I felt the barest hint of a touch run along my spine and down to my tailbone. I exhaled with delight. I tugged at his untamed hair, feeling him grow hard against my aroused groin. I led him to the bed, and he softly lay me down, caressing me in every secret place, overloading my senses. Sexual excitement flooded me, as I pulled him on top of me scratching his neck unintentionally. I wanted him inside me so badly, and I think he knew, yet he didn't give in. Even when I reached for it, he held my arms gently above my head and said breathily, "Let me give you your birthday present."

I closed my eyes and I felt his hair brush against my inner thigh. His warm tongue slipped between my labia and slid over my clit. Now I knew why he'd made sure he was so clean-shaven just before I arrived. The first few licks were exploratory, taking in the smell and taste of me. The licks sped up a bit, making me throw my head back and groan with pleasure. Without thinking, I grabbed his hair hard. Then I heard Ritchie's breath quicken and felt a gush of air when he breathed out heavily. I relished every second of this build-up to ecstasy. My heartbeat sped up with every slide of his tongue. I wailed noisily without restraint and panted as a huge wave of gratification hit my body.

"Oh, crap," I heard Ritchie say, unexpectedly.

I looked down and saw that he had climaxed also. I knew it must have taken some effort trying not to get turned on, but he was only young.

"It's okay. It doesn't matter," I consoled unsuccessfully.

"It's not okay. This wasn't supposed to happen," he replied, looking distraught.

I sat up, held Ritchie's face in my hands, trying to search his eyes, and said, "That was great. I enjoyed it and so did you. There's nothing to be embarrassed about."

He seemed to calm down a bit and a moment later, he said, "I better clean this up."

He returned with a towel and I stood up so he could remove the stained sheet. He looked so annoyed with himself and I wished that he wouldn't. I didn't know what else to say, as I understood that a lot of men would feel embarrassed. So I just freshened up in the bathroom and got dressed. He did the same. I sat there quietly, and Ritchie plonked himself on the bed beside me, but facing away from me.

Finally, he said, "I'm sorry. That's not the way I planned it."

"I know, but I really enjoyed it. I was so turned on; I had such an intense orgasm. One day, I'm going to ride you into oblivion, Ritchie."

From what I could see of his profile, a smile crept onto the corners of his lips.

"Well, I'm not sure how to respond to that. Probably wouldn't take very long, knowing me," he replied, with a mixture of humour and self-pity.

"Forget about it, Ritchie," I commanded.

Next, he reached over to the bedside cabinet, opened the drawer and took out a small box.

"This is your other birthday present," he announced as he handed the box to me.

It was another jewellery-sized box, and I tried to guess what was inside before I opened it. I froze when I saw that it was a black pearl ring. I absolutely loved black pearls.

"Oh my god, this must have cost a fortune," I said as a lump started to form in my throat. I suddenly felt quite emotional as I slid the ring on my fourth finger. I moved my hand around so that the pearl captured the light, highlighting that opulent peacock sheen. It was large – around eight or nine millimetres – and surrounded by sparkly stones on either side. I suddenly felt the sting of tears. I quickly held a hand up, half covering my face in an attempt to control my emotions and mask my expression. I managed to regain my composure for a second.

"Don't worry about the cost. I wanted you to have something to remember me by when you leave for Canada. This way, I hope you'll never forget me."

So he too had accepted our doomed fate.

I remained silent, unable to find the words. A rogue tear managed to escape before I could prevent it.

"Please don't cry, Francesca," he said, while putting his arm around me. "I've been such a pain in the arse recently. I know I'm hard work. I don't know how you've put up with me." His voice cracked on the last part.

I wiped away another rogue tear and said, "Sorry, this is so embarrassing." I hated crying in front of people.

"No, what I did a minute ago was embarrassing." He paused, turning to look at me. "Do you know what I love about you? A small gift means so much to you."

My heart skipped a beat when he used the word *love*. I suddenly felt afraid to hear anymore, not wanting to feel this deeply and not wanting to reveal too much. I knew I loved him, but I wasn't sure I could take hearing that he loved me too. I squashed and pushed this storm of feelings deep down inside. It was funny how being physically intimate was less intimidating than being emotionally intimate. I urged myself to say something before it was too late.

"Thank you so much," I was finally able to say.

Ritchie gave me an affectionate squeeze and I think he may have sensed my unease. At times I sensed that he was holding back like I was too. I wasn't really built for this double life. Once I moved away, maybe I would be normal again, not in constant limbo. Because that is what it was – a constant state of confusion and pain. I relished it, yet I wanted to avoid it. It was like a drug. I had an addiction that I couldn't shake, or an incurable disease. Perhaps I did need professional help to enable me to move on, as I lived in this confused heaven and hell daily.

I squeezed his hand in acknowledgement, sharing my silent thoughts, and he asked, "Do you like Malaysian food?"

Grateful for the change in subject, I replied, "Definitely."

We sorted ourselves out and took a cab to the restaurant, which was quite far, so that we wouldn't bump into anyone we knew. We sat in silence during the cab ride, having too much to say, yet nothing at all, not really knowing how to express what we were feeling. Tumultuous feelings swirled around us aimlessly, but we ignored them, straightened up, and looked ahead. I was actually genuinely hungry now and couldn't wait to eat.

As we travelled through the city, I caught sight of the moon, who smiled mockingly yet again. Venus shone brightly nearby – she was my only hope. Ritchie turned in my direction to see what I was looking at so intently.

"What's that bright star, Francesca?"

"The planet, Venus," I replied.

"Really? How do you know?"

Pleased that he was showing an interest in something that I had a passion for, I answered enthusiastically, "Venus is the brightest 'star' in the sky and is usually visible fairly low down in the sky due to its proximity to the sun. Sometimes, it's known as the evening or the morning star."

He nodded with fascination. "I've never seen a planet before," he said.

Most people I knew had no interest in space, so I was glad to have a chance to talk about astronomy. I continued talking about it until I got fed up with the sound of my own voice. I realised that it was partly nervousness. I needed to get out of my thoughts because talk of love had shaken me a bit. If I didn't talk about something, I would have driven myself insane.

Luckily, the food didn't take too long to be served and tasted great. I allowed the fragrant spicy food to invade my senses, so that was all I could feel. Once we'd had a drink, Ritchie became a bit chattier, and this time we both blabbed on about food and my plans for the following day with John.

Ritchie's plans for the weekend involved meeting Casey. In a way, I was glad that while I was with John he wouldn't be alone and contemplating anything that had happened this evening, but I also felt that familiar stab of jealousy. I did try to be positive and supportive though. I'm sure he also felt envious when I mentioned John, which was understandable. We both realised that to keep seeing each other, we had to behave as normally as possible. Especially after that close call we'd had recently.

To keep up appearances, he had agreed to go on another date with Casey. He promised to be a bit more accepting of her and to give her a real chance. I suggested that he practice his sexual techniques on her, and I stared with disbelief as he actually considered using her for this. He hoped that it would make him a better lover. There was ruthlessness in the way he said it, and I knew I had that side to me too. We would stop at nothing to make sure we carried on our secret life for now.

Eventually, our time together was over. I decided to take a bus home, and even though he suggested I take a cab with him, he didn't insist on it. He wasn't ignorant to the fact that I had a lot on my mind. Despite my outward appearance, I was battling with my feelings inside. Maybe he was too. He was very perceptive, and I couldn't really keep anything from him. After sharing a quick embrace, we separated.

I drowned out the world by putting my earphones in, but every song reminded me of him. By some bizarre twist of fate, it seemed as if every word was written for us. I was so wrapped up in my own thoughts, I ended up missing my stop, although the cold night air was a welcome relief.

Thank goodness John was out with his colleagues that night. He would arrive home drunk and would be oblivious to how I was acting or feeling. I had planned a nice day out with him the next day, and I just hoped that I would be able to pay attention to him. The bad part was that I no longer felt guilty about cheating on him. It was a necessity now. I just had to find ways to keep up the charade.

Countless questions popped into my head. *Why don't you leave John and be with Ritchie? If Ritchie had me, would he still continue to want me? What about Ritchie's future – his family and reputation? What about my future job prospects?*

I couldn't deny Ritchie's right to be truly happy with someone who could totally dedicate herself to him. It wasn't fair, expecting him to give up everything for me. Maybe one day in the distant future, in some faraway dream, we'd reunite. Maybe, when the dust settled, we would become one and rekindle that flame. When it had all been said and done, maybe we could pick up the pieces and move on. There were a lot of maybes, which all depended on whether Ritchie had come to his senses by then. Absence from one another and time apart would be a test we would have to take. No matter what pain we put ourselves through. A steely determination pushed away the doubts and I resolved to continue our forbidden love. I'd let the shadows be my only witnesses, and in the darkness, my secrets would be kept.

Chapter Fourteen

There was one more week until the Easter holidays. We would have two weeks off, but apparently I would be tutoring Ritchie for one of those weeks. John was a little disappointed as he had hoped to go abroad for a week or so. I had to remind him yet again that we couldn't afford it anyway. I didn't have enough to pay for the both of us, as I had on previous occasions.

Beth had made it clear that she expected Ritchie to keep up with his coursework requirements and exam revision. He'd been making good progress and, understandably, she didn't want things to slip. To his credit, he'd been really focused, worked hard in class and during our tutoring sessions. We both understood the importance of academic success; it was his ticket out of St. Pauls. Perhaps Beth shouldn't have insisted that he stay to finish his GCSEs. It may have been more beneficial to him if he had studied at a local college, but if he had changed schools, we wouldn't have met. I just hoped his nerves wouldn't get the better of him on the exam days. It was for this reason that Beth requested that I be present during all his exams, as a scribe, reader or motivator. Ritchie was more than pleased when the school willingly agreed.

This was the week Ritchie received some awful news. Monday morning arrived, but he didn't. I assumed he was sick, and then I was informed that his grandmother had passed away in the wee hours of the morning. This would be a huge blow to Ritchie, as he actually got along well with his grandmother.

I spent the morning clock-watching, wondering if I should call Ritchie. I didn't know what I would say, but I needed to hear his voice to see if he was alright. I held off calling and somehow I lasted until lunchtime. How I felt his absence. Finally, giving in to my nagging thoughts, I took my mobile out of my bag intending to send him a message. To my surprise, he had already sent a long text explaining that he would be in Bath for a few days for the funeral. He had even taken the time to say that he would miss me and would call me that evening when he was alone.

I felt an overwhelming love for him. His grandmother had just died and he was still thinking of me. I didn't have time to reply to his message just then. It would have taken a while, as I wanted to carefully consider my words first. I would wait for his call that evening and I hoped he would have time to speak to me. How I dreaded spending the next few days at school without him. I guess I would support some of the other students in his classes. I was tempted to pull a sickie or two, but that would be suspicious, coinciding with Ritchie's absence. And it might only add to the emptiness and concern I felt. I wouldn't be able to bear being home alone, wallowing in loneliness and longing. I did that enough already. The last thing I needed was to exacerbate the feelings which were already too much for me to handle at times.

I managed to survive the day by dragging myself through. Like a zombie, I headed home. My thoughts rendered me oblivious to the world. I was glad that John was working late that night as I wasn't sure if I could maintain normalcy. I hoped Ritchie would call while John was at work. We had devised a way of communicating that wouldn't arouse suspicion. We often kept our phones on silent when we sent texts, and we'd often ask, "What are you up to?" If either one of us replied, "Nothing much," we knew it was a good time to call.

We had always been fairly careful, but after that meeting with Sue, we had deleted all messages. I had stupidly been keeping copies of all texts and emails from Ritchie on USB, which I liked to read from time to time. I was still debating about whether or not to keep them. I couldn't bring myself to delete them yet. My obsession was causing me to take unnecessary risks now. I knew it was a bad idea and that my luck was running out. I could only imagine the looks on everyone's faces and the hellish nightmare we would have to face if we were found out.

I got all the laundry done as soon as I arrived home, ate a rushed dinner, and got ready for bed early. I lay there with the television on yet paid no attention to it. I held on to my phone willing it to ring, willing Ritchie to hear me. Eventually, I fell into a fitful doze until my phone rang. Startled, I dropped it on the floor and swore at myself. My heart thumping loudly, I picked up my phone and heard his voice.

"Francesca?"

"Oh, Ritchie, I'm so sorry for your loss."

"Thank you. I can't believe she's gone. It feels so weird," he said emptily.

"How's your mum taking it?"

"You know how she is – she's not the crying type."

"She's probably really upset, but some people just don't show it. I liked your grandmother. She seemed quite friendly when I met her."

"She was nice to everyone. She would always ask how I was and take the time to speak to me. She actually cared."

"Was the end peaceful?"

"I guess so. They said that she died in her sleep due to natural causes." I heard a slight hitch in his voice. He was trying not to cry. He'd probably had to hold it in all this time, afraid to show any emotion in front of his family.

"I wish I could say or do something to comfort you."

There was quite a long silence as he tried to contain his composure. I waited it out. I hoped that my presence, although over the phone, was consoling. After a while, I heard him take a breath.

"Wish you were with me. I was tempted to ask if you'd come. You knew her. The school would give you time off."

"Sorry, I don't think that's a good idea. It's your time to be with family."

"I know. I just miss you," he mumbled.

"I miss you too." *More than you know*, I thought.

"I need you to hold me, Francesca," he said thickly, suddenly revealing way too much. I felt those words deep within my core and it shook me. I tried to think of a good response, but I had none.

How hard it would be when we finally separated forever. Now, I couldn't even bear to spend a few days without him, especially because he was in pain. At the beginning of all this, at least I was able to spend some time away from him, like I had during the Christmas holidays when I'd had an inkling of self-control left. I had let my feelings get the better of me, controlling me, suffocating me.

"Francesca? Are you still there?"

"Sorry, yes. I was in my own little world for a minute there. I guess you better get to bed," I suggested, in an attempt to end the conversation. "Please pass on my condolences to your mother."

"I will do. Good night, Francesca." He hung up, sensing that he'd said too much and that I wasn't ready to hear it yet. It had also been a long day for him, dealing with everything. I hoped the next few days wouldn't be an ordeal. I desperately wanted to call him back, even if it was just to hear him breathe. We'd done that already anyway. I resisted the urge by leaving my phone on silent and on the floor. Knowing me, I'd probably end up checking it later, and that was why I didn't turn it off. I willed myself to forget it, to switch off and sleep, but sleep didn't come.

***

Joseph and Stuart were ecstatic when I told them they would be getting extra support until Ritchie returned. I have to admit that did put a smile on my face. It was nice to be appreciated. I found most pupils responded well to extra support from adults, while some found it a little embarrassing, worried about their reputations. However, they were only in Year Seven, so they still had some of the innocence of primary school aged children.

They had minimal behavioural issues, although Joseph tended to be silly and a bit cheeky. Most of the staff found it irritating but endearing at the same time. Stuart was different. He was very quiet and had difficulties communicating. He often spent lunchtime in the library and didn't have many friends. I wondered if he felt lonely sometimes. I had thought about asking him to join us at lunchtime, but I didn't want to share Ritchie. My time with him was precious. There may have been the odd occasion when Joseph joined us, but I had a feeling that Stuart would end up sitting with us all the time, oblivious to the fact that he was a third wheel.

I managed to keep myself busy for the next two days, but there were moments when I stopped and wondered what Ritchie was doing or what he was thinking. I hoped the funeral hadn't been too hard on him.

He called me every night he was away just to say good night. Our conversation still contained lots of long silences, though. He was obviously quite shaken by the death of his grandmother, and in an effort to be polite, I didn't want to change the subject or talk about myself for fear of seeming unsympathetic. During the silences, I could feel that there was a lot that needed to be said concerning us, but we just couldn't find the words. Even when he did return, I doubted that we would be able to describe our feelings and how deeply we felt those things. We'd always been afraid of saying too much, of revealing too much, because that would really make things difficult.

On Wednesday night, Ritchie announced that he would be returning the next day. He was worried about missing too much school and he had a test on Friday. Beth had decided to stay in Bath until Monday – something about the reading of the will.

When I arrived at the LSU, he was sitting inside. He had his back towards me, but I would recognise that gold mane anywhere. Sue waved me over before I made my presence known.

"As you know, Richard has had a rough few days, and I'm not convinced he's ready to return. The slightest thing could set him off. Could you have a chat with him and see if he's okay."

"No problem. Of course, I will."

"Luckily, he's in the LSU first two periods anyway. I know you're not timetabled to support him this morning, but you can stay with him if he seems a bit wobbly."

I walked over to an anxious looking Ritchie, who was probably wondering why he was missing registration. Guessing that he felt uncomfortable talking in front of Sue, after greeting him, I asked if he wanted to go to the one-to-one room.

As soon as we entered, we sat down and he asked, "Is there something wrong?" Understandably, he seemed a bit perplexed.

"No, they just wanted me to make sure that you're okay to return to lessons today. I know this is a silly question, but how do you feel?"

He absentmindedly started fiddling with a bit of glue stuck to the table. "I don't know," he answered honestly.

"Apparently, I can stay with you in the LSU during first period, if you want?"

"You know I want you to stay with me," he said quietly. He shook his head sadly, and added, "Aren't you supporting Stuart this morning?"

"Yes, I'm meant to be supporting him, but if you need me, I'll stay with you," I replied. I didn't want to neglect Stuart, as he had English, but I wanted to be there for Ritchie. He seemed to sense my dilemma.

"I'll be okay, Francesca. You do enough for me already." Seeing the look on my face, he added, "Don't worry, I'll revise for that science test."

"You shouldn't have to do that test tomorrow. I'll ask them to reschedule your test for Monday, although you might have to do it after school," I warned. "I can help you study for it over the weekend."

He visibly perked up at the thought of that and asked, "Do you really think they'll let me do it on Monday instead?

"Well, you've got extenuating circumstances, so I don't see why not," I reassured encouragingly. "It would be nice to spend some time with you over the weekend too."

He reached over, took my hand, giving it a gentle squeeze, and said, "Thank you."

The bell rung for first period and Ritchie returned to the LSU. I explained to Sue that Ritchie wanted to work independently for a while, revising for that test. She doubted that there would be a problem rescheduling his test either.

I knew Ritchie would be fine working alone in the LSU, although I wasn't one hundred percent sure if he was ready to return to actual lessons. I wanted to give him the benefit of the doubt and hoped there would be no incidents. Teachers were aware though, so hopefully they would be more vigilant to any possible aggravations.

As I sipped my tea in the staffroom during morning break, I glimpsed Ritchie sitting on the railing by the steps outside. Alone as usual, but somehow looking more alone than ever. I wanted to go to him and tell him that he wasn't alone. I really felt for him, but I debated whether or not I should go to him, fearing that it might fuel rumours. Inevitably, I gave into my urge.

"Hey, Ritchie," I said as I walked towards him. I must have woken him from his thoughts, as he took a moment to focus on me.

"Francesca," he responded, while giving me a sad smile.

"I saw you sitting alone out here and thought I'd say hello."

Instead of responding, he just looked down at the floor. My chest tightened when I saw the forlorn look on his face.

I waited, but he said nothing. I took a step closer, intending to physically comfort him. Remembering where I was, I stopped. Finally, I asked, "Are you okay?"

"The world goes on, doesn't it? When we die, it's like we never existed," he contemplated morbidly, though I had often thought this myself when I had experienced the death of a loved one.

"It's harsh, isn't it?" I said. "The way the world is. You just want to ask – does anyone give a shit?" And the answer is usually no.

"That's exactly how I feel," he said absentmindedly.

His eyes glazed over, staring into space. A few moments passed. He took a deep breath and asked, "How did you cope with death in your family?"

We'd had a conversation in the past about how many family members I'd lost during my lifetime. I had gone to so many funerals that I'd almost become numb to it.

"I don't know really. I guess I tried to celebrate their lives. I sort of feel that they never really left; that they're still here and I might see them again one day."

He listened intently and seemed to reflect on what I'd just said. I just hoped it helped in some shape or form.

"I'm going to try doing that. Thanks, Francesca."

"If you ever want to talk about it, I'm here for you." How I wanted to hold him against my chest and not care what the world thought, but I stood there, frozen, as the bell went.

Despite missing three days, he mostly kept up with everyone else during geography with a bit of prompting. His classmates stared at him conspicuously, but thankfully he didn't seem to notice. He was probably preoccupied with thoughts of his grandmother and the growing mound of work he had to contend with. He was extremely quiet after our chat earlier, but I didn't push him. I tried to be supportive as well as give him enough space to absorb everything that had happened.

"I've spoken to the head of the science department and they have agreed for you to do the test on Monday, which means we'll have the weekend to prepare. It will be during class time. I'll withdraw you as usual to be your reader."

Ritchie nodded almost imperceptibly as he played with his lunch. I wasn't completely sure that he'd heard me until he replied, "Sorry, I wasn't really there for a minute. That's good news."

Changing the subject, I asked, "Are you attending swimming club today?"

"No, I can't face it. Do you have plans this evening?"

I knew he wanted me to come over after school.

"I can't make it this evening. I have an appointment. I'm not sure how long it's going to take." His expression said it all. He was disappointed, although he didn't say it. I desperately wanted to make him happy. "I can cancel if you want?"

"No, don't cancel because of me. I know your back has been giving you problems recently. It's important that you go. I just wanted to see you," he explained apologetically.

"I'll see you tomorrow night. I have to go home first. I'll probably be there around seven-ish."

After school, whilst at my appointment, I was preoccupied with thoughts of Ritchie. During my assessment, the doctor had to ask the same questions more than once.

I was worried about Ritchie being alone. As soon as I left the surgery, I sent a text checking up on him. No response. I tried calling, but there was no answer. I couldn't help but feel the panic rise in my chest. Hours later, my phone rang. John looked at me questioningly as I took the call in the bedroom.

"Hi, Ritchie. I sent a message earlier," I said, relieved that he had called me back.

"I just saw your message now. Sorry. I passed out on my bed for a couple of hours as soon as I got home from school." It must have been an exhausting few days.

"No, it's okay. I just wanted to check that you were okay." There was a bit of a silence, but I sensed that he had more to say.

"I don't know, Francesca. I'm not doing all that well. This is the first time I've slept in the last few days," he answered honestly. I wasn't surprised.

"Didn't you sleep last night?"

"Not really. I spent most of the night on my laptop playing games, trying not to listen to the voice in my head." I hoped that he didn't mean literal voices in his head. I made a note to ask him some more about that another time.

"Why didn't you tell me before that you were having trouble sleeping?"

"I thought I'd be able to deal with it on my own," he said quietly. I knew what he meant – he was fed up with getting support for everything.

"But you don't have to deal with this alone, Ritchie."

"I know. I just wish you could stay with me tomorrow night. I need you, Francesca." It had taken a lot of courage for him to admit that he needed me. Sometimes, I wanted him to need me. That way he wouldn't leave me. If he stopped needing me, would he still want me? The truth was that I needed him too.

"Believe me I want to, but I'm not sure how John will feel about that." How would I begin to explain why I wanted to stay overnight?

He often said that he trusted me; it was other men that he didn't trust.

"I know it's a lot to ask. Just say you're helping me out and you're staying in the guest bedroom."

I would certainly try.

"What would your mum think though?" She could sense something between me and Ritchie – would she suspect anything? That was probably the last thing on her mind. Even though she might not show it, she must be devastated about the loss of her mother.

"She won't mind," he said, trying to reassure me.

"Well, I'm not so sure about that. You might have to ask her, but she's got a lot to deal with at the moment, so I'm not sure how she'll take it."

"She'll be fine with it. I'll ask her if you want, though."

"I've got to go now, Ritchie. I really hope you sleep well. Put the TV on and just drift off if you have to. It works for me."

"Don't go yet. Talk to me some more," he pleaded. I could talk to him for hours on end. Despite the long silences, it was the next best thing to actually being with him. If I couldn't be with him tonight, then at least I could still speak to him.

"I would love to hear the sound of your voice for longer, but John's coming to bed soon."

We reluctantly said our goodbyes, and soon after, John came to bed. I briefly explained that Ritchie's grandmother had died and he needed someone to talk to, which was mostly true. I tried to find the right moment to suggest that I stay at Ritchie's house. I never did.

***

Throughout the day, I kept clock-watching, counting down the minutes until I would be alone with him. I was still worried about telling John, especially if he knew that Ritchie's mother wouldn't be around to supervise us. I guess I could pretend that she was, but then again I needed to convince him that Ritchie was truly alone. It was different when I'd gone to Bath, as it had been a family gathering. I'm surprised we hadn't been caught. In hindsight, it was painfully clear that we'd been reckless; our feelings had got the better of us. Well, I would be pushing my luck once again.

When I arrived home, John was sitting at his computer. After saying a brief hello, I discreetly packed some small items for an overnight stay. I still couldn't bring myself to tell him about my plans, but I did manage to explain that Ritchie needed help studying for a test on Monday, as well as moral support. He didn't seem too bothered at first, as he was preoccupied with an online game.

I headed to Ritchie's house at around seven. Ritchie opened the door with a relieved expression on his face.

"I thought you were going to change your mind. What did John say?"

"I haven't told him yet. I'll tell him later," I said briskly.

Both of us were not in the mood for studying that evening. We didn't do much, just watched television. Ritchie quietly lay with his head on my lap. I gently stroked his hair away from his face. After a while, I fought the urge to keep touching him, thinking that I was overdoing it.

"Don't stop," he said. He seemed so vulnerable and young then. He must have spent his childhood craving affection from his cold father and distant mother. He'd mentioned before that there was one nanny who had been kind towards him when he was very young. He didn't remember her much, because she had decided to move back to Poland. He had missed her terribly, so he had kept his distance from every other nanny that followed. After the age of twelve, he was looked after by what I would describe as more of a live-in housekeeper who supervised him and prepared meals for him. Now that he didn't need supervision, the latest housekeeper was purely there to maintain the house and prepare an evening meal. She was usually gone by four o'clock.

By nine, I knew I had to call John. When he answered, I could hear the background sounds of a pub.

"But you spend so much time helping him already," he grumbled.

"Does it really matter? You're out at the pub anyway."

For the first time, I heard a note of anxiety in his voice when he asked, "Do I have anything to worry about?" He had never asked me that before. He was a simple, honest man who was innately good-natured, so it was a shame that I had to lie. Guilt passed by like a fleeting whisper but dissolved in a flash.

"John, what kind of question is that? You know you can trust me." The lie came so easily that I didn't even have to think. It felt natural — like breathing. The person I used to be was no more. No one would have recognised the person that I had become.

"I do, but what about him? Can I trust him?" Why did everyone think that Ritchie was the one to watch out for? Did I really come across as being morally just and decent, while he came across as being some kind of unstable deviant? Maybe it was because I used to be good, while

Ritchie had always had social problems.

"Of course you can. He's just grieving and he needs someone. His mum isn't around and he shouldn't have to be alone. It's not fair," I proclaimed strongly.

"I'm not sure why you care so much. He's not family. Just promise me that if he tries anything you'll come straight home, okay?" He seemed genuinely concerned – not just jealous. It was sweet in a weird sort of way, but he was out drinking yet again. *Silly old man*, I thought. We'd been through a lot together. It must seem strange how I needed them both. When things ended between me and Ritchie, John would be the one I'd end up running to. I doubted I could cope with being alone after we went our separate ways.

A wave of tiredness seemed to hit both me and Ritchie at the same time. For me, all the tiredness from the week converged on Friday night, which meant I rarely stayed up late. My body clock seemed to adjust to school time – early mornings and early bedtimes.

As we both lay in his bed, I guided him towards me, so that his head rested on my chest. I wondered if he could hear my heart race faster or feel my body temperature rise as I held him.

After a while, he said, "I'm so glad you're here." His voice was heavy with emotion; he'd probably been holding it in all week. I didn't want him to feel that pain. I said nothing and held him tighter. I'm not sure how long we stayed like that. Eventually, his breathing became deeper. I closed my eyes, until we breathed in rhythm with one another.

I woke to the smell of food the next morning. I guessed that Ritchie was making breakfast for us. I had a quick shower and went downstairs. Fascinated, I watched him concentrate, as he carefully placed the fried eggs on the plates. I loved these moments when he didn't know I could see him. I stared with appreciation at his muscular arms and his strong shoulders. Even the way he used his hands interested me. He swiped his hair back frustratingly as it cascaded over his eyes. It was my fault that it was getting long now. I had selfishly asked him not to cut it. I just couldn't bear to see it cut.

Deciding to make my presence known, I announced, "Morning, Ritchie."

"Oh. Morning, Francesca," he responded, slightly startled.

"How did you sleep?" I hoped that he hadn't got up too early because he needed the rest.

He put the plates on the table and sat down, making sure to give me eye contact as he answered.

"I slept really well." He reached out to stroke my hand. "Because you were there with me. Thank you." I had a flashback of the night before, of me holding him close against me, and a warm feeling spread through my body. His eyes were intense as his pupils dilated; the irises became thin rings. Just then the kettle finished boiling and he got up to sort out tea.

Although we ate quietly, he looked up at me frequently to see if I was enjoying the breakfast. As if he was desperate to please me, worried that he'd done something wrong. I reassured him that it was delicious. When we'd finished, he loaded up the dishwasher. I followed.

Standing behind him, I reached up to touch his hair and said, "It's too long for you now, isn't it?"

He stiffened, but not from discomfort. My fingernails grazed across his scalp, and I could see from his profile that his eyes were closed as I ran my fingers through his soft curls. Did he crave my touch the way I craved his? The very thought made my chest flutter. Then I was in his arms and his lips were on mine. I wanted so much more, but he ended it by saying that he needed a shower. I guessed that what he needed more was my understanding, so I forced myself not to be upset by it.

It was wrong of me to be selfish when he had a lot on his mind. I couldn't help but wonder when he would feel better, so that I could touch him like that again. I'd have to wait until he initiated, until he felt ready.

Revision went well that day. I enjoyed being in his company, despite the fact that he was quiet and we were working. When our knees touched, sparks shot through me. Bare minimum contact seemed to light a fire, and I found myself staring at Ritchie while he studied. I felt a hunger growing inside me. I could smell him and feel the heat emanating from his body. I yearned to touch him, but I had to keep giving myself a mental shake, because I had to give him space. It was hard though. I didn't dare try to initiate anything, fearing that he might push me away. I forced myself to turn away from his beautiful face and to focus on the task at hand.

Evening came quickly. I managed to convince John about staying another night, as it made sense, considering that I was going to tutor Ritchie the following day anyway. John made me promise to come home by lunchtime, though. I think he missed me, which was funny because we often didn't spend much time together during weekends. We were like strangers sometimes. Maybe the thought of me spending time with another man made him jealous.

That night, Ritchie snuggled up to my chest like the night before and fell asleep. He seemed so peaceful in my arms. I stroked his silky soft hair and kissed him lovingly. At least he would let me hold him while he slept.

When I woke up, I decided to have a bath while Ritchie slept. He seemed to be sleeping peacefully. His body needed the rest and so I left him be.

I stepped into the largest bath I had ever bathed in and relaxed. I almost dozed off, but then I heard a knock on the door. Hesitantly, Ritchie walked in. While he asked me if I would like some tea, he stared unflinchingly at my breasts. He ran his eyes along my body and I drank in his voyeurism. I loved the way it made me feel.

Our eyes locked.

"Why don't you join me?"

I just had to ask. I had been holding it in for what seemed like a long time and I desperately wanted him to touch me all over. He answered by removing his clothes and smiling. Finally. How long had I waited to see him smile like that again? I didn't smile back. I just stared back lustfully. *Touch me, take me*, I pleaded.

He sat behind me and I positioned myself between his legs. I brought both of his hands to my breasts and then he needed no more guidance. I had successfully coaxed him back to life. I threw my head back while he kissed my neck and squeezed my breasts, igniting the fire between my thighs. I felt his breath on my damp skin sending shivers through me. He played with my nipples and nibbled my earlobe. I touched myself as he touched me. I wanted gratification right away. I rubbed my clit slowly at first, increasing speed as I got closer to climax. My heart hammered against my ribs as I gasped loudly. Pure bliss washed over me. Ritchie became still, focusing on every moment while I came.

"Oh my god, you're so sexy," he said.

"I've been holding that in since Friday night."

"I was a bit out of it yesterday, wasn't I?"

"Don't worry. I understand."

Unfortunately, it was back to revision as soon as we were finished because I was planning to return home fairly early. A little bit before I left, we heard Beth pull up in the driveway. She had arrived sooner than expected. Ritchie quickly made the guest bedroom look like it had been occupied for the last two nights, ruffling the sheets and putting all the toiletries he'd so kindly bought for me in there. Although I doubted she would notice much after what had happened.

I made my way downstairs and told Beth that I was sorry for her loss, and she thanked me for supporting Ritchie. I explained that she didn't have to pay me for the weekend due to what happened. I had done it for Ritchie as a supportive gesture, though I told John that I had got paid.

Beth stepped into the kitchen to put the kettle on, and Ritchie grabbed one last kiss just as I walked out of the front door. When I left, all I could feel were his soft lips on mine. I could still taste him when I arrived home, and when John leaned towards me, I turned my head so that his kiss landed on my cheek. I wanted to preserve the taste of Ritchie that night.

Chapter Fifteen

Sadly, the first week of the Easter holidays came and went without me seeing Ritchie. John had taken a week off and he had managed to book plane tickets to Barcelona. I found out afterwards that he had used his overdraft to afford it, which caused an argument as usual. He claimed that he would be able to repay the overdraft after he got paid at the end of the month. I still gave him half towards the cost, as I knew he would struggle to pay it back. I just knew him too well.

The holiday itself, however, was actually quite nice. We spent the week eating tapas and sipping cocktails. Ritchie had encouraged me to go and have a relaxing break, insisting that he felt a lot better and that I needed a holiday. I found my mind wondering often, wishing to speak with Ritchie, constantly checking my messages and hoping that there would be one from him. I became ridiculously giddy every time he sent one. Despite John becoming intoxicated one evening, he was fairly well behaved for the majority of the week. Basically, he was slightly more considerate than usual.

I missed Ritchie terribly, and by the time I returned, I couldn't wait to see him. With John back at work and doing a long shift, we decided to study at my flat. Science and geography had been going well, so we thought it best to stick with literacy. English was the big one anyhow.

He arrived half an hour after John left for work, careful to get the timing right. He was in a good mood. I could tell, because he was making jokes, teasing me and being ever so touchy-feely. Evidently, he had missed me too.

We spent a good few hours on coursework, which made up thirty percent of the total mark. It involved comparing different representations of Macbeth in film. As part of the assignment, we had to watch specific scenes over and over again. Eventually, we just ended up in giggles and the chemistry between us intensified. I caught his eyes on my mouth quite a few times and it wasn't hard to guess what he was thinking.

I decided it was time for a break.

Cheekily, I showed him some sexy underwear John had bought for me years ago. I hadn't worn it for years. It still fit, and seeing as I was in a naughty mood, I put it on jokingly. I tried to dance seductively, but I couldn't keep a straight face or take it seriously. I even had Ritchie laughing with my silly antics – something I had not seen often recently. It was great to see him like that.

I dragged him into the bedroom and we frolicked, falling over ourselves onto the bed. Using Shakespearean quotes, we pretended to talk dirty. It reminded me of a corny porn movie without the sex. He tickled and fondled me with a vengeance until we were both in hysterics. Becoming seriously aroused, I ended up straddling him on his growing erection. I felt the hardness against me between my legs and I dry humped him. I raised my arms, holding my mane of hair up because it emphasised my figure. I wanted him to feast his eyes on me. I slid off, pulling him on top of me.

Laughter ceased. Lust took over.

We kissed over and over again – the feel of his tongue touching mine made me wet between my legs. Interlocking my ankles, I wrapped my legs around him, pulling him closer. It would be so easy. All he had to do was slip it in. I imagined the smooth head penetrating me and him thrusting hard.

"I want you inside me, Ritchie," I whispered.

He looked at me with a mixture of shock and anxiety.

"I can't," he answered breathlessly from all the kissing. "What if I'm not good?"

"I'm not going to lie to you; you might not last long the first time, but there's other ways of satisfying a woman."

He considered this for a moment.

"I want to. Believe me, I want to. More than anything."

He seemed so anxious, and I didn't want him to be. He was so worried about disappointing me, but there was no reason to be. Trying to relax him a bit, I wrestled with him playfully, forcing kisses all over his face until he laughed.

"I want to try something," I said as I removed my underwear. I straddled his face, tugged his boxers down and slid my mouth onto his rigid member. He caught my drift, knowing what I wanted. I felt his hands on my buttocks and his tongue on my clit and sliding inside me. As I sucked, he moaned with pleasure, but I didn't want him to climax yet. I paused, taking a condom out of the bedside cabinet and handed it to him. I wanted him to make the final decision, but I was expressing my intentions clearly. He swallowed nervously, took it from me and looked up at me. Within seconds, his veil slipped away and once again I felt immersed in green and gold. Dappled sunlight flickered through a shower of autumn leaves and his eyes came alive with passion.

He had me captured in his world yet again.

He took a deep decisive breath, ripped open the wrapper and slid the condom on slowly. I lay on my back, anticipating him. My body throbbed violently as he positioned himself between my legs. He leaned forward to kiss me long and deep. Already lost in this blissful moment, I felt his smooth head slip inside me. I gasped loudly with arousal. I had been waiting for this moment for so long. Ritchie moaned with pleasure as he thrust slowly at first. Once he found a rhythm, he increased the force of his thrust.

"Yes. That's it. A little harder," I guided breathlessly.

His body tensed as he reached orgasm. He panted uncontrollably into my hair. I looked up as he raised his head to look at me.

"Sorry," he said dismally, a dark expression cast upon his face.

He slipped out, but before he stood up, I pulled him back towards me.

"It's okay. Now finish it," I whispered in his ear. I guided his hand downwards and he eased his fingers inside, firmly thrusting in and out. He took his body downtown and I felt his tongue on my clit as he simultaneously stimulated both areas. It didn't take me long to have a really intense orgasm. There was a look of both relief and a hint of satisfaction as he watched, devouring the scene and burning it into his memory forever.

***

As John's alarm sounded, I yawned loudly. I'd barely been able to sleep; thoughts of Ritchie occupied every corner of my mind. When he asked me why I'd been so restless, I had no answer for him. Yesterday had been like a dream. I had to blink a few times and ask myself, *Had we really done that?* Yes, we definitely had. Because if it had been a dream, I would still be with him now.

He had left soon after. He had been embarrassed about his

performance, but it didn't really bother me, as it had been his first time and he was a passionate man. He put his all into everything, and he had opened himself up to the experience. It was just a matter of learning and experience. He was only young, so I could easily forgive him. Knowing Ritchie like I did, I knew that he would feel down about it for a while.

John interrupted my thoughts when he turned around to give me a cuddle. I returned the affection and snuggled his chest, imagining it was Ritchie's. They certainly didn't feel the same though. Over the last few years, John had not only piled on the weight, he had also aged rapidly. He barely resembled the man I initially fell for.

Half an hour later, John left for work after a rushed shower. I realised I had received a text earlier. My phone was on silent so I hadn't heard it. Ritchie had cancelled studying for that day. He was meeting Casey.

My heart sunk.

I so wanted to continue "educating" Ritchie. I wanted more and more to teach him and to guide him. It looked like he was going to be with Casey instead. For the first time, I felt myself feeling annoyed with him for abandoning me. I had to remind myself that it was I who had so strongly advised that he have a girlfriend and enjoy the perks that come with it. I couldn't help but wonder if he was indeed avoiding me. Had our time together been so terrible? Would he really let embarrassment cut him so deeply?

It wasn't until Wednesday morning that I received a call from Ritchie. We made small talk for a while, but deciding to cut to the chase, I asked, "So how did it go with Casey?"

"It went fine," he said mysteriously, without giving anything away.

"Aren't you going to tell me?" The line went silent because he could tell I was upset. "Were you avoiding me?" When the silence continued, I knew it to be true.

"No, I... Maybe I was. I'm sorry," he answered sadly.

"It's okay, Ritchie. I thought you knew that. I know it's about what happened on Monday. Well, it's a common problem that people face sometimes," I tried to explain.

"It was shameful. Premature ejaculation at my age is ridiculous. I couldn't face you."

Why did he have to think in such a negative way? I wish he didn't feel like that. Every time he hit a wall, he would try to avoid it rather than face it.

"Please stop being like this. It will get better – I promise. Just don't shut me out. You're making me feel like it was so awful for you."

"Oh Francesca, I never meant to. I've never felt so close to you. I just wanted to be better for you, but I'm not good enough."

He had such a cataclysmic way of thinking – *I've got to be the best or I'm not good enough.* There was no middle ground. My patience was wearing thin. I wasn't going to understand this time. I felt bubbles rise to the surface.

"Well, if you put it like that, I've never been good enough for you. Maybe you are better off with Casey," I said bitterly. Without thinking, I slammed the phone down. A few seconds later, I felt the sting of tears threatening to escape. Panic set in as I began to regret what I'd said. I wasn't ready to end it. What had I done? I spent the next hour replaying the scene in my mind.

The doorbell ringing brought me out of my stupor, and to my immense relief, it was Ritchie. I stood there, unsure of what to say, unsure of how he felt.

"Please don't leave me," he choked out.

"I don't want to, but maybe I'm not the right one for you. I can't make you happy."

His eyes sparkled as tears formed in his eyes.

"No, Francesca. You do make me happy." Taking a step closer, he looked me in the eyes and placed his hands gently on either side of my face. "Believe me."

I wondered if the moment had presented itself. Had the time come? Was it time to end things? Break away now, so that it would be easier to move on? He remained still, waiting for me to respond, willing me to understand. I couldn't. I couldn't turn away from him. Rather than speaking, I kissed him. That kiss alone conveyed a lot more than I was able to say that I was sorry for hanging up; that I understood; that I forgave him.

We talked for quite some time about his anxieties. He promised to try and be a bit kinder to himself. It wasn't going to change overnight, but I hoped that one day he would be happy in his own skin and proud of his achievements, no matter how small.

Apparently, he had felt a bit awkward when Casey expressed an interest in going all the way. I was surprised that he had turned her down – he was a young man, after all. Perhaps the way he'd imagined his first time wasn't the actual way it had turned out. I suggested that he'd put way too much emphasis on the importance of it. Throughout all those years, feeling alone and frustrated, he had imagined all kinds of scenarios and developed farfetched fantasies. Reality had kicked in and he wasn't ready. A kind of misguided loyalty to me was preventing him from being truly intimate with Casey. I hoped that I hadn't pressured him into sex the other day. Maybe he really wasn't ready.

I had always assumed that men only ever thought about one thing. His anxieties were a huge barrier to his fulfilment. I decided that I wouldn't pressure him again. Let him initiate. That was exactly what I'd tried before, but I had let my desires get the better of me.

It had been suggested in the past that Ritchie receive professional help. Maybe he did need it to change the way he saw the world. Part of me was afraid that he might accidentally reveal what was going on between him and me. I couldn't risk that, but he did need some kind of help. His neuroticism needed to be tackled before he reached true adulthood.

He made an effort to be open with me, and we talked for so long that we never did get around to studying. I made him promise that he study hard for the rest of the week. John was going to be home at around six, so Ritchie left at around half five.

What a strange week it had been so far. In some ways, we really had opened ourselves up to the pleasures and the pains of a real relationship. I tried to understand that things would be difficult for Ritchie. I remembered what I had been like during the first year of my relationship with John – so immature, arguing and getting upset over nothing.

John came in drunk that night yet again. I wished that Ritchie had stayed later. I still sometimes questioned myself as to why I was still with John, but I knew why. I just wanted Ritchie here instead – whose speech wasn't slurred, who wanted to be with me and at least communicate with me in some way.

Once John fell asleep, Ritchie and I sent messages to one another for hours. We chatted about random topics and ended up quoting from our favourite movies such as *Star Wars*. We must have sounded like a couple of nerds, but I found it comforting. After yawning quite a few times, I reluctantly ended the conversation, imagining him lying in his bed as I lay in mine, and I slept.

As soon as John left for work, Ritchie was at my door. He seemed unusually happy, as if a huge weight had been lifted. I was so glad. His moods could last days, even weeks. I understood that things had been difficult for him as a child and there were a few issues he needed to talk about one day, but for now I was glad he had a smile on his face.

"I hope you're ready to study," I said teasingly.

"Do I have to, miss?"

I loved it when he called me miss, and he often said it to be provocative. Even when he said it at school, it felt like foreplay.

"Unless... you'd rather be punished?"

He smiled coyly, looking at me with his sexy eyes, enjoying the banter. My face started to become hot with arousal, even though he'd only been standing there for a minute or so. I grabbed his hand, led him into the living room and made him sit down at the table. Then we both giggled.

"You've got to be a good boy today," I said, half meaning it. We really did have to be on our best behaviour – like little school children.

He sat with his elbows on the table, his chin leaning on his palms, and stared at me wistfully. "Maybe I want to be punished." He chuckled as I playfully slapped his arm.

It took us a while to get into study mode, but once we'd found our flow, he bent his head down in concentration. I watched as he carefully read from his textbook and yet again I found myself observing him rather than scanning the text with him. He became aware of it, turning to look at me and returning my gaze.

"Have I ever told you that you have beautiful brown eyes?"

That was another reason why we were attracted to each other. In terms of looks, we were opposites. His white hand contrasted against my tan coloured hand, my dark Mediterranean features against his pale Nordic features. We both seemed exotic to the other. Our different backgrounds were interesting to one another. What we had in common was our passion for one another. It wasn't just skin deep. We had seen beneath the surface and had experienced each other's inner worlds.

The scent of him lingered once again that evening. I found myself unable to stop talking about him when John came home. I was full of endless praise for him, but the expression on John's face made me stop. I realised that I was going on too much. I forced myself to change the subject, asking about his day instead.

***

It was nearing the end of the Easter holidays and I went to Ritchie's house for the last day of studying. Beth greeted me like an old friend, like part of the family, which felt a bit strange. She invited John and I to a family event that would be taking place, date yet to be confirmed. Relatives were visiting from America, so Beth had invited a 'small' group of family and friends over. She also said that she would like to meet John. This so-called small get-together sounded like a grander affair than that. I noticed that Ritchie shifted uncomfortably on his feet, and when Beth left us to it, I had to ask what was wrong.

"Casey will be there," he said. When I didn't respond, he continued, "So I won't be able to spend much time with you."

"That's okay, because John will be there too. I'm sure it won't be that bad." I tried to sound positive, but I had no idea how it would go.

Chapter Sixteen

I sat beside Ritchie during mass, which had been changed to Tuesday, due to it being an inset day the day before. He almost forgot where he was, leaning towards me as if to give me a kiss. Just in time, he seemed to realise it was the wrong time and place. He cringed apologetically.

"I saw Casey on Sunday," he whispered. He watched my face as I responded – like he needed my approval.

"Great!" I replied with feigned cheerfulness. "How are you two getting along?" I tried to keep my expression and tone more neutral.

"We're up to third base now. Sort of," he said, while searching my face with his eyes, trying to gauge how I was feeling. I made a mental note to check what third base actually meant. I wasn't really up to date with baseball euphemisms.

Keeping my game face on, I replied, "Sounds like you're making progress. I'm glad you haven't been alone. How do you feel about her?"

Just then mass started. We'd have to continue our conversation later. I didn't want to know, yet I did want to know. I wanted him to be happy, but I didn't want him to leave me. He had to be a normal eighteen-year-old. He had to experience life. Sometimes, I felt like I was standing in his way of finding true happiness. The thought of them together was hard to take, but I'm sure the thought of me and John together was difficult for Ritchie too – yet he had never complained. I was a conflicted woman. That was for sure.

He glanced at me a few times during service, but I purposely didn't look back. I would speak to him when the time was right.

As we sat in English class, I thought about how far Ritchie had come. He had come a long way. Michael had deliberately made comments when Ritchie entered the classroom. Ritchie must have heard them, but he didn't respond. At first glance, he seemed to act as if he hadn't heard it. On closer inspection, I noticed his jaw clenching.

While the graded first drafts of the coursework were being handed out, I asked, "Are you alright?"

He nodded, replying stubbornly, "I'm fine." Just then, he received his assignment back. He'd got a B minus for his Macbeth piece. Although I'd helped him put it together, it was ultimately his work. I had merely been a tool. It was one of the best grades he'd ever got in English. Any momentary flashes of anger were forgotten and quickly replaced by a look of pleasant surprise. He never thought that he could achieve that.

"Tell me, am I seeing things?"

"No, you really got that grade. Well done. I'm so proud of you." I gave his arm a light squeeze. This was about all I could do in public. I wanted to give him a congratulatory hug and kiss, but I held back for obvious reasons. Maybe I could later. His joy was marvellous and it seemed to have a knock-on effect. He carried it with him. It was infectious. It was great seeing his confidence growing.

A lot had happened since returning to school after Easter. It was a successful time for Ritchie. His grades had improved, and he was engaging in a real relationship with Casey, but not letting it conflict with his studies.

Her family were really keen on a future marriage between the two. Beth was ecstatic that things had been going so smoothly. I got the impression that he had given me all the credit for his improved life. Beth had unexpectedly thanked me profusely for all my support, insisting that he wouldn't have given Casey the time of day if I hadn't encouraged him. I couldn't have asked for a more convincing cover story.

I was happy that he was leading a seemingly normal life, but I couldn't help but see Casey in a negative light. He often went into great detail about his relationship with her, which made me cringe with envy at times. But I needed to know, just in case his feelings for me were changing. My usually good mood plummeted when he said that her demeanour had softened and she'd become more submissive in many ways.

However, he was quick to say that he preferred strong women who didn't value money over love. Strangely, he became even more affectionate towards me, as if to reassure me that I was still as important to him. I kept waiting for the day that he would confess his love for Casey and realise that he no longer needed me. That day had not come yet, but the seeds of paranoia had been planted.

He had been exploring sexually and had finally gone all the way with Casey. He'd described it as good practice. Apparently he was not so self-conscious about his performance with her, coldly admitting that he didn't care about how she felt. He complained that she wasn't a very active participant during sex. She lacked passion, he said; there was no intensity, he insisted. This pleased me greatly, until I realised that he had been careful not to penetrate me since our first time. I wondered what he was waiting for. This added to my paranoia big time. I was swinging from one emotional extreme to the other. I felt like a yo-yo.

My feelings were put to rest the night of the party. It was completely unplanned, unexpected, and entirely risqué.

***

Beth welcomed me and John as soon as we entered the house. Some people had already arrived. Ritchie spotted us, and together with Casey he proceeded to greet us. My eyes immediately settled on Casey's arm linked with Ritchie's and I couldn't help but feel a little bit sad, thinking that he was becoming more and more out of reach.

We were introduced to quite a few people, who spoke to us enthusiastically. I recognised an older gentleman from Ritchie's grandmother's party, and he politely engaged me in small talk. The food was great – tasty canapés galore. Glasses were kept full too. I had rosé, which was a bit more bearable than standard wine for me.

I decided to go into the living room and sit on one of the plush velvet couches while John went to the loo. I wasn't aware of Ritchie following me until he was standing in front of me. As he sat down beside me, I couldn't take my eyes off him now that I had time to drink him in. He looked incredibly handsome in a tailored black suit, and his hair was combed back, but nothing could tame that wild mane. He locked eyes with me as he sat a little bit too close to me, whispering, "You look beautiful."

I was wearing a red trouser suit, having decided against wearing the dress Ritchie had bought me, since I'd already worn it to a family thing. His eyes dropped down to my cleavage, then he returned his gaze to my eyes. I felt exposed, like he was caressing my body, and I loved every second of it. I forgot where I was. All I could see were his eyes, and I automatically leaned in towards him, intoxicated by his presence. We were rudely awakened by the sound of Casey's voice and the spell was broken. Shortly after, John joined us too. He made polite conversation with Casey as Ritchie and I spoke quietly.

There was a live instrumental band playing familiar pop songs in a sort of classical style. So when a song we all recognised started, Casey suggested that we all dance. It took some convincing to get John up – he was like a dead weight sometimes; the spring in his step had long ago died. Ritchie sat waiting for our decision. I don't think he would have agreed if I hadn't agreed.

The next minute we were all up slow dancing. Not my cup of tea, but a bit of fun. I couldn't help glancing over at Ritchie as he stared over Casey's shoulder. I wasn't sure if there was something in the air or not, but I could feel Ritchie's desire from across the room. No doubt he could feel mine too. The atmosphere felt heady and dreamlike. I looked on enviously as Casey leaned her head against his chest. I had to turn my head.

I then felt a tap on my shoulder and Ritchie was standing there with Casey, asking if he could have the next dance. It was almost amusing the way we swapped partners. Casey and John smiled at each other awkwardly, while Ritchie and I relished the opportunity. He held me a bit too close, so close that I could feel his body against mine. We were walking on fire, dancing with fate. I could feel his breath on my face, and it took every ounce of control not to look up and kiss those soft lips.

"Excuse me, I need the bathroom," he announced, while indicating with his eyes that he was intending to go to his room. He wanted me to follow. He left and I quickly scanned the room. I saw that Casey was already chatting away to another girl around her age that had just arrived, and John looked like he was raiding the buffet. I quickly made my way upstairs, wondering what Ritchie wanted.

I stepped into his unlit bedroom. I felt someone grab me and shut the door, locking it. Of course, it was Ritchie. Whether it was me seeing him with Casey, or Ritchie seeing me with John, or the fact that we were just enjoying the risk factor – who knew? All I know is that something came over us. We kissed in a frenzied moment of pure lust, breathing heavily. He touched my body as I touched his. We unbuttoned each other's clothes in a blur of sexual anticipation. He slipped his hand into my underwear and I held it there, pushing it against me. I whimpered, uninhibited, almost crying. I had wanted him inside me again for so long, like an itch I couldn't scratch. I couldn't hold it any longer, and I would have begged if I had to.

His chest heaved up and down violently. Pulling my underwear down, almost ripping them off, he lifted me onto his chest of drawers. I caught a glimpse of the look in his eyes. Something dark and animalistic was brewing. They bored into mine unflinchingly. The intensity was very nearly intimidating, but I wanted it and he knew it.

He thrust himself inside me hard. He was so deep inside that I gasped, yet I wrapped my legs around him and pulled him even closer. I cried out – not caring anymore. He'd obviously had some practice recently, the way he moved his pelvis against mine. We were so into it, we both unleashed a chorus of moans. He just kept thrusting deeply over and over again.

Then all I could feel was a rush, a force, a release so strong, I could hear the blood racing in my ears. I felt pounding in my head, just too much to contain, like I was going to explode. The momentum subsided as our heartbeats slowed down. Ritchie leaned his head against mine.

The whole thing had probably only lasted a few minutes. However, I felt slightly disorientated, as I had lost track of time. As the fog cleared, it suddenly dawned on me that in the throes of passion, I swore I'd heard him say that he loved me. Though I said nothing as he quickly freshened up.

He went back down to the party first, but I stayed for a minute to adjust my skewed clothes and attempted to disguise the sheen on my flushed face. Luckily Ritchie kept some of my things in his room. I guess Casey hadn't spent as much time here as I thought she had.

I told John that I had gone to the bathroom, but he seemed none the wiser. He was enjoying the food, his plate spilling over and his wine glass full. I don't remember the rest of evening much at all. My mind was adrift in a murky haze.

***

I tried to act as nonchalantly as possible in the days after. Sometimes I would spot Ritchie staring in class; he would swallow and his face would change colour. Perhaps the memories of that night might be embarrassing for him in hindsight, especially if he had said the L-word. We didn't talk about the incident, possibly because we couldn't find the moment or because it had all been so surreal.

I still couldn't believe the risk I had taken that day and I felt myself growing hot when I replayed the scene. Did we really do that? Should we talk about that night or should we leave things unsaid?

Almost a week later, we were studying in his dining room because we needed to use the large table to sort through his work. His mum had left to meet a friend and we were finally alone. I took this opportunity to broach the subject.

"About that night, Ritchie. I can't stop thinking about it."

I could see him visibly tense, but he answered honestly. "Me neither."

"It was mind-blowing. You've obviously learnt some new skills," I said, not quite sure how to word that.

There was a look of relief on his face. "Let's just say I've been practising and improving my knowledge. I just wanted to be good for you."

"Is that why you wouldn't... I started to... I thought that you didn't want me anymore." I thought I sounded so needy and vulnerable then. I looked down uncertainly.

"Oh my god, is that what you thought? Why didn't you tell me before? I didn't want to disappoint you, that's why. I had to make sure I knew what I was doing."

"I didn't know—"

Before I could finish, he asked heatedly, "Seriously, Francesca, don't you know how much you mean to me?"

"That's kind of what I wanted to ask you. The other night, I thought I heard..."

I trailed off, unable to finish asking my question and not quite ready to hear the answer. I decided to change my question.

"Hope you don't mind me asking. Is it like that with her? Is it as intense?"

He looked at me suspiciously, noticing the change of subject, but he went along with it. "No, it's different with her. I'm not sure how to explain it." He paused. "She's dead in the eyes. Like a Barbie doll. I guess I could describe it as mechanical. What about you and John? I've always wanted to ask."

"I close my eyes and pretend it's your face that I'm seeing. It helps to relieve some of the loneliness when I'm not with you," I answered honestly.

His eyes softened. "Do you really?"

"That's what I try to do, but it's not good enough. We barely get physical now. I really want it to be you. It's so hard sometimes."

"Please remind me why we're not together, Francesca."

Not realising that he meant this rhetorically, I began to answer, "It's because—"

Abruptly he clamped my wrist. "No, don't answer that. I know the reasons and I'm sick of hearing them," he said, clearly distressed.

I leaned over to hold him and he gathered me in his arms affectionately. He took a deep breath, as if all our feelings were just too much to handle. And sometimes they were.

He stroked my hair soothingly and lightly kissed it. "Well, we're together now, aren't we?"

Cupping my chin, he tilted my face upwards so that I was facing him, and he kissed me so tenderly. That kiss meant so much more than words, and it occurred to me that I didn't need to ask him what he had said that night, because I already knew.

Consumed by the kisses, I felt that all too familiar heat coursing through my veins and that moistness between my legs. My whole body throbbed for him. He stood up, pulling me with him. He undressed me slowly – no rushing this time. With one sweep of his arm, he pushed all his books onto the floor. He kissed me fervently, whilst nudging me back until he lay me down on the dining table. He slipped his fingers inside me, brought his hand to his lips and tasted me. He inhaled my scent deeply. He indulged in the pure simplicity of the act. He took me right then and there. We never did return to studying that evening.

On my way home, I thought about how he had changed from the painfully shy boy I had met at the start of the school year. He was more than ready now. In his spare time, he'd studiously learned a few techniques, and now he had a lot more confidence about initiating sexual contact. He'd undergone a kind of metamorphosis into a passionate and mature young man. He still fascinated me, and I was in awe of him.

When I finally lay down on my bed that night, I could still feel his hands all over my body, his weight on top of me, and him sliding in and out of me. We had experienced a level of true and real intimacy. I smiled as I touched my lips and caressed my breasts, trying to imagine what he had felt, because I damn well knew what I had felt. I hoped that, through my kisses, he could tell that I felt the same way.

Maybe he would decide not to feel awkward about it and not to waste time on that. We only had a short time left together, so we had to use it well. And he could have me – mind, body and soul. I'd deal with the consequences and damage later. Self-destruction was what

I had to look forward to. The future was bleak. Who knew if I'd ever recover? I couldn't just walk away. I already knew that this short but sweet affair would end soon, but Ritchie was right. We shouldn't dwell on the reasons why we couldn't be together. It was too painful to even talk about, opening a wound so deep. Best to put it off for as long as possible. Maybe pain was what I deserved for doing this to John, for breaking the rules and for having a single-minded desire. What goes around comes around, they say. Was a short time of pleasure worth a lifetime of suffering?

I felt tired on Monday morning after yet another sleepless night, but the thought of seeing Ritchie made me feel good. When I saw him during mass, he smiled openly, and I felt butterflies in my stomach. Neither of us had any interest in what the chaplain was droning on about. I was hyper-aware of our closeness, while he glanced at me often and gently rubbed his leg against mine. We had to be more discreet than this.

I was determined to ensure that Ritchie focused on his work. We were meant to do it over the weekend, but we both had got distracted in a big way. I had to make sure it didn't happen for the time being. His final exams were coming up next month. He'd completed most of his work, the first drafts anyway, but we had to focus on revision now. I'd have to remind Ritchie of that, and remind myself.

There was the counselling to finish also. I was still well aware that I wasn't the best person to do it, but he was opening up. However, I noticed that he still wasn't entirely comfortable about revealing personal information, even to me. The problem was, and this reminded me of a saying I'd once heard, that we would end up closer than close. We'd be drowning ourselves in each other, immersed in one another's anxieties to the point where there would be no communication. We could often read each other without verbal dialogue. Only silence.

Seven hours later, we were sitting in his room at his desk. He had insisted on working in his room, so I had a feeling that he wanted to get me alone. I attempted to focus entirely on the task at hand. I saw what I recognised as Ritchie's game face – firmly set jaw and eyebrows drawn in concentration, as he tried to remember details about the civil rights movement. We then looked at practise exam questions and he managed to successfully complete a question comparing and contrasting different approaches that had been taken. Studying went on past six and I realised that we'd got there without being distracted. I was pleased. I believed that, in the end, he would do well in his exams.

"I better go. John's dad is visiting from Canada and I promised to meet them for dinner."

"Wait, is it that time already?" He sounded disappointed. I nodded in response. "I haven't had a chance to kiss you yet," he said as we both stood up. Wrapping his arms around my waist, he kissed me longingly. I almost lost my senses. He always got my blood flowing. I avoided his eyes because I knew that would be the end of my resistance. I quickly left before I had time to think and change my mind.

The dinner went fine, but I wasn't really myself. I tried to be polite by suppressing my sometimes lurid sense of humour. By the end of it, I just wanted to go home and have a hot shower.

John had drunk too much as usual, and my patience had run out when I finally settled in for the night. I forgot why I was playing this game. Why was I still with John? Why didn't I just end it? Couldn't I just be alone after Ritchie? Would I be able to live a single life when Ritchie started a new one? Probably with Casey – their future marriage had pretty much been arranged anyway. I would be out of the picture soon. Was it really worth it? Starting anew with John in Canada? What about my dreams of living a different life and pursuing my career goals, which I had hoped to do in Canada? A mass of questions bombarded my brain.

As John came to bed, I felt more confused than ever. I wanted to have exciting life experiences, travel the world and see what else was out there. Maybe it wasn't meant to be – not with John anyway. If I didn't want to be with John and I couldn't be with Ritchie, then what? I guess the only logical answer was to go solo.

I had some painful decisions to make soon, and I wasn't sure if I'd be able to cope. I wanted to call Ritchie, declare my undying love for him, and hope that everything would fall into place. But then, there would be no future for me. Accusations galore would follow. What was I to do? I was plagued by an inner conflict and I dwelled on it for most of the night.

***

The reflection staring back at me in the mirror was drawn from my emotional hangover, like a residue. Even my legs felt heavy, like dead weights, as I dragged them to work.

However, with learning objectives to focus on and an eager Ritchie to tend to, my worries were stifled. I must have looked like crap, but

I couldn't conceal the blotchiness and the tiredness, and I hoped that Ritchie wouldn't notice.

During my planning time, I thought about our upcoming and last one-to-one session. I felt it was time to face and tackle the big issue, though I had no idea how. I decided that I was going to attempt a *Good Will Hunting* scene.

I hadn't really stuck with the programme throughout our sessions, and even though I wasn't really meant to, I was going to go there. It was highly unprofessional and unrealistic, but I wasn't a psychiatrist, and Ritchie would have refused to see one anyway. My unorthodox approach had worked in the past, though, due to the good rapport I normally had with students. I knew I could use our closeness to my advantage. I would just flat out ask, and he would feel obliged to answer.

***

"So, this is our last counselling session," I announced. "I may ask you some difficult questions. I hope that's okay?"

To my relief, he nodded. "Okay. I think I can do it now."

"Thank you. I know it has been difficult and I appreciate your openness."

"You want to ask me about my childhood, don't you? I've always wanted to tell you, but I was afraid to. Do you have to report what I say?"

"Whatever you say is confidential, unless you're currently at risk."

All staff had child protection training at least once a year, and we were always told never to promise to keep a secret. Although, technically, he was an adult now.

He looked off to the side, deep in thought, and inhaled deeply, like he was trying to pluck up the courage to start. A look of steely resolve planted itself firmly on his features, though he didn't return eye contact.

"He was violent, you know," he said distantly. His eyes glazing over as his memories took over.

"Your father? Towards you or your mum?"

"Both," he replied, returning eye contact.

I reached over to hold his hand for encouragement. We were seated like we normally were – two chairs facing each other, no table in between.

"It's okay, you can tell me."

He took another deep breath – this time a bit more shakily. Obviously, this was hard for him. "He hurt my mum, and she would leave me with him. He would hit me and tell me I was worthless." His voiced cracked a bit and my eyes began tearing up.

"You're not worthless, Ritchie. I hope you know that."

He squeezed my hand almost painfully and carried on.

"I had a nanny – Isobelle. She was so kind to me. He was having an affair with her, and then all of a sudden, she left. I had no one. I was devastated. I heard that he made her pregnant."

He looked down and sobbed suddenly. Taking deep breaths, he tried to control his emotions. A few minutes later, he regained his composure. I admired him for trying, and for his determination.

"I tried—"

He stopped short, face crumbling, unable to maintain his composure. He covered his face with his hands.

I put my arm around him and said, "You don't have to say anymore if you don't want to." My voice was thick with guilt, knowing that I was making him relive this.

Shaking his head profusely with disagreement, he replied, "No, I have to do this." Despite his breath catching, he wiped the tears away. "I was so afraid that I was turning into him every time I hit someone." In a strangled voice, he added, "I-I wanted to kill myself *and* him. For years I thought it was my fault he died because I wanted it so much."

At that moment, I really felt his pain. I let my tears fall for him and he reached out to wipe a lingering tear on my cheek and said, "I didn't mean to upset you."

"Don't worry about me. What about you? Are you okay?"

"It's strange, but it feels like a huge weight has been lifted. My mum never told anyone. I'm glad I finally did."

"Maybe that's why she is the way she is. She's working through it her own way."

"Maybe, but I don't know if I could ever forgive her."

"I'm so sorry you had to go through that." I truly felt privileged that he went through the trauma of dredging up the past to tell me what happened. "Thank you for telling me."

"I needed to do it. It's been holding me back for a long time," he said, while he stared at me with red-rimmed eyes.

His vulnerability was beautiful to me. I just wanted to protect him, care for him and keep him forever. Leaning forward, I kissed him softly on the lips, tasting the salt from his tears. I knew I shouldn't have, as it was a dominant gesture, but I felt empowered. I knew I had a hold over him, but in many ways he had a hold over me. He was a complicated person and I wanted to throw myself into his complex universe full of twists and turns. I could spend a lifetime exploring him, forever entangled in the thorns. He harboured a darkness that responded to mine. I didn't want to be free.

In the days that followed, I had to touch him, taste him, feel him. I couldn't get enough of him. I smothered him. And for some reason, he responded, letting me indulge.

The haunted look in his eyes began to fade, though it didn't fade completely.

Chapter Seventeen

It was May and exams were fast approaching. Ritchie had completed most of his coursework, getting either a grade C or B. Beth was pleased but insisted that he work harder on revision. The good news was that I would be his reader during all exams apart from Art and English, though I would be present during the English test as a motivator.

I proudly flicked through Ritchie's art books before they were to be submitted for marking. His technical skills had improved immensely. I had taught him some new skills, but the basic talent was already there. He even had a chance of getting a grade A. Some people didn't place much worth on an art GCSE, but at least it would add to the total number of passes.

Every time I told him that I was proud of him, he responded with a lovely, almost modest smile. I couldn't help but love him, and he was nothing but loving towards me. I often wondered why someone as beautiful as him was still interested in me. I had promised him that I would try not to question his interest in me, yet I still couldn't believe that he'd chosen me from the many he could have chosen.

In contrast, my relationship with John had been a bit stressful recently. He had just gone through a disciplinary for being under the influence at work. Although I was really upset with him, when I saw that dejected look on his face, I didn't have the heart to leave him. Not when he needed me most. The whole thing had reminded me that I hadn't completely turned into a cold, calculating and heartless woman who was having an affair.

An affair. What a strange way to describe something that was so natural, I thought. In a way, John was having an ongoing affair – with alcohol. The way I was beginning to see it was that John had drink and I had Ritchie. We both had our drug. After John's disciplinary, he seemed to question me less and less when I spent more and more time with Ritchie. Maybe he knew but wanted to keep me still.

Unfortunately, but necessarily, Casey was back in the picture a bit more. Ritchie tried to see her on Sundays because he liked to reserve Saturdays for me, whilst John was at work. Even though I saw him at school, during the week, and sometimes on Fridays, it was more in a tutoring capacity. Saturday evening was often the only day we could get any uninterrupted quality time together.

There was still that element of coldness and detachment from Ritchie towards Casey. As she wasn't a particularly warm person, it seemed to work for the both of them. According to Ritchie, she still seemed uncomfortable about his relationship with me. He'd explained that there was a bond that wasn't to be severed. Hopefully, she saw it as a sister-brother thing or a mother-son thing.

Beth would ask me questions from time to time, as Ritchie didn't volunteer much information at all. The expectation of a marriage between them was as strong as ever. It was partly down to an unusual clause in Ritchie's father's will. The release of an immense fortune was only due if certain terms were met. It seemed that his father still retained control from beyond the grave. However, it was one hell of a fortune.

I felt that Ritchie should maintain a relationship with Casey anyway. It took some pressure off him and me, knowing that people were less likely to discover the truth. The addition of a fortune would only help him anyway. He would be able to do whatever he wanted, and Casey wouldn't question it as long as she could live well. She would be well taken care of. If money was what she wanted, then that is what she would receive. What did love have to do with it?

Beth had made a similar decision, or sacrifice, some might say. Although she had benefited in the end after the death of Ritchie's father, she felt alienated from her son, and he was the one who had suffered the most. I just hoped that Ritchie wouldn't resent receiving his father's fortune – that was how he saw it, anyway. Actually, I now knew it was old money. It was something to do with ownership of major real estate, primarily in London, as well as various other locations. The lineage went way back, and the wealth had continued to amass.

I must admit I didn't know much about it and I had never really asked. It was like he was ashamed of his aristocratic roots. It was irrelevant anyway, but in some ways it wasn't. Ritchie had always shied away from such conversation, enjoying what precious moments we had together.

Knowing that exams were coming up very soon, Beth was around a lot more. She had been in regular contact with the school, ensuring that he would have the required amount of support. She was desperate for him to graduate from high school. I think she was afraid that a stigma would be attached to him, though I was afraid that it had already happened within the family. His learning difficulties were common knowledge. It appeared that he'd redeemed himself somewhat by dating Casey, appearing more normal and behaving like a Cunningham.

Part of me couldn't wait until it was all over so that we could spend more quality time together, but on the other hand, it meant that time was running out. There was increasing pressure on Ritchie to go to California to learn about his deceased father's business – yet another thing Ritchie didn't talk about, but Beth had mentioned something about stocks and shares. It all sounded pretty boring, and I'm sure he found it boring too. It was like everyone else was planning his future, but it was a secure path. With me, he would have had an unpredictable path filled with stress, possible financial worries, and no hope of producing children. I'd been told long ago that I couldn't have any. He would be shunned by his family before he had even aged enough to understand the consequences of his actions.

There was also increasing pressure on me from John and his family to relocate to Canada. I'd have to give up on my pipe dreams and make some very real decisions soon. Maybe neither of us would return to London or to each other once it was all said and done. Maybe we would adapt to our new lifestyles, and our fling would be a long-forgotten dream. A thing of the past. Ritchie would move on and we would both come to our senses.

I often found myself thinking about how I could keep seeing Ritchie after we moved away. It was easier to cope with the inevitable when I had some kind of hope. Could we still meet from time to time, considering that we would be on the same continent? Was it even possible? How would it work? Wouldn't it be a bit too obvious? Would all the secrecy be too much in the end?

How I wished things were not so complicated. Ritchie had once asked if we could just up and leave together and just go anywhere, but there would be no future for Ritchie that way. I had to do what was best for him, even though it didn't feel right.

***

Exams would be commencing just after the May holidays, which were only two weeks away. Interaction between me and Ritchie would be mostly business. I felt as strongly as Beth that he passed.

Even with his head bent down in concentration, Ritchie was still the most beautiful man alive to me. It took all my control not to initiate contact or more. I think we intentionally dressed in our most unflattering clothes to prevent distraction. Although he still had self-esteem issues, he knew what he did to me and how I responded to him. We saw the desire in each other's eyes, but we kept going, plodding through revision until he knew the information well. It was twice as hard for him to revise due to his difficulties processing text, so we often used images or colour coding, associating it with a piece of information that he could verbalise.

The school had agreed that I could take on the role of amanuensis – a scribe – as long as he could verbalise the correct answer exactly the way he wanted it written, word for word. Despite our bond, I wouldn't give him the answers or anything like that. I believed he could achieve it by himself, and he was too proud to cheat anyhow.

In no time at all, exam week arrived. Ritchie was so nervous, his voice even shaking at times. I reassured him to the best of my ability, constantly reminding him that he had the knowledge. All he had to do was stay calm and apply the mnemonic strategies he had practised.

The first exam was the dreaded English test. We were assigned the one-to-one room for the test. I wasn't allowed to read anything. I was there merely as a timekeeper, motivator and scribe if needed.

He cautiously opened the test paper as if it was a precious manuscript. He breathed deeply a few times and proceeded to read the text. I told him that he could read aloud if that helped. Slowly, but surely, he read the first section and managed to answer the questions.

Time began to run out, and I reminded him to move on or to try and work just a bit faster. He was doing well, but at a slow pace. I worried that he wouldn't get it all done and that his true ability would not be reflected in his grade.

"You have fifteen minutes left, Ritchie," I announced.

"I don't think I can do the last two questions before then," he said anxiously.

"Which one is worth more marks?"

"The second one," he replied.

"I think you should just focus on that one because you probably won't have time to do two," I suggested. It was that dreaded long answer question.

"Okay, let's do it."

With me writing as fast as I could, he managed to complete two pages before the time ran out. Then it was finally over. Ritchie sat there mentally drained, and I sat there with a stiff hand.

"Sorry to do that to you, Francesca," he said, referring to the fact that both my hand and neck were in pain. I'd tried not to show it, but I'd had to self-massage in between questions.

"I guess you owe me a massage then."

"I owe you a lot more than that," he replied, almost reverently. I didn't feel that he owed me anything though. It was my job; his mum had paid me to tutor him, and anything other than that had been my choice.

"No, you don't. I think you should give yourself more credit, Ritchie. You have been so focused and I admire the determination you have shown," I responded truthfully.

I hadn't meant to, but I realised that I had overwhelmed him with that statement. He hung his head while shaking it slightly. He was about to respond, but I interrupted by tilting his chin upwards so that I could see his eyes and said, "No, Ritchie. Don't downplay your achievements, and I'm talking about all of them – academic, social and personal." With added emphasis, I continued, "I'm very proud of you."

My words seemed to have an impact, and although I could see he wanted to say more, he didn't. He knew I wasn't in the mood to let him put himself down.

***

Ritchie's final exam was over. We'd been sitting in the one-to-one room, struggling through a particularly difficult history exam. It was the only test that I wasn't confident that he would pass. I kept my thoughts to myself, though.

I stood up, pulling him for a congratulatory embrace. He immediately put his arms around my waist and pulled me close. I nuzzled his neck, inhaling his scent and forgetting where I was for a minute. He stepped back, stroking my hair. His eyes closed, and he kissed me tenderly. I reached out to stroke his cheek and traced the outline of his soft lips, surrounded by a bit of stubble. I rarely saw him with stubble, as he was usually quite meticulous about shaving almost daily, but I have to say I enjoyed the slightly rugged look it gave him.

Looking into his stunningly bright eyes, I said, "I missed you." Even though I had seen him very often throughout this whole exam period, it felt like I hadn't really been with him. We'd been physically close, but I'd purposely turned away and avoided eye contact at times to keep things on track.

"I think I know what you mean. I missed you too," he whispered.

Something in his eyes changed suddenly. His gaze becoming more intense, hungrier. He placed his hand suggestively just below my navel, skimming over my clothes and over my mound. I felt his hand between my legs and his fingers slid along the seam of my trousers purposefully. I immediately gasped, my heart rate skyrocketing. He drank in every moment.

"I love the way you respond to me," he whispered, his face flushed with excitement.

I looked down at his bulging erection and replied cheekily, "And I like the way you respond to me."

We giggled as we gathered the finished test papers and waited for his erection to calm down. We were about to leave the room, when he squeezed my bum, giving me a nonchalant expression and feigning innocence. I slapped him playfully and he flinched, chuckling to himself. We tried normalising our expressions as we stepped out.

Now that the exams were over, I realised that we would be seeing a lot less of each other. So I went straight to Ritchie's house after school. Thoughts of time running hung negatively over my head, but I pushed it away, promising to myself that I would still see Ritchie as often as I possibly could.

I was greeted by a huge smile and mischievous eyes. He had his uniform on, but no shirt underneath his blazer. At first I thought it odd that he was walking around like that, but I vaguely remembered Beth saying that she would be travelling to Paris for the weekend. I guess that was her way of celebrating the end of Ritchie's exams.

Seeing the realisation finally dawn on me, Ritchie said, "Mum's not here. It's just us."

I then allowed myself to finally enjoy the view. I'd never admitted to myself until that very moment that seeing him in his uniform really turned me on. I would honestly miss seeing him in his uniform, and I suppose that meant that I was truly depraved after all. His exposed flesh underneath was tantalising to me and I extended myself the privilege to caress that chest.

"I knew you'd like it, Francesca," he said, obviously enjoying watching me watching him. His lips parted slightly with anticipation. We'd been barely controlling ourselves since the end of that history test. We could finally allow ourselves the passion we'd been suppressing for what felt like ages.

His eyes devoured my lips – like a ravenous beast, he kissed me, as if he'd been starved of affection for years. While he kissed my neck, I asked, "Does it make me some sort of degenerate?" I knew it was the wrong time to ask that, but I was slightly worried that a school uniform got me so hot and bothered.

Breathlessly, he answered, "What? You liking this? Of course not. It's a reminder of when we first met."

"How did you know I'd like that?" I hoped I hadn't been that obvious, that my lurid stare had not been seen by anyone else.

In between kisses, he replied, "I know you, Francesca. I'll do whatever you want. Anything." His words were filled with so much intensity, so much conviction. I felt his need for me, because that was exactly how I felt towards him.

Somehow, we ended up in the living room. He unbuttoned my shirt and my nipples hardened in response. He nuzzled my breasts, squeezing them together as he eased his face into them. He licked my cleavage greedily. Maintaining eye contact, he played with my body, making me feel sexy and desirable – like a goddess. Then he unzipped my trousers, pulled down my knickers and slipped his fingers inside me whilst showering me with kisses on my neck.

"You're so wet. You're always wet for me," he said throatily. He ran his hand over his face, licking his fingers to taste my juices. His breathing became deep, his chest heaving up and down. My groin throbbed for him, so I pulled him close, rubbing against his thigh, letting the animal inside take over. Pure lust. He held me firmly against his manhood.

"You don't know what you do to me, Ritchie. I want you so much. Take me now. Fuck me," I begged.

"Oh my god. You're so fucking hot."

I threw what clothes I still had on all over the place and pretty much ripped Ritchie's clothes off. I pushed him roughly onto the settee, climbed on top of him and then he was inside me. He gripped the cushions, obviously enjoying the rough stuff.

Throwing my head back, I groaned, almost whimpering. My feelings overwhelmed me and my body could barely contain them. I didn't know how to release them. So I drove down harder on Ritchie until he was deep, deep inside me. I felt like I was possessed by a creature with primal, basic urges.

As I pushed down, he gripped my hips and moved his pelvis upwards, his movements in unison with mine. I could feel my sweat trickling down, merging with his sweat as we continued our lustful frenzy. Our movements sped up as we neared climax. I felt the build-up deep within my groin, which travelled through my body, exploding through my chest. An outburst of heavy breathing and gasping escaped us, as ecstasy washed over us. It totally shook my world.

It was too much to hold in, this amount of desire. We had waited too long. We needed to be with each other more frequently, because this type of sex was on another level, both physically and emotionally. We threw ourselves into it like it was our last hour on Earth, desperate and mad.

I looked down at my captive Ritchie, falling into those eyes. They looked darker somehow. Smouldering. I finally got off and lay next to him, balanced precariously on the edge of the settee.

"That was… Wow," he said.

"I know. That was mind-blowing. I mean, look at me. I'm shaking." I felt as if I was on a come down after doing hard drugs.

Shaking his head, he responded, "You don't know what you're doing to me, Francesca. I want you so bad. I can't get enough."

We eventually stumbled off the settee and picked up the scattered clothes off the floor, on the cabinet, under the table. And when we finally got to his room, I lay on his couch and passed out.

Sometime during the night, I was positive that I heard Ritchie speaking with John on the phone. I realised that Ritchie had called John to explain that I'd fallen asleep and asked if it would be okay if I stayed the night. Without asking too many questions, it sounded like he agreed. I suspected that John really did know what was going on. Maybe he was allowing it to sweeten me up to the idea of moving to Canada – sooner rather than later.

Chapter Eighteen

"When's the exhibition?"

I was keen to see all Ritchie's work displayed. Schools often did a huge exhibition at the end of the year after the artwork had been moderated.

"Think it's next week. I'll have to return at some point to back up my artwork and put it up on the display board."

"Okay, I'll look forward to that. What are your plans for the rest of the week now that you're officially off?"

"I want to take you away for the weekend to say thank you."

My heart leapt at the thought of spending time away alone with Ritchie. We could indulge our fantasies, pretend that we really were a couple.

"I'm not sure how John will react to that, but I could say I'll be travelling with you and your mum."

A slightly worried look marred Ritchie's face. "Please try, Francesca. I want to be with you in the open without worrying about who might be watching."

Although we were in the LSU, it was empty. I placed my hand on top of his, replying, "One way or another, I'll come."

The bell went and it seemed to symbolise the end of what had been an eventful year. I would be seeing less of Ritchie, but I hoped we could continue this somehow. He pushed his hair back while he bent to pick up his rucksack.

"Meet me at Paddington Station tomorrow morning at ten," he said as he stood up to go. I wouldn't be seeing him later that evening, so I embraced him quickly. Neither of us wanted to let go, and I was painfully aware that anyone could walk in at any moment. Eventually, I tried to step back, and he released me.

"Look forward to it."

He smiled at me, and I couldn't help but smile goofily back. I watched him leave the LSU. Life would be different at St. Pauls now that Ritchie didn't need to come as he'd finished his exams, except maybe to collect his artwork. I would be given a few new students to support in Years Seven and Eight for the remainder of the academic term, as well as some extra administrative duties. I'd expressed an interest in mentoring during my performance management, and now that I'd had some basic counselling training and had successfully applied those skills, they had asked me to work with two other students on a one-to-one basis.

It seemed as if I had found a niche of some sort at St. Pauls; nevertheless, I just couldn't bring myself to continue in September knowing that Ritchie would never return. Every classroom and corridor would be a lonely place without him and would remind me of his absence. I hadn't informed the school yet, but I was planning to find a new job by September. I decided to return to working in primary schools. At least I could do no harm then and return to being a normal rule-conscious person again.

That evening, I had a hell of a time trying to explain to John that I would be going with Ritchie and supposedly his mother on a surprise weekend trip. I genuinely had no idea where. He knew I wasn't going to take no for an answer and didn't give me too much hassle, probably because he'd been nothing but trouble recently. Sometimes I didn't know why I felt so responsible for him, like he was a child that needed looking after. I was seriously in two minds now. I found myself trying to convince myself that I would be happy with John when all I had was John. Maybe I should just give up, follow Ritchie around like a lost puppy for the rest of my life, no longer being a person, but an empty shell. I didn't have a clue what to do, as confusion had really set in.

I managed to push all the nagging thoughts to one side when I went to meet Ritchie. As soon as I saw him standing there, he took over my whole world. I rushed over to him, not worried about who could see, and kissed him on the lips. I could sense that he felt a bit taken aback at first, but then kissed me passionately back. We grinned at each other, but there was something else behind those eyes.

I noticed that we boarded the first-class section of the train. That was definitely a first for me. "So, we're going to Cornwall? What have you got planned?"

His eyes shifted mysteriously, smiling slightly. "Well, it wouldn't be a surprise then."

When he saw the look on my face, he elbowed me playfully and we giggled, despite looks of annoyance from some of the other passengers, which only made us laugh louder.

A few hours later, we were travelling in a taxi to the hotel. When the hotel emerged, I couldn't contain my excitement as it was a hotel designed for astronomy. It even had its own observatory. I had read about places like this, but had never had the chance to visit one before. I practically dragged Ritchie into a huge embrace, almost knocking him to the ground. He laughed while he struggled to maintain his balance.

"Thank you so much. This is perfect," I said gratefully.

"You're welcome. A boring gift just wouldn't cut it. I thought that an experience would be more valuable to you. And me," he explained. I loved him more than ever then.

Once we were settled in, we spent most of the day there exploring our surroundings. I couldn't wait until the evening, because I could tell that it was going to be a clear night with few clouds. Now I knew why he'd insisted on coming this particular weekend. In England, you had to grab clear nights when they came. And I wasn't disappointed. I took two steps onto the stepladder to look into the fourteen-inch scope and witnessed the most beautiful view of Saturn that I'd ever seen. Even Ritchie seemed fascinated, and it was lovely sharing this experience with him. Unfortunately, the clouds eventually thickened up.

There were two other couples there, but we didn't hang out with them, eager to get back to our room. Being tired didn't stop us from being intimate that night. As the warm water trickled down our faces, he sucked on my bottom lip as we kissed. It wasn't as frenzied as the last time. Taking our time, we had sex in the shower, really savouring each sensation. Our encounters were quite varied; sometimes we just couldn't control our intense urges, at other times we flowed naturally to a rhythm. But every time, we gave ourselves up fully to the experience.

We went down to breakfast the following morning, sitting by one of the other couples. Ritchie really shocked me when he introduced himself as my partner. I watched their reactions carefully. After a brief look of surprise, they quickly continued their conversation. It just seemed to confirm what I thought all along – that Ritchie was too good for me.

Late that night, we lay on the grass, looking up at the dark sky. It was a bit chilly, but I didn't care, as long as I was with him. I hoped that this moment could last forever. We lay in silence for ages, having so much to say, but not saying a word. It had been a heavy burden to bear. Maybe now we had to confront our true feelings, but I couldn't bring it up.

I'd fallen for him.

Hard.

A silent tear ran down my face before I could stop it. It wasn't fair on John and it just wasn't fair on Ritchie. My breath hitched as I tried to stifle a sob.

Immediately sitting up, Ritchie asked, "Francesca, what's wrong? Are you okay?" He looked so concerned.

"I'm fine," I said quickly. "Thank you for all of this." I gestured. Taking a deep breath, I sat up too.

"You don't have to thank me. You've been so good to me. You kept me out of trouble. Kept me sane. For that, I can never repay you."

"I'm going to miss you, Ritchie."

He opened his mouth to respond, but when he saw me shivering, he quickly wrapped his arms around me.

"You can cut your hair if you want to," I added randomly, as I reached out to remove a leaf from his hair.

He looked down at me sadly, as he knew I was intentionally changing the subject. He played along. "No, I'm keeping it long for you," he whispered, almost painfully.

He held me in his arms that night, stroking my hair, the silence extending from earlier. He probably knew what I was thinking. I think he tried to respect my silence for a little while, but he couldn't stand it anymore.

"I'll give it up for you, Francesca. We don't have to pretend anymore." A surge of hope rushed through me, but I couldn't be selfish.

"No, you can't give that up," I insisted.

"I don't want my father's money. I don't need it."

"It's not your father's money. It's been passed down, generation to generation. Once you have it, you can do what you want with it and then you'll be free. You deserve it after all you've been through. It's *your* money."

"Francesca, I know that you think that I'm too young, that I don't know what I want, but I—"

"No, you have to live your life. You've got too much to lose," I interrupted, trying to convince myself more than him. "Please, let's not talk about this anymore."

He sighed frustratingly. "Okay, whatever you want. But I promise you I'll prove to you that we're meant to be."

***

John asked me a whole load of questions when I returned, and I robotically responded to each one of them. He seemed to suspect something, but I didn't care. I needed to recover from my own feelings.

During the week, Ritchie tried calling over and over again, but I deliberately avoided speaking to him. I was determined that he live his life. Old feelings cropped up. I still felt that he might change his mind about me if he was away from me and occupied. I felt awful about ignoring him, but I genuinely believed it was the best thing to do.

I decided that the distance had to be greater between us, so I finally lodged that visa application. I had prepared most of the documents already, so it was just a matter of uploading them and paying the fee. John was really pleased and maybe his suspicions were put to rest then, as I was showing *commitment* towards him, or so he thought. I was mostly doing it for Ritchie.

Ritchie gave me space for that week, texting only on Friday to suggest we meet on Saturday. However, I'd already made plans with John. Over the next few weeks, he'd text occasionally in an attempt to get me to see him, but eventually, the texts became less and less frequent. I worried that he might turn up to the school or at my front door, demanding that I speak to him, revealing all to John. My concerns were put to rest when he sent a text at the end of June saying that he'd be staying in Jersey for a little while with his uncle. Apparently, his uncle had organised a series of work placements and his mother was keen on him getting work experience. I wished him luck and briefly explained that I'd been busy job hunting, though that was not the reason why I hadn't been in contact. Ritchie responded with an extra-long text providing all his contact details in Jersey if I needed to contact him via any means and invited me to stay with him in August. It was just an invitation, not demanding a response, an exact date or confirmation.

I went to work as normal, but I had finally informed them that I was looking elsewhere. I attended two interviews, turning down the first offer, but accepting the second. I would be working at a primary school in Camden come September. It was easy to travel to, offered a better pay scale and less working hours. I obviously didn't mention that I had applied for a visa and might not be there for the whole academic year. It was a huge relief knowing that I wouldn't be returning to St. Pauls.

I gave in, texting Ritchie to let him know, and he immediately sent a congratulatory text back. He wanted to know the specific address of the new post, as if I was trying to run away from him. I also asked him how the placement was going. Apparently, it was boring, but different. Not as bad as school though. Thinking that was the last text, I hadn't expected another. I stood there frozen as I read the words *I miss you*. Unsure of how to answer, I left it at that.

It became clear that Ritchie would not be able to return for the art exhibition. I took it upon myself to prepare his work for it. I backed the large pieces and sticky backed the sketchbooks to keep them in good condition. I helped the art teacher staple everything up along with all the other students' work. I took a photo, because he probably wouldn't get a chance to see his work displayed. I'd probably end up collecting it too when the exhibition was over. Otherwise, I would just keep it. It would make me feel close to him, even though I was attempting to distance myself.

I hoped that his absence would subdue my feelings, but all it did was make me feel alone. I wondered if Ritchie felt the same or if he was getting used to being away from me now. I thought about him every day and at all times of the day. Every moment that I wasn't busy, he snuck into my thoughts and invaded my senses, as I remembered things about him. Sometimes, it was a memory of us making love or a fleeting flash of his smell or the colour of his eyes.

When I slept, I dreamt about him. They would fluctuate between worst-case scenarios and ideal situations. I would wake up feeling anxious, not knowing exactly why, but knowing that it was partly because of what I had dreamt.

I became increasingly on edge, snappy and irritable. My reasons were simply that I wasn't feeling well or that I was stressed about John's drinking problem, which wasn't entirely untrue anyway.

At other times, I became sexually aroused, almost unbearably so. Sometimes when John was out, I would close my eyes, visualise Ritchie and touch myself. I lost all interest in sleeping with John, offering any excuse to avoid it.

The worst thing of all was the crying. When I was alone, I would call his name and break down in tears. I would clench my pillow, wishing it was him, and sob. Every time I looked in the mirror, I was drawn and tired. People just thought I'd been under the weather. When it was too much to take, I would pull out a photo of him and fall asleep with it in my hands. It did little to comfort me.

It was a haunting reminder.

Then the obsession set in – the constant checking of my messages to see if he had sent anything or just to check the last time that he'd been active. Knowing that he'd been active moments ago was comforting to me somehow. Sometimes, I would just end up rereading all the messages we had exchanged, not caring about deleting anything anymore.

I kept myself as busy as I could by visiting family, constantly catching up with friends and spending time with John. I also found myself cleaning unnecessarily and signing up for any overtime opportunities. I thought that the less time I spent with myself, the less time I would have to think about how I was feeling. Inevitably, no matter how busy I was, I still ended up listening to my tumultuous thoughts. I held my head in vain, as there was no cure for my illness. Even sleep gave me no comfort. Despite all the distractions, including a sick grandmother, a disabled mother, an unstable boyfriend and work, there was no respite for me. Not for the wicked. Maybe fate had decided that this would be my punishment.

For loving Ritchie and living this lie.

And so I roamed aimlessly, like someone with a soul possessed. I was physically standing there, but I wasn't really there.

***

The end of term neared, and I had no idea how I dragged myself through the last month. I tried to convince myself that once I started the new job in September, all would be well. It would be a fresh start.

I'd almost convinced myself that Ritchie was finally starting to forget about me, until one morning, a package arrived. I opened it, wondering what I had ordered recently. To my surprise it was a plane ticket to Jersey, and with it was a card. I instantly recognised the scrawl. It was Ritchie's handwriting.

Francesca,
Please join me in Jersey
I miss you so much
Love,
-R-

Also enclosed was another smaller envelope. Inside was a fine silver bracelet. My heart thumped violently, because despite my intentions, he hadn't forgotten me. It was a charm bracelet containing a star, a moon, a planet, a comet and the sun. Each charm had some kind of small crystal inlaid, or were they diamonds? There was one charm that appeared to be a logo of some sort. On closer inspection, it looked like the initials R and F combined in cursive script. It was so beautiful, and the fact that he'd had that symbol designed made my heart burst with a mixture of elation and pain.

I held my phone for a long time while wondering whether I should use that ticket to Jersey or if I should at least say thank you to Ritchie. My heart got the better of me, and I decided on the latter. Even though I wanted to call him, I sent a text, but I could hear that John was up now.

Ritchie sent a text back a minute later asking if he could call me. I refused, explaining that it wasn't a good time. He replied a second time asking when I would be able to see him. It was an open ticket, but he knew that I only had a couple of days left at St. Pauls and that I would be available. I purposely didn't respond, honestly not knowing what to say. I pictured his distraught face and felt like an awful person. He deserved much better.

John went to do his weekend shift and I was finally alone. I fetched the package from under the couch and put the bracelet on, touching it every so often, hoping that it could somehow bring me closer to Ritchie. I had kept a T-shirt belonging to Ritchie and found it hidden at the back of my wardrobe. I inhaled it deeply, hoping that his scent still clung to it. I lay on the bed and played with my breasts, imagining that I was him. With my eyes shut tight, I envisioned him on top of me, touching me in every secret place. I desperately hung on to the mental image of him as I gasped and sighed.

Yet again, I was lost, so totally lost. Desolate and without hope, I yearned for him, but I could not be selfish anymore. I had to let him go. I had to be free of my obsession.

I finished my last few days at St. Paul's. Joseph and Stuart were sad to see me leave, buying me lovely gifts. I said my goodbyes to the staff but opted not to go with them to the pub, instead choosing to go home and drown in my sorrows. Leaving St. Paul's was like leaving Ritchie, even though he wasn't even there.

I intended to destroy the plane tickets when I got home because I was so tempted to use them. And I had to remove that temptation. I stood there, scissors in hand, about to cut them up, but something stopped me. A small nagging feeling surfaced, and I never did destroy them, though I wasn't sure why.

Chapter Nineteen

I spent the first week of my holiday in Sheffield visiting a cousin who I hadn't seen in years. I was so busy seeing the sights and catching up with her that it was a welcome distraction. On the journey back to London, my dark thoughts took over and I decided my only solution was to go out as much as possible to avoid being alone.

However my idea did not go to plan. One afternoon, I received an unexpected and distressed phone call from Beth.

"Francesca, I'm afraid I have some bad news." She sounded upset. There was a pause and then she took a deep breath. I immediately thought that my worst fears had come true. All I could do was remain silent and grounded to the spot. "It's Richard – he's been in a car accident."

Shock and horror hit me full force. I froze, unable to answer.

"Francesca? I think he's going to be okay, but I'm in Paris at the moment and can't get a flight until tomorrow. Could you please go to him? He would want to see you."

There was no other choice. "Of course I will," I managed to say, half choking on my words.

"Thank you. I knew I could count on you. I'll text the details. Please call me when you get there."

There was no way I was not going to him. Nothing could have stopped me. Now I was glad that I hadn't thrown out the plane tickets; it was like something had told me to keep them even though I hadn't really intended on using them.

After sending John a quick text, I hurriedly threw some items into my small suitcase, not really paying attention to what I was chucking in. I had no idea how long I'd be in Jersey. I wasn't the praying type, and I didn't know what to pray to, but I prayed for Ritchie.

How awful the decision I had previously made was. How could I have ignored him like that? Imagine how he must have felt? Then a morbid thought popped into my head, *What if he had done this on purpose?* Please, no. Who knew how deep his pain ran and how severe his mental instability was.

Sooner or later, I managed to get on that plane, and when I arrived at the hospital, I practically ran whilst dragging my suitcase behind me. The person at reception directed me where to go. I managed to get in by saying I was a relative and then I was told where his room was.

I stood, shocked at the scene before me. I actually stopped breathing while my brain tried to process what I saw. There lay a shell of a man. His shoulder and arm were in a cast, he had a neck brace, and his head was bandaged. Worst of all, I could make out a huge gash with stitches along the right side of his face.

I wept. I wept for his beautiful face and for my treatment of him. I collapsed into the chair beside his bed and let the tears fall, not caring who saw. I hated to grieve in public, but this was beyond my control. It was bigger than pride. That had disappeared hours ago.

Moving my chair closer, I held his hand willing him to open his eyes, just so I knew he was okay. The nurse had already tried to reassure me that he would make a full recovery and the neck brace was just a precaution, but I just had to see it with my own eyes.

After the initial shock of seeing him with bandages, I saw that his beauty was indeed still there. I just had to see his bright eyes sparkle and I had to know that he wasn't upset with me. I also wanted to know the exact details of the accident.

I stroked the back of his hand, standing up to brush a strand of hair away from his face. The tears threatened to start up again and I felt a sudden urge to speak to him. Unsure of whether he could hear me or not, I let it all out regardless.

"I'm so sorry. You deserve much more. You mean so much to me, and if you were gone, I wouldn't know what to do. Because the truth is—"

A sob forced me to catch my breath and almost prevented me from going on, but I pushed through.

"I love you. I love you so much." My tears fell upon his face, so I quickly took a step back to recover myself.

Slowly but surely, his eyes opened, as if on cue. His voice thick with grogginess, he said, "Please don't cry for me, Francesca."

I placed my head gently on to his chest and sputtered, "Ritchie, I…"

I didn't quite know what to say, having temporarily lost the ability to form words. I felt his hand stroking my hair.

"Is it that bad?"

When I heard that, I immediately stood up, deciding that my over-dramatic behaviour was worrying him further. He lifted a shaky hand to his face and felt the bandages, and an expression of fear haunted his features.

"Oh my god. It is bad."

"Taking his hand away from his face, I pulled myself together and said, "No, it's not bad. They said you're going to be fine. It looks worse than it actually is at the moment."

He didn't seem convinced, obviously and understandably really concerned about the scar on his face.

"You still look beautiful to me." I leaned down to kiss him lightly on the lips.

I took a deep breath, looked into his eyes and added, "I'm sorry about everything."

"Stop saying sorry. You don't need to."

Realisation dawned on me. He watched my face intently and we both understood. "I heard what you said," he confirmed. "I love you too, Francesca. Always have."

It was all out in the open. There was no denying it now.

***

Hours later, a healthcare assistant came in with a trolley holding a tray of food. She set it down in front of him and asked if he would like help eating. I said I would help him, and then she left.

He eyed the food hungrily and he actually attempted to feed himself. His face grimaced in pain as he discovered that he may need help after all. I cut up some food and he reluctantly allowed me to feed him. Obediently, he opened his mouth and, obviously extremely hungry, he ate quickly.

While I fed him, an overwhelming sense of love engulfed us. I knew then that whatever happened, I would always be there to take care of him. No matter what.

I turned, sensing a presence behind me. Beth had stealthily walked into the room. How she had done that wearing heels, I had no idea. Maybe, she'd been there for a while, as Ritchie wouldn't have been able to see her from his angle with my body blocking the view.

"I came as soon as I could. Thank goodness there was a cancellation.

I was so worried. How are you feeling?" She nodded to acknowledge my presence but made no attempt to hug or kiss Ritchie.

"Battered and bruised, but I'll survive. Is Uncle David okay?"

"He's in surgery now. Nothing too serious though. He'll be fine," she replied vaguely, probably not wanting to worry Ritchie.

"How long will I be here?"

"I'm not sure," she replied. Turning to look at me, she continued. "Thank you for getting here so fast. You're welcome to stay at my brother's house, Francesca."

"Thank you, Beth."

"No. Thank you."

After a particularly long silence, Beth went to get a cup of coffee. I wondered if they would ever repair their broken relationship, and part of me worried that I was getting in the way, making the atmosphere worse. I suggested leaving to give them a bit of space, but Ritchie wouldn't hear a word of it.

"I have just got you back. There's no way you're leaving me."

"But it's awkward. What about you and your mum?"

"That's not your problem. I want you to stay, Francesca. Please?"

For the next few days, I stayed at David's house. I spent most of my time at the hospital though. It turned out that David's injuries weren't too bad. They had managed to save his leg, which had almost got crushed by the force of the impact. He was a bit shaken by the experience but seemed to be recovering well. Ritchie insisted that he wanted to return to London. Both David and Beth agreed, as soon as he was able. After about a week, he was declared fit for travel, as it was only a short flight back to London.

***

John had not been happy when I'd popped in to drop off my stuff and announced that I would be staying with Ritchie. He hadn't put up too much of a fight when I stubbornly said that this was the way it was going to be. I hadn't meant to be unkind, but there were more important things on my mind. I must admit that I felt little sympathy while he sat there drinking himself to death.

Back at Ritchie's place, we faced a dilemma. We were downstairs in the kitchen and Ritchie said, "Well, I need to have a shower."

I realised what he meant – the HCA must have cleaned him back at the hospital. I had to help him into his clothes earlier that day. He wouldn't be able to wash himself properly with his shoulder and arm in a cast.

"I can help clean you," suggested Beth hesitantly.

"No, Francesca will help," he insisted.

Beth could not quite hide her shock and answered as if she didn't quite trust what she'd heard. "Are you sure?"

"Yes, mum, I'm really sure I'd rather Francesca did it," he reiterated.

Once we were standing in his room, I helped to undress him. I felt how much I missed touching him. He seemed oddly at peace as he watched my face when I took his clothes off. I guessed he had missed it too. He didn't take his eyes off me as I undressed too.

Awkwardly, we tried to get positioning in the shower right, so that his cast wouldn't get wet. The bandages had been removed from his head and face days ago. I attempted to lather up the parts of his skin that were exposed.

The water trickled down his scar, which I had learnt to love. Although it was large, running along his cheekbone down to his chin, I had never found Ritchie more attractive or sexy. It gave him a tough edge, bringing more masculinity to his beautiful features. Any boyishness that had been there was now gone.

I caressed the shower gel into every contour that was exposed – left arm, buttocks and muscular legs. As he tilted his head, leaning to one side, I lathered the shampoo gently through his hair, which was so long now. It felt oddly sensual, and Ritchie was enjoying the sensation, judging from the expression on his face. I deliberately tugged on it to see if he still enjoyed that. He took a deep breath and shuddered slightly. Feeling aroused, I pushed him back, so that the water was falling on me and kissed him long and deep.

Putting some more shower gel into the palm of my hand, I gently cupped his testicles, cleaning them at the same time. It was plain to see his growing erection, which I massaged with soapy hands. I got down on my knees and put it in my mouth, slowly sucking. When I heard his breathing speed up, I increased the speed of my suction and he gasped with pleasure, laughing at the same time.

"Ow. That hurts," he said as he grimaced in pain, the orgasm and the laughing aggravating his cracked ribs. Nevertheless, it had been a while since I'd seen him crack a smile.

"What's so funny?"

"Shit, I'm glad you washed me, instead of my mum."

"Well, that's the way I do it," I said grinning.

I turned the shower off and dried Ritchie. I helped him into a T-shirt and shorts and into bed. We were both feeling tired, so I joined him without a second thought. I was past caring what his mum thought about me staying over.

I constantly checked if he was okay, annoyingly so, until I drifted off myself. For a moment, I was in heaven, falling asleep next to the man I truly loved and who needed me. I found that I had enjoyed taking care of Ritchie. He really was mine, but how long would it last? Was I deluding myself? And had I been deluding myself all along?

***

Treading softly, I left Ritchie's room and headed down to the kitchen to make some breakfast for us. Whilst I was whipping up an omelette, Beth wandered in.

"How's he feeling?"

"He was in a bit of pain last night, but he's okay."

Beth was silent for a minute. "You really care about him, don't you?" It was more of a statement than a question.

"Of course I do," I said as I removed the pan from the stove and turned around to face Beth. Ritchie definitely shared his mother's ability to read a person, and her direct stare.

"Obviously, I know something is going on."

I stopped breathing then, afraid of what this was leading to. She carefully observed my facial responses, but when I didn't say anything, she continued.

"You love him, don't you?"

In a moment of sudden clarity, I answered, "Yes." It was barely a whisper, but I meant it with all my heart. "But I've always asked him to do the right thing, Beth," I said, my anxiety rising, worried that all would be revealed.

To my complete and utter shock, she just replied, "I know."

The tense atmosphere was broken when we both heard Ritchie slowly walking down the stairs. Seconds later, he appeared in the doorway.

"Good morning. What's all this?" he asked gesturing with his hand. Just seeing him standing there out of the hospital was enough to make me smile. All the risks I'd taken, I decided, were worthwhile when he smiled back.

"Breakfast, of course," I announced cheerfully.

Weirdly, it felt like a weight had been lifted after speaking to Beth. She discreetly left as if she wanted to give us some space. It was the strangest thing. She seemed supportive, but I didn't know what was really going through her head. She could report me for unprofessional conduct, because technically, my contract didn't end until the last day of August.

Or was my connection with him or my *power* over him the only thing that had prevented her from taking it further? I didn't know. I didn't mention any of this to Ritchie. I would tell him when the time was right.

"You look beautiful, Francesca," he said unexpectedly. Whenever he complimented me, my heart still skipped a beat, because to me his beauty surpassed mine. It was a privilege to be loved and admired by this young man, maybe a privilege I didn't quite deserve.

I put my head down shyly. Even after all this time, he still made me feel this way.

"Thank you, Ritchie."

Obviously still in pain, he sat and ate. Refusing any help, he ate slowly and unsteadily, but determinedly.

I decided to stay with him for the next few days, even though John disapproved. I just couldn't deal with him, or Casey. She turned up a few days later, seemingly eager to see Ritchie. I decided to leave then, although Casey spied me descending the stairway and sent daggers through me with her cold snake-like eyes. Understandably, she wanted me out of the picture. I honestly understood her frustration, but if she just wanted to use Ritchie, then she deserved whatever she got. I doubted that she really understood what real love was. She had certainly taken her time coming to see Ritchie after his accident.

After that, I returned home to John, who at first seemed very quiet. Perhaps he'd realised that he had to hold on a little tighter and appreciate what he'd had for years. He then became unusually attentive and helpful, offering me just a glimpse of what I was initially attracted to. My fondness for him, and our companionship, hadn't quite died, but friendship was all that it was now. The results of my visa application would soon be approaching, and I had until then to make my final decision. Would I stay or would I go?

***

The weeks passed and Ritchie's health improved vastly. The cast was removed and the scar on his face was no longer an angry red gash but a light shade of pink, adding character to an otherwise almost flawless face.

Up until now, he'd refused to cut his hair, asserting that it was what I wanted. I managed to convince him to trim it. I loved it long, but I knew that he had only kept it long to please me. Although I could be bossy at times, particularly with John or my parents, I didn't want that kind of relationship with Ritchie.

August arrived with GCSE results. He waited until I got to his place before he opened them. Beth sat with us and we nervously watched Ritchie open the envelope. He'd got an A for art, B for English, Cs in science and geography, and a D for history. He glowed as he proudly read them out. Years of struggling had finally paid off. Beth didn't seem as pleased as she should have been, but four out of five was better than nothing.

I rose to give him a congratulatory hug. I hadn't seen him beaming like this for months. His smile was infectious. Unexpectedly, Beth followed my example, awkwardly giving Ritchie a brief hug. He stood stiffly, accepting the gesture, probably shocked at her rare display of affection.

"Well done, Richard. I'm proud of you," she said robotically, but I think she might have really meant it.

"Thanks, mum."

"You've finally got out of that place now, Ritchie," I piped in.

"Finally! Thank you, Francesca – I wouldn't have done it without you."

Beth disappeared for a moment, reappearing with a cheque which had my name on it. She handed it to me and said, "For everything, Francesca."

It was a cheque for one thousand pounds! I couldn't believe my eyes. I honestly thought she put up with me only to keep Ritchie happy.

"No. Please – I can't accept this. I did it for Ritchie."

"Are you sure you won't take it?"

"I'm sure, Beth. Thank you so much."

We spoke for a while about future plans. Beth mentioned that David was expanding the business overseas to California. As soon as Ritchie had fully recovered from his accident, the expectation was that he would go and assist with the business. That way he could continue his family's legacy when he returned to the UK. It sounded like a great opportunity.

Throughout the conversation, he sat quietly. I knew him, so I knew that he was worried about being away from me. I would be there for him for all time if he ever needed me. This would be the ultimate test. That was what I tried to tell myself anyway.

We had tried the distance thing before Ritchie's accident. It was hard, but we'd managed to do it. However, that had been just for a month or so. Perhaps the distance or amount of time hadn't been great enough for him to forget about me. I started to believe that after this major separation, he might reconsider everything. I marred his view. I was always there as a reminder and maybe he felt he owed something to me. I didn't know. We said that we loved each other, and I knew that I certainly loved him, but could an eighteen-year-old really understand real love?

How I wanted to believe that he loved me, but as was always the case, the claws of reality started tearing at me and the seeds of doubt were planted. How I dreaded the day when he no longer wanted me.

I watched his expression become more and more anxious until he abruptly stood up and announced, "I'm tired. I'm going back to bed."

Beth exchanged a worried look with me and said, "Can you talk to him please?"

"I think I know what's bothering him. Don't worry. I'll try to make him see."

"Please see that you do, Francesca. You use that influence you have because you can't be there for him forever."

"I know. Trust me – I know."

Ritchie lay curled up on his bed, his face buried in his pillow, so that I couldn't read his expression. I didn't have to see his face to know what he was feeling, because the truth was that I felt the same way. I was just trying to view things with a bit more clarity and reality.

I sat beside him and said the only thing I knew that would make him respond.

"Do you want me to go?"

A few minutes later, he stirred and turned onto his back, staring up at the ceiling.

"No," he paused. Taking a deep breath, he continued, "You think I should go to California?"

"Yes, it's a chance to explore and see different places. I don't want to hold you back. Don't stay for me. If I wasn't here, you would go."

I lay on my back beside him. Memories of when I first lay on his bed flashed before my eyes. I remembered him saying how he wanted me, not Casey. I'd experienced one of the sweetest kisses I'd ever tasted that fateful day.

"Actually, that's probably true, but it doesn't mean I have to like it though."

"Believe me, I want to keep you all for myself, but it wouldn't be right. I'll see you when you come back anyway." *That is if you ever come back.*

"And I will, Francesca. You can count on that."

We lay there in silence until all we could hear was the clock ticking and each other's breathing. Without saying a word, Ritchie held my hand. I don't know how long we lay there. We lost track of time, lost in a world of our own.

I managed to keep my composure until the moment I arrived home. Large, hot tears released themselves from my eyes. I'd told Ritchie to be strong, but I felt far from strong myself.

We had already attempted this in the past. I had urged him to have a girlfriend, to move away, yet we always found ourselves in this impossible situation. I forced myself to face up to what I had done to John, the lie that I had been living. I looked myself in the mirror and willed myself to do this. It was time for Ritchie to spread his wings and time for me to prepare for my future in Canada.

***

I started my new job at Camden Lock Primary School. My experience at St. Paul's began to feel like a dream. Ritchie's wounds healed, but our separation loomed ever closer. I didn't want to lose him again, believe me, but he had to go. Beth now expected me to support her expectations of Ritchie and I knew I had to keep her on my side. I had to encourage Ritchie to do right by his family. I was afraid of what would happen if I didn't agree or if he changed his mind. She knew that something had gone on between us and she had the power to make my life difficult if she chose to.

Maybe this was what I deserved. Because of what I had done, I had to suffer my greatest pain: to live as a shell of my former self. John would be oblivious as usual, lost in a blissful, drunken stupor. Obsessed with his gaming, he never noticed any changes in my demeanour. We'd even stopped being intimate. Had he even noticed that? Maybe it was the perfect cover. We could both wallow in our broken worlds because that was all we had. At least we weren't entirely alone.

All our subsequent encounters were a bit more sombre, and we spoke less. The spoken word was too painful to bear. Ritchie and I held each other in the increasing darkness, listening to all the sounds of the night.

I resolved to see Ritchie as much as possible before he left – after work and during weekends. For some reason, John hardly questioned me, and I no longer needed to explain why I needed to see him so much. Each night that I lay next to John, I cried silent tears of acceptance, because I had finally started to accept what needed to be done.

In some ways, I knew that the distance might disperse any suspicions that people may have had, and I'm sure that there were a few. No one would ever truly know. There were records of correspondence via phone, but no evidence of what was actually said. Neither of us would ever break. Ritchie's lips were clamped firmly shut and I knew with all my heart that he wouldn't tell a soul. And we never actually admitted anything to his mother, despite her very accurate conclusions. Still, that was one loose end. I guessed she supposed that as long as he was under my influence, it was better to stand with me rather than against me. Plus, what we had done wasn't exactly illegal, especially now that we'd both moved on from St. Paul's. In the eyes of the law, he was a consenting adult. Even though that was a somewhat comforting thought, I still didn't want a stigma attached to either of us. Ritchie's life was just beginning.

Ritchie's last night arrived. We stood frozen with loss on the doorstep until he stepped aside, his head hanging sadly. We walked up to his room one last time and closed the door behind us. My eyes had welled up before I had even arrived, and when he turned to look at me, his eyes also shone with grief.

"Oh, Ritchie," I said as I reached out to stroke his cheek along his scar which I had grown to love. He held my hand there like his life depended on it and his face crumpled a bit as he tried to control his emotions. "I love you. I always will."

"I love you too, Francesca. Please don't forget me," he croaked.

Cupping the back of his head, I brought him towards me, kissing him softly on the part of his face I loved to kiss, just about where his temple was, where the skin was softest.

"How could I ever forget you? My beautiful man," I whispered, my voice cracking, a painful lump having formed in my throat. He gathered me up into his arms and held me for a long time. I nuzzled his chest, listening to his heart beating. Our breathing became one. There was no me and no him.

Becoming aware of my tears dampening his T-shirt, he guided my chin up towards his face and kissed me, our silent salty tears mingling with our kisses. I felt a longing need, a desperate passion in Ritchie's lips. Then we were lying on his bed caressing one another, his skin warm against my naked flesh, and then he was inside me. He was deep in me, but I pulled him further inside, gasping. Each time he thrust himself inside, I pulled him in with my legs. Our heavy breathing became louder. Our bodies became moist with sweat as we clung to each other. We kissed frenetically, wanting to taste as much as we could, to savour it, to hold on to it and to remember.

How I loved him – mind, body and soul. I wandered his dark landscape, as he explored mine. Our minds entwined forever. Memories burned into our brains. Our shared experiences flashed before my eyes and I stacked each one away, never to be forgotten and to remember when all hope was lost. The evening went by in a blur.

I decided that I couldn't stay the night. I couldn't prolong the pain, and so I prepared to leave. Ritchie looked more and more distraught, and I felt more and more empty. He stood in front of the doorway, blocking my way as I tried to leave.

"Ritchie, I've got to go. We've got to say goodbye."

All of a sudden, a violent sob burst through him. He'd obviously been trying hard to control it, but he lost the battle with his own mind.

"No, I can't let you go!" He said it with so much raw grief that I felt so bad for what I'd done.

"I'm sorry, Ritchie, I should never have done this to you," I choked out, having finally lost control of my own grief. I attempted to lead him away from the door, but he wouldn't budge.

"Don't you say that. You saved me, and now you're leaving me." He collapsed on the ground, firmly planted in front of the door.

"But you can do it without me. I promise you will."

He didn't answer. He just put his head in his hands, in vain. I collapsed in a heap beside him and held him until our sobs subsided.

Eventually, Ritchie raised his head and whispered, "I'll come back for you, Francesca."

"And I'll be waiting for you, Ritchie."

He stood up then, putting his hand on the doorknob. I mistakenly thought he was going to open it, but his hand remained there. I put my hand on top of his in an attempt to turn it, but his arm tensed further. Rock hard strength gripped the knob.

"Please, Ritchie. For me," I asked.

He took a deep breath and abruptly let go. I leaned toward him, standing on my tiptoes, and kissed him lightly on his scar. And finally, without a word, I turned and left.

Chapter Twenty

Ritchie

It was the hardest day of my life was when I had to say goodbye to Francesca. She had been my rock for a year and I'd fallen for her.

I didn't know what to expect when I had first met her. She'd gone way above and beyond the call of duty. I'd told her that she had saved me, and I'd meant it. I really don't know what would have become of me if she hadn't been around. She was the only person who had given me the time of day, becoming not only my best friend and my soulmate, but also my lover, showing me an intimacy I didn't know existed.

The time had come for me to leave. It was hard, so hard for me to let her go that day, but she had been strong. I had to be strong too. I wanted her to be proud of me. I was determined to use my time away from her to better myself, so that when I did return, she would be proud of me. And hopefully, I wouldn't be so pathetic anymore. That was even if she was remotely interested in me still. I was nothing before she came, struggling with school and struggling with life. The only thing that brought me the slightest bit of joy was music and sport, but even they had lost their charm. She came, and suddenly the world seemed brighter.

So I left London with a heavy heart in pursuit of a career. I had to do something with my life, and I could feel the pressure increasing from my family. Whatever I did, I couldn't get the image of her out of my mind. I would try not to think of her, but it was pointless. I needed her like a drug, like I needed air. One year seemed so long. How would I survive?

But I had promised I would try and try I would. I forced myself to at least attempt to appear like I could cope. It should have been exciting though, travelling and learning new things. Uncle David had been good to me, trying to involve me in the business, even when I wasn't overly enthusiastic. I would put the effort in because I felt as I had no other choice. I knew that I would never be able to get a decent job on my own, so I had to take this opportunity.

When I had accepted, I'd seen what looked like hope in my mother's eyes. She'd almost lost hope when I failed most of my GCSEs the first time around. I think I gained some kind of respect from her when my retake results came in. I'm so grateful that the school allowed Francesca to sit by me during most of the tests. She'd had a calming influence, helping me in a way that she couldn't possibly imagine.

All these thoughts flashed in my mind as the plane travelled to my destination. And when the plane landed, the distance between Francesca and me seemed greater and more permanent. I tried to brush my feelings aside, but things that Francesca said kept popping into my head. *You're an intelligent guy with dyslexia who feels things deeply. I can't hold you back. I'll miss you. I love you.* I wished I had an off switch so that my brain would shut down and leave me the hell alone.

As Uncle David drove me from the airport to his apartment, I checked out the scenery. Whenever I saw something interesting, I imagined that Francesca was sitting beside me and that we were sharing the sights we saw.

The following day I started work, and I was glad for the distraction. David showed me around, introducing me to the staff. I was then instructed to shadow someone for the day to get the hang of working for the company. It wasn't too bad, but it was boring.

Some things were quite difficult to get my head around, but I tried. Francesca always told me that I wasn't stupid, so I sure as hell had to prove her right, though I often felt stupid. The staff would give me this 'you don't get it, do you?' look. She was right, though. I had to experience real life. The more I experienced it, the less I liked it. Maybe it was just me. Couldn't we just run away and be together, Francesca and me?

And that's how it was for months. I would go to work like a drone, do what I was told, and come home and pine for Francesca. Nights were the worst. Eventually, Casey came to stay. I had no idea what she did during the day when I wasn't around, probably shopping or getting her nails done. I never asked and she didn't tell me. There was a coldness about her that reminded me of my mother. She was there, but not really there. We had sex, but it felt like she was doing it because she had to, to somehow keep me interested. I don't even know if she enjoyed it. She willingly lay there while I masturbated inside her. I used her to satisfy my needs. A means to an end.

There were times when I almost called out her name. I could see Francesca in my peripheral vision, like a ghost, and I would hear her voice in the darkness. When I was alone, I found myself talking to her as if she were in the room. I would have a full-blown conversation with myself.

On my days off, Casey would insist that we go to the beach, take selfies to show off to her friends, and go to dinner, pretending to enjoy holding hands. It was weird. Why did Francesca want me to be with Casey? Was it to please my family or to see if I would forget about her? Why did she say, *I should never have done this to you?* What did she mean? What did she do that was so awful? None of it made sense to me. The way I saw it, we should be together, no matter what anyone thought. I may have only just turned nineteen, but I could definitely understand real love and how I loved Francesca. If she had asked me to go to the moon and back, I would have done it. She had asked me to do this, and I would see it to the very end. She didn't believe that I would come back for her. I had seen it in her eyes when we said goodbye and it had hurt, knowing that she didn't quite believe me or trust me. It had hurt a lot. Maybe that was why I was even more determined to do this.

I don't think I could ever tell her what went through my mind that day. It was the first time I had ever felt resentment towards her. I even considered telling John everything. That way, she would be mine, I figured. In the end, I couldn't bear to see her light fade and to see her turn into the miserable person I usually was. No, I couldn't do that to her. I didn't think she would ever forgive me after all the promises we had made. I would keep our secret to the end.

I hoped that one day, there wouldn't be a secret to keep. I would go along with this charade for now to get my inheritance and satisfy the requirements of my father's will. Once it was mine, I would leave Casey and my whole family, take Francesca and run away into the sunset. And she would be mine forever. Grey hair or not, she would be truly mine.

How I hated my father. I never thought I would tell anyone, but I did. I told Francesca everything. I had cried like a baby telling her all about it. She had a way of piercing the root of any problem and tackling it. I didn't want to talk about it, but I felt that the time was right. I had bottled it up for far too long. I was ashamed, but she had just held me.

Despite facing up to my issues, he still controlled me through his will and my mother. As soon as I could, I would try to sell that business. I tried to tell Francesca that I didn't need the money. I would have given it all up for her, but she insisted she didn't want to be the cause of that. It was a lot to throw away, she'd said. I found a lot of what she said to be frustrating. I didn't always understand, but I knew she had my best interests in mind.

I had considered going back home for a short stay over Christmas, but Mum had actually come over to see me for a week. It was strange not seeing Francesca, so I sent her a gift.

I had a moon-phase watch custom made with a kind of wave design in mother-of-pearl. Just a small gift. She was never impressed by diamonds, but I asked for a small diamond to be put on the full moon.

She had also sent me a gift – a drawing of me. She had sketched me so accurately. Her talent still continued to astound me. The drawing made me feel a little embarrassed, kind of exposed. That's how it was with her. She exposed my core and she had somehow captured my vulnerability in that drawing. I hid it and yet I treasured it. Calling was too painful, so we exchanged emails instead to say thank you. Neither of us could have brought ourselves to pick up the phone.

I never told her, but I wrote a song for her. She had asked me a couple of times to sing to her. For some reason, I never did. I was scared. My feelings for her were so raw, I felt that I wouldn't have been able to say the words. And when it had been time to leave, I just couldn't bring myself to do it. Maybe one day I would record it and send it to her. I could probably do that. Maybe it would convince her that I do care for her and it would remind her of me, because I was afraid that she would forget about me. I worried that somehow John would get her to move to Canada sooner rather than later, and by the time I returned to the UK, she would already be gone. Like a madman, I would stalk her, and then she would turn around and say that it had all been a huge mistake. My worst nightmare would come true.

Christmas had brought back a lot of memories, as our first kiss had happened the previous Christmas. I had been both flattered that such a great woman liked me and overwhelmed because it was the first time I'd tasted a woman's lips. I was bombarded with a whirlwind of emotions and it had been a wonderful discovery. Afterwards, looking me dead in the eye, she'd told me that she had feelings for me. Finding out that someone actually liked me was amazing.

I had been through a hell of a lot in the last year or so before that. I'd had a rocky start, and I had been on a seemingly downward spiral. Then she came along. She'd been supportive and a bit pushy actually, but I'd needed it. I remembered all the times she'd kept me out of trouble and stuck up for me. Every little thing had bothered me. I must have seemed like a right spoilt brat having temper tantrums, but she never judged me. She had understood.

She made me want to be a better person. I wanted to be strong like her. Not physically, but mentally. I tried, and she said that she was proud of me. I had never heard those words before, not directed towards me anyway. I didn't feel as worthless as I did before. Although, now and then, I felt myself sinking into that familiar pit. A number of times, I gave into my urge and dialled her number, only to hang up before she answered. I withheld my number, so she wouldn't know it was me. I felt like an immature school child, losing my control and my sanity.

As the months went by, I learnt more about stocks and shares and how my father and his father had made so much money. Surprisingly, David was alright. He didn't get in my face, giving me space when I needed it. Even though he wasn't directly related to my father, he had stepped in when he died, and he had certainly benefited. I wondered if he was nice to me because he hoped to get a cut of whatever. Nevertheless, I could tolerate him.

I was glad when Casey decided to return to England in February. I missed the sex a bit, but I certainly didn't miss her boring small talk or her corpse-like stare.

Unfortunately, I was alone with my thoughts once again as a result. I often found myself reminiscing, reliving my steamy encounters with Francesca. Damn, she was beautiful. She was a woman in every sense of the word. Her almond-shaped eyes, so dark and beautiful. They would suck me in like a black hole, and I lost all awareness of time and space. Her eyes, like a leopard about to pounce on me and consume me, screamed: I want you. We needed no words. I felt her hands on my body and her lips on mine. So bloody sexy and irresistible.

Watching the water cascading down her breasts in the shower, I had felt like the luckiest man alive. Flickers of memories replayed over and over again, and I would close my eyes, attempting to experience them all over again. Many a time, I would grab myself and imagine that I was inside her. We used to lose ourselves totally, living the moment, totally consumed with the other. I loved seeing her gasp with pleasure, and knowing that I had caused that pleased me greatly.

At night, I would lie awake staring at the ceiling, seeing her face in the shadows. I could almost feel her lying next to me in the darkness. I could even smell her when I concentrated hard enough. I loved her odour, especially after we had sex. It would linger in my bed and I would smell her pillow, inhaling deeply. I was so totally obsessed. I knew it wasn't healthy, but I didn't care. I didn't want to forget her. I wanted to remember all the times that we'd shared, and if it meant replaying scenes or creating new fantasies in my head, then that was what I would do. I often wondered if she ever thought of me too. Did she miss me as much as I missed her?

I thought about that time in the hospital after my accident, when I opened my eyes and there she was, like an angel. She'd said that she loved me for the first time as I lay there, battered, bruised and scarred. She was the first person to show any kindness, respect or love towards me.

She had walked amongst the shadows and the light in the deepest recesses of my soul, uncovering feelings that no one else understood. She taught me something I had never experienced before. Without her, I struggled to exist as a single entity.

Epilogue

I heard the school gates click shut for the last time. It had been a good year at Camden Primary School. The relaxed atmosphere had been just right for me. The positive nature of the staff, students and parents helped me to cope, after all that I had experienced.

I had arrived to work every morning smiling, throwing myself into everything I did, even volunteering to run after-school activities. I found that being around children and staff who enjoyed my company and who had a great sense of humour enabled me to survive without Ritchie. It had all helped dull the pain I felt each and every night. I dreaded weekends most when my subconscious would dredge up painful memories.

Although my visa to Canada had been granted months ago, I had decided to end things with John. Receiving the visa confirmation letter was what finally pushed me. It seemed a shame after investing so much time and effort applying for it, and wasting a good chunk of my savings on a visa that I would never use, but I'd decided that I could no longer live this lie. After yet another argument about his drinking, I finally told John that I didn't love him anymore and that I didn't want to go to Canada with him. He had looked at me with hurt in his eyes and silent acceptance. He just walked out and went to stay with a mutual friend that night. The very next day I arranged to move back in with my parents until I found a place to live. They were upset and confused as they had seen John as part of the family. He was also a good friend to my father.

I never told him about what happened between Ritchie and me, because that was the last time I ever spoke to John. We made no attempt to call one another, and he moved back to Canada without the English Rose he'd promised to bring with him. I think he knew in his heart that it had been over some time ago, and I started to see that I'd never really loved him. Not the way I should have anyway.

It was strange how I saw things much more clearly when Ritchie left. Not a day went by that I didn't think of him. I believe a part of me truly died when I left Ritchie. I feared that I would become an unfeeling robotic shell, devoid of any emotion, because I had experienced this for a brief time. Now I was oddly at peace with the whole situation. At least I had experienced true love for a while, and I would treasure the memories forever. I doubted that I would ever find anyone to replace Ritchie, my beautiful angel.

I handed in my notice at work, accepting a job in a completely different borough on the outskirts of London, and managed to find a small studio flat nearby. I wasn't able to keep the flat John and I had rented due to the cost. Plus, I didn't want any reminders of bad memories. I wanted to start anew. I wanted a fresh start. It was obvious that Ritchie had moved on, hence his silence. I always knew that it would happen. He had finally come to his senses, as I suspected he would.

As all these thoughts raced through me at an incredible speed, I thought I caught sight of Ritchie at the corner of my eye, like an afterimage. I guessed it was my mind playing tricks on me. I expected the phantasm to disappear, but it didn't. I was afraid to look at it directly, as it would mean that I really had lost the plot.

Slowly, I raised my eyes and turned to face it head on. There Ritchie sat, as clear as day, on the wall opposite me. Had it really got to this point? Did I genuinely need psychiatric help? The thought scared me terribly.

Then he stood up.

It really was him. I couldn't believe my eyes.

Like a hurricane, all the emotion locked up inside hit me full force, so much so that it manifested as a sharp pain in my chest. I took a ragged breath, and my eyes stung with unshed tears. I stood there frozen with disbelief.

He had come back for me.

The End

About the author

F. Burn was born and raised in Central London, which has been an inspiration for her stories. She writes fiction which explores the dark side of the human psyche.

F.Burn wrote songs and poetry before shifting to novelettes and novels. When she is not writing, she spends most of her time reading horror books, watching sci-fi movies, painting, going for long walks and cooking.

If you would like to know more about F.Burn and her blog, please visit her website at https://fburn2020.wixsite.com/website.

More Black Velvet Seductions titles

The Brute and I by Suzanne Smith
Home by Keren Hughes
Only A Good Man Will Do by Dee S. Knight
Secret Santa by Keren Hughes
Killer Lies by Zia Westfield
A Merman's Choice by Alice Renaud
All She Ever Needed by Lora Logan
Nicolas by Callie Carmen
Paging Dr. Turov by Gibby Campbell
Out of the Ashes by Keren Hughes
A Thread of Sand by Alan Souter
Stolen Beauty by Piper St. James
Mystic Desire - Anthology
Killer Deceptions by Zia Westfield
Edgeplay by Annabel Allan
Music for a Merman by Alice Renaud
Joseph by Callie Carmen
Not You Again! by Patricia Elliott
The Unveiling of Amber by Viola Russell
Husband Material by Keren Hughes
Never Have I Ever by Julia McBryant
Hard Limits by Annabel Allan
Anthony by Callie Carmen
Paper Hearts by Keren Hughes
The King's Spy by L.J. Dare
More Than Words by Keren Hughes & Jodie Harrold
Lessons on Seduction by Estelle Pettersen
Rigged by Annabel Allan
Desire Me Again - Anthology
Mermaids Marry in Green by Alice Renaud
Holy Matchmaker by Nancy Golinski
Joshua by Callie Carmen
Whiskey Lullaby by Keren Hughes
Forgiveness by Starla Kaye
When the White Knight Falls by Virginia Wallace
Cowboy Desire – Anthology
The Bookshop by Simone Francis

Our back catalog is being released on Kindle Unlimited
You can find us on:
Twitter: BVSBooks
Facebook: Black Velvet Seductions
See our bookshelf on Amazon now! Search "BVS Black Velvet
Seductions Publishing Company"

Black Velvet Seductions

Printed in Great Britain
by Amazon

64972366R00116